Praise for V

"A complicated, beautiful, heartbreaking, and hilarious story.... Gipe manages to craft characters who look around and see drug addiction and extractive industries and dysfunction—and who are funny and fierce and reflective."

— *Appalachian Journal*

"The dialogue, with its distinct Appalachian dialect, charges Gipe's illustrated story of a tight-knit community in coal country, in which people struggle to make ends meet, raise families, maintain friendships, and survive the opioid epidemic. The many cartoons add emotional complexity to the evocative language and terrific character development."

— *Booklist*

"When [Gipe's] prose is coupled with his cartoon-like drawings in which the characters tend to stare directly at the reader, the effect is similar to watching a documentary film. ... This strategy imbues his work with a kind of realism that is not quite traditional fiction and not quite a graphic novel but engrossing nonetheless. His characters come a cross as absolutely real, simultaneously funny and heartbreaking."

— *Chapter16/Knoxville News Sentinel*

"Robert Gipe is the real deal: a genuine storyteller, a writer of wit and style, wisdom and heart. His characters are as alive as anybody I know, and his sentences jump off the page. I find myself reading them out loud to whoever's handy and saying, 'This is how it's done.'"

— Jennifer Haigh, author of *Heat and Light*

"*Weedeater* is about how to go on when your heart is broken. With a style worthy of Ray Hicks, author Robert Gipe makes his characters Dawn and Gene stare straight at you and tell what they have to tell. It is impossible to turn away from them. Their compelling tale of current Appalachia, told through true and vital language and with great compassion, is necessary reading for everyone."

— Carrie Mullins, author of *Night Garden*

Praise for *Trampoline:*

"*Trampoline* is a moving account of working-class Kentucky mountain people who live in an environment dominated by mountaintop removal coal mining. *Trampoline* is also the most innovative American fiction to appear in years. The story, the characters and the writing style are startlingly new, as in: original. *Trampoline* adds a fresh consciousness to the enduring conversation about the Appalachian region. Pathos and humor are present in about equal measure."
 — Gurney Norman, author of *Divine Right's Trip* and *Kinfolks*

"Dawn Jewell is one of the most memorable and endearing narrators I have ever read. She's like a combination of Scout Finch, Huck Finn, Holden Caulfield, and *True Grit*'s Mattie Ross, but even more she is completely her own person, the creation of Robert Gipe, an author who has given us a novel that provides everything we need in great fiction: a sense of place that drips with kudzu and coal dust; complex characters who rise up off the page as living, breathing people we will not soon forget; and a rollicking story that is by turns hilarious, profound, deeply moving, and always lyrically beautiful. I think *Trampoline* is one of the most important novels to come out of Appalachia in a long while and announces an important new voice in our literature. I loved every single bit of this book."
 — Silas House, author of *Clay's Quilt* and *Eli the Good*

"Gipe's powerful sense of place will seep into teen readers' lives. This is a killer debut of one teenager's flight from destruction—strong stuff tempered with humor and love."
 — *School Library Journal*

"There are the books you like, and the books you love, and then there are the ones you want to hold to your heart for a minute after you turn the last page. Robert Gipe's illustrated novel *Trampoline* is one of those—not just well written, which it is; and not just visually appealing, which the wonderfully deadpan black-and-white drawings make sure of; but there is something deeply lovable about it, an undertow of affection you couldn't fight if you wanted to.... Gipe deftly avoids every single cliché that could trip such a story up, which includes having a pitch-perfect ear for dialect and making it into something marvelous."

— Lisa Peet, *Library Journal*'s "What We're Reading"

"A story that left my heart at once warmed and shattered, *Trampoline* rides the razor's edge of raw beauty. This is Appalachia illuminated with a light uniquely its own. I dare say Robert Gipe has invented his own genre."

— David Joy, author of *Where All Light Tends to Go*

"In 1980, John Kennedy Toole's classic, *A Confederacy of Dunces*, was published by the Louisiana State University Press. The following year it won the Pulitzer Prize in fiction. That may have been the last time a university press introduced a major American voice—the last time, that is, until now…. *Trampoline* is a new American masterpiece."

— *Chapter16/Knoxville News Sentinel*

"Fascinating, honest, and sometimes darkly comic…. The consciousness of the mountain itself and the animals on it become the quiet heart of this loud and heartbreaking book."

— *Orion*

"Rare is the novel that delivers on all that is promised by fans or by the carefully curated blurbs featured on its cover. But, in my mind, *Trampoline* fulfills these promises, portraying Appalachia in a manner that falls prey neither to the demeaning stereotypes nor the romanticized clichés that are commonly associated with the region and its literature."

— Zackary Vernon, *Cold Mountain Review*

"I fear this book. I'm in love with this book. I'm laughing out loud at this book. I am knocked to my knees in grief by this book. One of the most powerful works of contemporary fiction I've read in years. I'll never forget Dawn Jewell. I'll never escape Canard County."

— Ann Pancake, author of *Strange as This Weather Has Been* and *Me and My Daddy Listen to Bob Marley*

"I believe it takes a special genius to create a story that is hilarious and poignant and eloquent all at the same time, and Robert Gipe has done just that in his amazing debut *Trampoline*. Gipe's is a voice like no other and I guarantee you'll fall in love just like I did."
— Pam Duncan, author of *The Big Beautiful* and *Moon Women*

"Robert Gipe has the most original voice to emerge on the literary landscape since Lewis Nordan. Dawn Jewell is a delicious heroine, whether she's shouldering her way through a community conflict or a family scrimmage. Geographically anchored, yet universally relevant, *Trampoline* is funny, serious, dark, radiant, and amazingly honest, filled with rich characters and a culture wracked with contradiction and heartbreak, but also strength and resilience. An excellent debut from a gifted and insightful writer."
— Darnell Arnoult, author of *Sufficient Grace*

"Robert Gipe has produced a one-of-a-kind masterpiece. Here's a narrator, Dawn, trapped absolutely in an Appalachian Gregor Samsa kind of way, surrounded by loved ones who are at times difficult to love. Dawn is precocious, bighearted, and fearless—a mountaintop-removal-fighting Mattie Ross. I couldn't put this novel down."
— George Singleton, author of *Between Wrecks*

"Billboards. That's what we need. 'Dawn Jewell is queen' on one. 'Jump on this Trampoline' on another. All of them shouting how good this book is. Read it, everyone, read it."
— Jim Minick, author of *The Blueberry Years*

"Quite possibly, one of the best books to ever come out of eastern Kentucky."
— *Huntington Herald-Dispatch*

"*Trampoline* is that rare kind of book, a first novel that feels like a fourth or fifth. It is a roaring tale that knows when to tamp its own fire—which is another way of saying that it is funny as hell but will hurt you too."
— Glenn Taylor, *Electric Literature*

"Gipe is the best of populists: generous of spirit but not smarmy. There are some deeply flawed people in Dawn's circle (she's one of 'em), but they're never all bad, never unchangeable but never unrealistically transformed. Gipe has a gift for staging tender reconciliations that you suspect won't last through the afternoon. To borrow from an old country song, *Trampoline* is ragged but right, and it builds to an effective blend of contrasting tones: world-weary yet hopeful, not too sentimental but — let's quote Dawn once more — 'soft, like the sound a Christmas tree makes when you throw it over the hill.'"

— *Minneapolis Star Tribune*

"Canard County is a fictional county in Eastern Kentucky. It's rural, poor, and white. Coal mining, unemployment, drug addiction, and religious fervor dominate the landscape and the culture. It is, in other words, straight-up Appalachia. But as *Trampoline* embraces its Appalachian-ness, it also questions commonly held notions of what it means to be Appalachian. Its combination of prose narrative and quirky illustrations delivers a unique storytelling form, and the insightful, hilarious, and honest protagonist Dawn Jewell makes *Trampoline* unforgettable."

— Cartel Sickels, *Southern Spaces*

Weedeater

WEEDEATER

AN ILLUSTRATED NOVEL

ROBERT GIPE

OHIO UNIVERSITY PRESS • ATHENS

Ohio University Press, Athens, Ohio 45701
ohioswallow.com
© 2018 by Robert Gipe
All rights reserved

Printed in the United States of America
Ohio University Press books are printed on acid-free paper ⊗ ™

28 27 26 25 24 23 22 21 20 19 18   5 4 3 2 1

First paperback edition printed in 2020
ISBN 978-0-8214-2406-3

Library of Congress Cataloging-in-Publication Data
Names: Gipe, Robert, author.
Title: Weedeater : an illustrated novel / Robert Gipe.
Description: Athens, Ohio : Ohio University Press, 2018.
Identifiers: LCCN 2017058087| ISBN 9780821423097 (hardcover) | ISBN
  9780821446256 (pdf)
Subjects: LCSH: Coal mining--Kentucky--Fiction. | Dysfunctional
  families--Fiction. | Drug abuse--Fiction. | Domestic fiction.
Classification: LCC PS3607.I4688 W44 2018 | DDC 813/.6--dc23
LC record available at https://lccn.loc.gov/2017058087

Dedicated to the memory of my mother

Barbara Jane Hale Gipe

1939–2016

Contents

~~~~~~~~~~~~~~~~

I

~~~~~

DREADFUL CRASH

GENE

First day of July I was thumbing the Caneville Road. I'd walked off another of Brother's cleanup jobs, mine sludge up to my pant pockets, throat raw, hands itching and broke out. For eight dollars an hour I told him I couldn't do it. Told him I'd walk back to Canard. He didn't like it and called me an ugly name, but I told him I'd make it up to him, and at the time I thought I would.

I got my first ride from a blackheaded man in a Chevy pickup. He set me out at the Caneville bridge, and I stood there a good while, till a heavyset preacher picked me up, but he got a flat before we got to Pic-Pac and had to call his wife to bring the spare. I went in Pic-Pac and got me a Popsicle, come out, started walking. I walked a half mile when a man stopped had the crazy eye. I told him I'd wait, and he gunned his silver Buick across the double yellow line into a red Ford heading the other way. The Ford flipped up on its side against the rock wall, and the Buick sailed down the ditchline toward Canard a hundred yards and hung up on a road sign, front wheels spinning, no skid mark in sight.

Such as that common in oh-four, back when the pain pills poured down like February snow. Same year one died in a bathtub dry and blue as a pool chalk. Another they found dead in the sewer ditch in front of the Frawley Headstart. A lady's heart give out, a needle in her arm, back of the Christian Church, and a teacher died at Kettle Creek School snorting a pill off her desk in front of a room full of kids. All that in Canard County in a single year.

When you're first one at a wreck, you can't believe how quiet it is. A woman had hair dyed orange come hollering out of the sideways Ford, but even still it felt too quiet. No police nor ambulance. Just you and what happened. A man with a winch on his truck come up, had a hat said "Blackbird VFD," and he went to work getting that Ford set down. Then a lady in her hospital scrubs stopped, tried to see to that screaming woman. After that, people gathered from every side—come out of their houses to say they seen it, cars lined up down both sides of the road full of people wanting to help, a man running for magistrate handing out cards. Pretty soon so many people had congregated, felt like a yard sale. One woman stopped to ask if anybody was selling baby clothes, but when the ambulance pulled up and she seen it was a wreck, she started to cry. I told her not to feel bad, told her I thought the very same thing.

When she settled down, I walked back to the Buick. They was several people crowded around, and I could barely see the driver the way the Buick was rared back on that road sign. I stood up on my tiptoes, and seen the man stir. He stared out the windshield at the white summer sky.

Somebody said, "You gonna make it, buddy?"

The man in the Buick leaned over on his elbow towards us, mouth hanging open, face white as the sky. His eyes opened wider, till they was like two bowling balls coming down the alley. He shook his head back and forth and said, "Nope."

Then he lay his head down on the car seat and didn't move no more.

Somebody said, "Did he die?" and I turned to see who it was. That right there was the first time I seen June. God, she was good-looking. I fell in love on the spot. I got to where I couldn't bear to say her name. I just call her That Woman.

That Woman stood there with a big tall girl, her niece, name of Dawn. When I didn't answer June about the man dying, Dawn said, "Say," so hateful all I could do was stand there and look at her big wild head of hair.

DAWN

"Say," I said, and Gene just stood there, his arms brown as bread, covered in gray mud, every other finger mashed up. He smelled like he'd bathed in lighter fluid and looked like he'd been drug through the landfill. He turned to us, eyes all misty. I thought he was fixing to cry.

I said, "You fixing to cry?"

Aunt June told me to hush. I was sorry for that man being dead, and I shouldn't have been hateful to Gene, but I was in a terrible mood. It was too hot to be married. But I was. To Willett Bilson, a man I'd courted on the Internet. I had my little girl Nicolette strapped in the car and Aunt June's yellow dog Pharoah pulling at the leash. Willett hadn't turned out like I hoped and I had moved to Tennessee for him and now this Gene was gawking at Aunt June, and they was dead people scattered all over, and it was too much. I'll just be honest.

I WAS NOT MY BEST SELF THAT DAY.

Gene walked with us back to June's car. "If I'd rode with him," Gene said, "this might not've happened."

I said, "Or you'd be dead too."

"I'm Gene," Gene said to Aunt June.

"Hello, Gene," Aunt June said.

Pharoah barked.

"She'll bite you," Nicolette said to Gene. Nicolette was four.

Gene put his hand down to Pharoah's mouth. Pharoah raised her lip.

Gene said, "That's a good dog."

June looked off at the Ford. The orange-headed woman standing beside it was screaming, "Save my baby. You got to save her." A woman in hospital scrubs had her arm around the orange-headed woman. A truck had winched the Ford back down onto the road.

"How'd you get here?" Nicolette said to Gene. "Where's your car?"

Gene said, "Aint got nary."

June said, "You need a ride?" June loved a project. She loved saving stuff.

I loved it when it rained and everybody stayed home. Gene moved to get in the car. Then he stopped and spoke.

GENE

"I don't know you want me in your vehicle," I said. "I aint what you call fresh."

That Woman said, "We aint that fresh ourselves."

Niece Dawn said, "What's that all over your pants?"

I said, "That's from helping Brother clean tanks."

Dawn said, "What tanks?"

The little girl said, "Army tanks."

I said, "Tanks held coal float."

Dawn made a face like she'd opened something spoiled, looked at That Woman.

That Woman spoke to her niece a minute and then That Woman took the dog and the little girl and Dawn opened the trunk and pulled out painter dropcloth plastic, started spreading it in the front seat. A Dabble County sheriff's cruiser pulled up and a deputy got out, asked questions of the people gathered, must have been fifty by then. Out the side of my eye, I seen the woman in the hospital scrubs pointing at me. The deputy come over and asked had I seen it, and I said I had. He asked what I seen and I told him and he stopped writing in his little book, folded it up, said, "Now what was it you were doing out here?" and looked me up and down like there might be something to find out about me, but there wasn't. I was just walking off a bad job like anybody with the least regard for theirselves would, and I don't know what I said to that deputy exactly, but he leaned his head forward like somehow I had some part in that bloody mess.

About then, That Woman said, "You holler when you're ready to go, Gene." When that deputy looked at That Woman, she leaned over, picked up that little girl and moved that dog leash to her other hand, said, "We'll be waiting for you."

The deputy flipped back through his notebook, said, "I can get ahold of you at this number," and turned the notebook towards me, showed me the number at Sister's house. I said he could. He nodded and I said, "It's OK for me to go?"

He looked at me, waved his hand had the little book in it, said I could go.

DAWN

You had to be hemmed up in the same vehicle with Gene to appreciate how bad he smelled.

I said to Nicolette, "Stop rubbing your nose." We were sitting in the backseat with the dog. Gene and June were up front.

Nicolette said, "I caint."

I said, "Yeah, you can," and set her hand down in her lap.

Gene said, "What's this?" He turned, reached across the seat, and held a piece of glass up between me and Nicolette.

Nicolette said, "Where'd you get that?"

Gene said, "Off the road."

The glass was blue-green clear, like old pop bottles, rubbed smooth like water'd been running over it, like it had been somewhere it could tumble. Glass going back to sand.

Gene said to me, "Can she have it?"

I said, "I reckon."

Gene reached the glass to Nicolette. She closed her hand around it, and then dropped it out the window. June didn't see it. Gene didn't say nothing. Nicolette grinned like a half-shucked ear of corn.

Aunt June said, "Where you going, Gene?"

"I'm staying at Sister's," he said. "My sister's."

Pharoah growled. Gene looked back at her.

"Be careful with her," June said. "She's liable to bite."

Gene stared at Pharoah. He had a face like desert rocks in a cowboy movie.

"That's a good dog right there," he said. "She's looking after you. That's what makes her growl."

Pharoah was a sweet yellow dog, but crazy as a bestbug.

"What's that on your face?" Nicolette said.

Gene put his hand to the cinched-up black spot on his cheek, said, "That's where they cut off my hairy spot. Said it had the cancer. Where I'm out in the sun so much."

June's eyes filled the rearview.

Gene said, "Something like that make you appreciate." His eyes stayed on us, blinking like somebody was squirting water in his face.

"How can you sit turned around like that?" I said. "Makes me carsick."

Gene put his hand to Pharoah. She laid her ears down, and he scratched between them. "Does me too," he said.

I turned and looked out the car window at a cornfield, at a yard full of scrap lumber and rusted car tops, at the hillsides so full of green they looked almost blue. There was a lot to appreciate. I wished I could.

GENE

It was nice in That Woman's car, but I needed a smoke. I was thinking of that dead man, the screaming woman and her baby.

SEEMED LIKE I SHOULD'VE STAYED LONGER

That Woman said, "Does your sister live in town?"

I said, "She lives in the green house next to Lawyer Dan."

That Woman nodded. "That's where you want to go?" she said.

"Yeah," I said. "I stay in the little house out back."

The yellow dog licked itself.

I said, "That dog might need to go to the bathroom."

That Woman said, "She was just out." She pulled the car to the side of the road.

The little girl said, "Mommy, I want my glass back."

Dawn said, "Little late for that."

Little girl said, "Help me find it."

That Woman hunted something in the floorboard. The dog fidgeted and grunted like this: "Unh unh unh unh unh."

That Woman said, "I can't find my phone."

I said, "You want me to walk your dog a little bit?"

She said, "Gene, yes, I would." Felt good to hear her call my name. Like somebody scratching between my ears.

The back door hung open where Dawn and her little girl had got out. They rummaged down the side of the road in the gravel. The dog sat there, head pulled forward. I got ahold of its leash. Dog raised its lip. I said, "Come on, Old Yeller, let's me and you sniff this place out." The dog come down out of the car. We got off in the grass, and she cut loose with the waterworks. I said to her,

But by then the dog was nosing in the gravel, trying to make her own sense of the world.

DAWN

Aunt June didn't care much for air conditioning. She liked to keep things natural. All the way to Canard the air whipped through that Honda and our stinks mixed up together—mine, Nicolette's, Pharoah's, June's, and Gene's.

On the way home, Gene filled June up with stories of every yard he ever mowed, stories more tedious than my husband's pimple-and-bowel-movement stories, more tedious than him telling me his dreams every morning and the plots of his comic books every night. Gene's weedeater stories about gas-and-oil ratios and how to keep grass clippings off people's porches and how he learned to tell the difference between weeds and stuff people had planted on purpose went on without end, and by the time we'd got back to Canard, June had him mowing my mother's yard.

When we finally got to the foot of the hill in front of Momma's house, Gene was going on about mowing over a nest of yellowjackets and I said to him,

Mamaw's Escort parked on the street in front of us, on the other side of Momma's steps. Mamaw got out, said, "Our Savior, arrived at last."

June sat both hands on her steering wheel, said, "I can't believe she's still driving that thing."

Mamaw came over and stood to where June couldn't open the car door without hitting her. Me and Pharoah got out and stood in the street while Nicolette got loose from her car seat. "Do it myself" were Nicolette's first words and she'd said them ever day since. Mamaw's eyes fixed on Weedeater, who couldn't get loose where June had the Honda jammed up against the bank. He'd got his shoulders above the top of the door, but his feet had got tangled up in all that plastic June lay down for him to sit on.

"Mamaw!" Nicolette hollered and ran to who was really my mamaw. Nicolette's real mamaw—my mother—had not been around enough in the past three years for Nicolette to name her. She just called her Tricia or Trish, which is her name—Tricia Redding Jewell.

Weedeater finally got out and stood on the sidewalk above the bank. He squinted up at Momma's house, which was at the top of seventy-three concrete steps, seventy-three steps pretty much straight up a hillside in downtown Canard.

Weedeater said, "Some yard."

Mamaw said, "Who's this?" standing close to June looking into the side of her head.

Nicolette looked at June like Mamaw was talking about some creature living inside June's ear. I tapped Nicolette's shoulder. She tilted her face up at me.

I said, "She's talking about him," pointing at Weedeater.

Nicolette looked at Weedeater, looked at June, then shot over to Mamaw and gave her a hug that might've knocked over some. Mamaw said, "Aint that something?"

Nicolette said, "I got to pee."

GENE

Me and that parade of women headed up the steps and by the top I would have eat that baby for a smoke. I was winded, but That Woman's mother, they called her Cora, wadn't even drawing hard. She was built like a roll of rabbit wire and didn't weigh much more.

"God Almighty," Cora said from the screened-in porch. The rest of us strung down the steps, me and Dawn furthest down, looking out over town. That Woman said, "What, Momma," and at the top we seen what.

It was as nice a house as I'd seen without a front door. It had big high ceilings and walls smooth with plaster. It was plain inside, no ductwork or drop ceilings. It was also a trashy mess—piles of frozen dinner and pizza boxes in the living room, clothes strewn, mail strewn. They was a line of sticky drips on the floor from the front door to a commode straight ahead against the back of the house. I tramped through the cans, the bottles, the shot-off fireworks, on my way to the bathroom. Once in there and going, I was afraid my pee would knock the commode through the rottenwood floor. That commode was one of many things not secure in that place.

When I come out of the restroom, Evie Bright stood in the door frame like it was our fault she didn't have wind enough to get up the steps.

DAWN

"God Amighty," Evie said. "There aint no point to that."

I asked her what happened to Momma's door. Evie was my age, but her and Momma partied together.

Evie said, "I don't know. Somebody took it."

I said, "Took a door?"

Evie said, "I don't know, Dawn. How would I know? I'm not the door-woman. You want to know where the door is, come home and watch the door. Caint see the door from Tennessee, can you? Caint keep an eye on the door from there."

I walked off. You can't talk to high people.

Even though she was half my size, Evie used to take up for me. But by the summer of oh-four, she was a quarter my size. And dwindling. In high school though, she's the one would fight when people would give me shit about how big I was or how I didn't listen to the right music, or didn't act like boys were interesting, or how I let my pit hair grow or whatever. Evie didn't care. In high school, she'd fight for me over stuff she didn't like about me herself. But it had been a while since high school.

Evie was also practically my sister-in-law though her and Albert never had been officially married. But between him and running around with Momma and ever other person that "partied," she didn't have much time for me. Truth be told, I didn't much want to be around her by that July, least not what she'd become since she'd been taking pills. She used to be fun. We'd sit in my room at Mamaw's house and wish warts on stupid girls' private parts and disfiguring accidents on their faces. We'd steal stupid girls' shoes. Steal their lunches. Steal their homework. Evie loved to tear up people's homework. She didn't care to key a car either. One time Evie stole a girl's lipstick and used it on a cat's butt and then put it back in the girl's purse. That was my favorite.

I did everything with Evie back then. I was the one took her to the ER when she banged her head on the bathtub when she passed out piercing her own nipple with a safety pin. I'm the one huffed keyboard duster with her. Once. Cause keyboard duster will make the sides of your brain so they can't talk to each other. Me and her would go to hear music every once in a while, always the music she liked. She liked rap and country, which I didn't. Only person we both liked was Nelly. But we never saw him. I'd go with her to stuff though, just to go with her. But that got less and less after high school and I started going more and more to Tennessee and she went more and more to drugs until we'd got to where we were that summer—her being aggravated at me all the time. And truthfully I don't know I missed her that much. That's bad to say and I know it is probably also a lie. I was mad at her to hide how sad I was. It was a loss losing Evie cause she'd been there in a way more than Momma, in a way different from Mamaw, a way I'd needed. So it was sad. But I couldn't show that, could I? Back then I didn't think I could. Back then I thought they'd got on drugs just to ruin my life. I thought they'd got on drugs just to break my heart. That's how stupid I was then.

"Where's Tricia?" Evie said to Mamaw.

Mamaw said, "Not here."

Evie said, "She's sposed to be here."

Mamaw pushed a spraypaint can into a pile of clothes with her toe and shrugged.

Evie said, "You gonna let us in your college class, June? I aint going to lie to you. I need the money."

June was teaching a summer art class at the community college. She'd got a grant to pay the students who took it.

June said, "Yes, Evie. Of course."

Evie said "Starts Wednesday, right?"

"Yes," June said. "No. It starts this coming Tuesday."

Evie said, "I'll be there Wednesday."

Talking to Evie was like somebody emptying a nail gun into the side of your head. I said, "You don't need to take that class, Evie. That class is for people who give a shit."

Evie said, "Why do you care then?"

I headed to the kitchen.

Evie said, "Tricia's taking it."

June said, "Taking what?"

Evie said, "Your class."

That summer Momma and Evie's shame was so gone you couldn't have found it with a pack of prison movie dogs. Momma and Evie could have cared less how it would make June feel for them to fart around in her summer class, how it might knock out somebody who might actually want to be in there.

I went upstairs.

GENE

That banty-rooster girl Evie said, "Who are you?" and I said, "Nobody," cause she come at me like a wad of yellowjackets, and caught me blank.

She said, "I can't say you aint." Then she was gone, quick as she come, and that old woman, Cora, looked at me and said, "Now, whose are you?" I told her who my daddy was and she said, "Why you here?" and when I pointed at That Woman, Cora said, "Yeah, I seen you get out of her car, but why have you come here?"

I said, "To mow the yard."

Cora said, "Well, that aint nothing to be ashamed of, is it?" She looked at Nicolette when she said it.

Nicolette said, "I don't reckon."

I'll just say it—the whole bunch made me nervous. I come from some ruckus-making people, so I try to avoid stir in strangers, and if it was most people, I'd of just cut the grass and not said nothing to none of them, just gone to That Woman for my pay when I was done. But That Woman was a bug zapper and I was the bug. I couldn't stay away from her nor nothing swirling in the area around her.

Cora said, "What are you looking at June for?"

I pulled my mouth shut and said I didn't know.

Cora said, "Come with me." We went through the kitchen to the back door. She took me out in the yard, said, "Is that all you do is mow?"

I said,

She said, "Come here."

She climbed up the rock steps wedged into the hillside past a flat spot held in place by a low stone wall, could have been a garden spot was it not all growed up. She took me to another stone wall on the far side of the flat spot. The second wall was higher than the first, made of creek rock. The old woman stopped short and I about run into her. She clamped down on my shirtsleeve, made me feel like a field mouse a bird had snatched up out of a field, said, "You see them hydrangeas?"

I said I did.

She said, "Anything happen to them hydrangeas I'll murder you."

I said, "Did you plant them or something?"

She looked at me flat as pavement, said, "Look at them."

They was four hydrangea bushes stretched out towards the kudzu that had took over the hillside behind That Woman's house. Cora said again, "Look at them."

I reckon what she was wanting me to look at was the wads of flowers, blue and purple at once. The shade of a big oak made the flowers look like something you'd see under the ocean on one of them coral reefs like I saw on TV in this motel one time in Newport when Sister and her husband took us to see the Cincinnati Reds play baseball. I'd never seen a TV that bright and clear. I'd never seen a coral reef neither and I couldn't believe how all them bright colors was waving in the blue water, and how bright and striped and spotted the fish were, and how all that bright actually helped them hide amongst that coral. I wanted to understand it more, but Sister's husband flipped the channel to try and find the UK football game.

That old woman said, "You got it?" I said I did and she said, "Well then, come over here." She darted off behind a snowball bush on the other side of the yard where there wadn't hardly no room to go.

I followed in after her. We come to the far side of the house. The air condition perched in an upstairs window dripped like a ice cream cone. That old woman had a walking stick painted with spots and stripes like a coral reef fish. She tapped me with it on my shins, said, "All that vine has got to go," and waved her stick from the back end of the house to the front. They was vine all over a trellis by the front porch and they was vine running up the electric meter and they was vine running up on the satellite cables and they was vine running up the power line feeding the air condition. At the base of the house, they was junk bushes, all thick and tangly with vine, out of which all the rest of that vine was spewing like some vine volcano.

I said to that old woman, "That's a mess of vine."

She said, "We need rid of it. Can you handle it?"

I looked back over the whole thing, believing I could, and when I threw back my head, they was a woman standing at the very peak of the roof. I couldn't make out much about her because the sun was behind her head, but I could hear a bird chirping and it was like a morning bird, a bird that had forgotten to wake up, which couldn't be cause birds don't forget to wake up.

That old woman hollered, "Patricia!" and it startled the woman against the sky and she threw her arms out to balance herself. The roof woman seemed thin and light, nothing but the center nub to her, which could have been a trick of the sunshine. She wobbled, one foot on either side of the peak, faced right straight out over us. She fell down on her knees, hanging on with both hands to the lip of the roof, looked down at us, said, "Smile, Momma. Don't be so sour."

DAWN

The upstairs of Momma's house wadn't no better than the down below. The air conditioner in the stair window roared like people on Fox News. All the other windows swung open on their hinges, waved in the wind like pothead beauty queens. A bird flapped through Momma's bedroom, bashed his head against the wall, pooped her bed, flung himself out into the glare. One wall was half-painted green. Another half-painted gray. There was a mattress on the floor, ashtrays on either side, a knocked-over lamp, scattered clothes—some sparkly, some tie-dyed—little clothes, way littler than mine.

Out the window, Canard rolled out to a pointy-headed mountain at the other end of town. The town looked pretty laid out there in the valley. Things had been too jacked up in Canard for too long for anybody to have enough money to ruin its old-timey look. I wondered about the man who built this house, back in the 1920s. I wondered did he think Canard would go on forever. I wondered did he care.

There was a clatter on the roof. Momma come around the corner, walking on the mostly flat spot that covered the porch. Momma swept the shingle grit off herself. The knobs of her elbows and wrists were scraped. Her hair rustled like willow branches in the breeze. She pulled a cigarette out of her pocket and lit it before she seen me.

When she did, she said, "What are you doing?" like she always did.

I said, "Come to wish you a happy birthday."

She said, "It aint my birthday."

I said, "I know it aint."

Momma blew smoke at me.

I said, "Why you on the roof?"

She said, "Come out here."

I said, "I aint." My whole life felt like I was a bug crawling inside a coiled-up garden hose—smaller and smaller circles, slick-dark and rubber-smelling, the only hope of escape something likely to drown you as save you.

Momma raised her voice, said "Come out here, Dawn."

I said, "I'm a mother now, Momma."

"Well," she said, "Who aint?"

The wind quit and Momma said, "Hubert's mad at me."

"How's he mad at you?" I said. "I thought he was in jail."

Momma said, "Come out here with me, Dawn." She turned from me, not too fast, not too slow. She didn't talk in a hurry. She seemed to be at normal speed, said, "Who's that with Cora?"

She didn't seem excited, didn't get all tangled up on her words, seemed to be saying what she meant to say. All this to say, she didn't seem high to me. But I didn't always know about high, didn't know about pain pills and what they did to you.

I knew Momma and Evie lived for them. Knew my brother Albert, my uncle Hubert, and a bunch of others sold them.

Pills were easier to stay away from in Tennessee. So was crazy. Easier married to Willett Bilson and his momma's houseful of fragile things, her house full of quiet sleep.

I pulled up the window screen and stepped onto the radiator under the window. Swung my leg out and straddled the window frame. Momma stood at the roof's edge amid loose siding and shingle scraps. Her shoulder blades come up out of her tank top like the oars of a boat, my name tattooed between them in cursive where she'd never see it. I got through the window and onto the roof without falling, but it was not a smooth exit. I am not a fireman nor a ballerina. I am big. I am an ox.

My mother sat down, her toes hanging over the gutter. She turned and looked at me over her shoulder, one leg straightened out, its foot out in the air. She patted the spot next to her with her cigarette hand.

I didn't know to sit there or not. Smothery heat didn't help me think. Two downpipes ran across the roof on either side of the window, framing the space where Momma sat. I guessed the shingles were hot and sticky.

I said, "How can you sit on that?"

"Used to it," Momma said.

"Momma," I said. "Are you high?"

Momma didn't turn around. She said, "No."

I said, "We seen a wreck on the Caneville Road."

Momma said, "Anybody die?"

I said, "Probably."

Smoke came out in a cloud over Momma's head. She said, "So June's down there?"

I said, "Yeah," pushed the window closed behind me, and sat down with my back against the wall. The shingles weren't so hot as I thought. I said, "You OK with that?"

Momma said, "With what?"

"With June coming back."

"Got to be," Momma said. Another cloud of smoke bloomed off her head. "I miss that tree," Momma said.

There had been a red oak in the front yard, big enough to have branches you could touch from where Momma sat, big enough that me and Momma could only barely touch fingers when we hugged it from opposite sides. Last time June got busy saving Momma, she had a man trim some limbs off the oak hung out over the street. Big storm a week later knocked the whole thing over. Bad roots, the guy from extension June called said. Thing blocked traffic, lay there a month across Momma's yard, right across the steps into Glenda's yard next door, before Mamaw got somebody to cut it up.

One old lady in the projects down the hill across the road from where the tree trunk lay went and lived with her daughter in Corbin waiting for that tree to get gone. She was afraid the trunk would get loose, roll across the road, and explode the illegal propane tanks between Momma's house and her apartment. Blow her to Kingdom Come. I don't blame her. Who can you count on? Thirteen pickup trucks of cut wood come out of that tree.

I said, "Lot hotter out here without that tree."

"Seems like," Momma said.

Down below Mamaw lined out more chores for Gene. Her voice was like radio static. Momma peered over. "Who's that guy?" Momma said.

"Some guy June picked up," I said.

Momma turned to look at me, her eyebrows riding up her forehead. "Do what?" Momma said.

"Hitchhiking," I said.

"Oh," Momma said.

"There she is up there," I heard Mamaw say. "Not the sense God gave a goose."

Momma said quiet and tough, "Geese are smart."

I said, "And they honk a lot."

Momma laughed, said, "Hubert's out."

I said, "Is he reformed?"

Momma sat quiet. "No doubt," she said with another puff of smoke.

I said, "Why'd they arrest him?"

Momma said, "Who knows?"

"You do," I should have said out loud instead of just thinking, but I'd been knowing a good while no point asking Momma for something she hadn't already give you.

The bedroom window pushed open. June held Nicolette back from climbing out there with us. "Hey yall," June said. Momma snapped a look over her shoulder, turned back to the sky, pushed out another cloud of smoke.

How cold Momma was made me hurt for Nicolette. Nicolette stood at the window, watched her grandmother like she was a biting dog or a flower she'd been told not to pick. I stood up, reached to Nicolette through the window. She put her hand in mine. Her hand was sticky and buzzed with energy, a beehive hand.

June said, "I'm taking her over to see Houston."

I squeezed Nicolette's hand. "You like that, honeypot?"

Nicolette said, "I aint no honeypot."

She let me put my hand on her hair. I curled my fingers over her ear. I lay my hand against her cheek, and that was too much. Nicolette knocked the hand down, said, "Momma Trish."

My mother turned around. "Hey, baby," she said. "You going to see your papaw?"

Nicolette said, "You can come too."

Momma said, "I can't today, baby. You hug that old goat for me. All right?"

"Yeah," Nicolette said.

June put her hand on Nicolette's shoulder. Our eyes met and June said, "We'll be back."

I nodded. They left. My mother lit another cigarette. In my mind, my mother's coal truck heart T-boned mine, a dreadful crash on an empty stretch of road, all shattered glass and twisted metal, no law, no ambulance in sight. I climbed back through the window, set on the stairs,

The air conditioner roared, and there was no way for Momma to know whether I cried or not.

2

RUCKUS

GENE

When Cora finished lining me out over what to do in That Woman's yard, Brother come got me and we went down to the jail, put twenty dollars on the commissary of this girl from church. I was still inside when I seen Hubert Jewell out in the parking lot. His hair ran across his head in stripes, his eyebrows wadded together like plug tobacco. He was rubbing his arm muscles, which was like rocks. Hubert Jewell wasn't tall, but he wasn't nobody to mess with neither. Cats walked the other way when they seen Hubert Jewell. His nephew, skinny Albert Jewell, stooped to talk in his ear and Hubert turned away. Albert was Dawn's brother. You'd see him in town, moving on all the store girls, gunning his big loud truck through red lights,

GENERALLY RIDING FOR A FALL.

I was going to stand there till they passed, but the jail woman said, "Is that it?" and before I thought, I said it was and went outside.

Hubert Jewell said to Albert, "If you don't know how to do it, you shouldn't do it."

I kept my head down, walked towards Brother's vehicle.

Albert said, "What are you looking at?"

I looked up before I thought and said, "Nothing," then seen Albert Jewell wadn't talking to me. Albert said, "I aint talking to you, old dude," and Hubert said something to him I couldn't hear.

When I got close enough, Brother said, "Get in the damn car." When I did, he said, "What are you thinking? It's a dumbass step in the middle of two Jewells arguing."

Brother fanned the gas, put the vehicle in gear, bounced over the railroad tracks, and threw gravel pulling out on the Drop Creek road.

"They's a hundred women in there," Brother said, pointing at the recovery center next to the jail. "A hundred women separated from mankind. Aint right." When I didn't say nothing to that, Brother spit his chewing gum out the window, said, "I heard Albert say that Tricia Jewell is ratting on Hubert."

I said, "Why would she do that?"

Brother felt of his back tooth with his finger, said, "I'm gonna take them rehab girls some chewing gum."

I said, "I might go back and work some more."

Brother said, "Let's go get some chewing gum for them women."

I said, "We could." Brother stepped on the gas. I said, "But I'd just as soon go work."

Brother looked at me, then at the road. He had his vehicle wound up to where I thought it would fly apart. Brother said, "You're a sight."

Brother took me back over to That Woman's. I started in on the ivy work and yard trimming. That Woman sat at a fold-up table on the porch, wearing a peach-pop tanktop and a flouncy flowerdy skirt, drinking a beer lit up by the sunshine, beer yellow as a caution light, out of a girl-shaped glass. She wrote in the book she was reading. I'd set a load of brush at the bottom of the steps and was heading back up the hill to the backyard. I wadn't going to say nothing, just walk on, get on with my business.

"Say, Gene," she said.

"Say," I said, squinting up at her.

She said, "Be careful," and I thought, shoo, I'd be careful with her, whatever she wanted me to take care with. I went on in the backyard, fired up the weedeater, let myself get lost in that.

Before long, Hubert Jewell come up the steps, Albert trailing behind, looking down at the muscles in his arms. I kept on weedeating. A while later, I seen them go back down. When I got done edging, I cut down ivy a while, hauled it off. I got the work going good enough I could give my mind over to think about things. Spent some time trying to think like a fish, so it'd be easier to catch fish. Thinking about having eyes on either side of my head give me a headache, and I had to stop thinking like a fish, least for a while.

Sun got close to the ridgeline. Bugs started to stir. I went to see if That Woman might still be on her porch. She wadn't, but when I come up the steps, she come out, stood in the empty doorframe, said, "Gene, what are we going to do about a door?"

I said I didn't know. She smiled and blinked real slow. She might have had another beer. I couldn't see it mattered much. She wadn't no drunk. You could see that.

She said, "How much I owe you?" I named a figure and she said, "OK."

She was easy to work with. Always was.

She said, "Do you want a glass of water?" I told her I could drink some water. She wasn't gone a second before she come back with a glass full.

I said, "You want, I could get Brother to hang a new door for you."

She said, "You reckon we could get it done tomorrow?"

I said, "I'm sure we could."

We stood there saying nothing. There's days I go without talking to nobody. I hadn't talked much at all, really, since Easter. Not since Sister died.

That Woman's eyes darted like dragonflies. I felt she had something on her mind, something she wanted to talk about. I figured it had to do with Hubert Jewell coming up there. Figured it had to do with what Brother said about her sister telling on people. That Woman's eyes settled off over my shoulder.

"I start teaching my class Tuesday," she said. "I reckon Monday's the holiday."

I said, "I reckon that's right."

She squeezed hard on the door hinge. I asked her did it bother her to stay there without no door.

"I don't reckon," she said. "Should it?"

I sipped on my water. "I'd keep an eye on you if you like."

She said she didn't need that.

I said, "Let me know. There aint nobody else there at Sister's."

She said, "They gone for the holidays?"

I said, "Something like that."

That Woman set on an old rocking chair with a fake leather seat.

I said, "I seen Hubert Jewell come up here."

The sun went behind the ridge and everything got darker in a way made my head light. In the dim, That Woman's face turned up at me, cool as the air from a coal mine.

She said, "You know him?"

I said, "Not really."

That Woman rocked in her rocking chair. She looked at me awhile and then she looked out over the town, said "Did you ever get in over your head, Gene?"

"Several times," I said. "Mostly out at the lake."

She smiled.

I said,

"Is that right?" That Woman said.

"Like a cinderblock with hair, she said."

That Woman said, "Mine too."

I was getting my talking ability back. I was about to sit down in the other rocking chair next to That Woman when she said, "Well, thank you, Gene," in a goodbye way. She gave me forty dollars. I told her when I'd be back with Brother to get her a door and I went up the hill and back over to where I lived, in the little house out behind Sister's.

DAWN

Friday night, I was going back to Tennessee, to be with my husband Willett Bilson and his parents for 4th of July. Aunt June took me up to Mamaw's, to get the Escort she said I could drive. June had to stay in Canard. Get ready for her college class. She said, "They might have me a job. If I do right." Before we left we went to see my grandfather, Houston Redding.

Houston didn't live up on the mountain no more. He lived in one big room in town. Houston was June and Momma's daddy. Since he'd settled down, they'd let him live in the High-Rise Apartments with all them other old people.

When me, June, and Nicolette got off the elevator in Houston's apartment building, there was a wall covered by a photograph of some Rocky Mountain scene—sharp mountains covered with snow, flowers in the meadow in the

foreground. Nicolette took off down the sticky carpet through the bleach stink
to Houston's door with its ribbons and toilet paper roll firecracker 4th of July
decoration done by somebody feeling good about theirselves for all they'd
done to cheer up old people.

Houston's room was twenty foot square. His bed was in the far corner, in
the shadows beside the window. It was a twin bed had an old quilt on it from
the little house around the bend from my grandmother's, the place she'd chased
him when his loafing and trifling got too constant.

There was a bookcase beside his bed. On top of it set a big boombox. On
the shelves beneath it set plastic boxes each holding ten cassette tapes. There
was twelve of those boxes on the shelves beside Houston's bed. There were
another twelve cassette boxes on the shelf to my right as we come in the room.
There were old dime store frames filled with oranged-out seventies-looking
pictures of my mother and grandmother and Aunt June. They hung next to
black-and-white copies of pictures of musicians in suits and fedoras from the
twenties and thirties, blurred pictures of pictures hanging in the same dime
store frames as the pictures of my mother and aunt and grandmother. A sorry-
looking meals-on-wheels lunch sat on a white foam tray beside the bed—syrupy
pear slices curled together on their side like people died in their sleep, a slab of
meat covered by a morgue sheet of gravy. There was a little kitchen set in from
the rest of the room painted the gold of strip mine mud, had nothing on its
counters but a box of devil food snack cakes and a ceramic man in a sombrero
holding a ceramic basket in front of him. There was a cactus growing in the
basket, placed so as to look like the ceramic man's penis.

Houston said,

Nicolette said, "Who is that?," pointing at one of the black-and-white
pictures, a picture of a man sitting spread-legged on a chair, his mouth a grim

stripe across his face, fancy socks showing where his suit pants had rode up, a banjo across his front.

"What'd you say?" Houston said, loud enough to be heard out in the hall.

Aunt June said, "Look at Houston when you talk to him, honey. So he can hear you."

Nicolette turned, said, "Who's that?," and she slapped her hand flat against the wall below the banjo man with the fedora and the grim stripe of smile.

"Dock Boggs," Houston said. "That's Dock Boggs." Houston marched up close to Nicolette and stuck his face in hers, said "You don't know Dock Boggs?"

Nicolette laughed and grabbed hold of Houston's ears. "No," she said and went to twisting the ears.

Houston turned over a milk crate and said, "Sit down there." Nicolette sat, and Houston pulled out one of the plastic boxes, taking out first one cassette and then another, holding them up to his face, pulling out slips of paper covered in typewritten names of musicians and songs paired the way they had been on the originals in his 78 rpm record collection. He settled on one of the cassettes and put it in his boombox. "You listen to this," he said.

The music was terrible old banjo plunking, singing like they was sparkplugs up his nose. I said, "Aint no way a daughter of mine going to sit still for that." And that's when I learned how I didn't know my own daughter, how rank a stranger she was to me, cause she set there and kept sitting there, fat little fists jammed up under her chin, elbows on her knocked-together knees. She set there and mumbled words to one song after another—no use for the red rocking chair—never had a dollar nor a friend—and Houston just looked at her like, finally here a child that will do right.

I said, "Nicolette, sit up straight," and she didn't even act like I was in the world, and when it switched over from Dock Boggs to Roscoe Holcomb, Nicolette wheeled around said, "That's a different one, Houston. That aint the same one, is it?"

I said, "Nicolette, come on honey. We got to go see your daddy."

Nicolette said, "Can't he come here?"

I said, "No. We got to go back to Tennessee."

Houston said to me, "Why don't you leave her till you get back from Cora's? She'd be good company."

I said, "Nicolette, you want to do that?"

"Yes," she said without looking. "Of course."

Houston said, "Look here," and when Nicolette turned he had a record cover had a skinny old-timer in a straw hat and a khaki shirt on the cover

standing in front of a barn. Houston said, "That's Roscoe Holcomb. That's
who's singing now."

Nicolette took the record cover out of his hands, held it up to her face the
way he'd held the cassette cases up to his, and said, "That's a good-looking man."

Houston laughed his wheezy laugh and I got Nicolette by the chin, said,
"You do what your papaw tells you."

She said, "He aint gonna tell me nothing."

I said, "Well, you do it anyway," and me and June left out of there.

We were halfway down the hall when Houston come out, said, "Misty
Dawn, let me see you for a second," and when me and June come back
towards him, he said, "June, you go on. I need to talk to Dawn a second."

June looked hurt, but she went on. Back in the apartment, Houston took
a pair of green headphones looked like they could've been Jesus's down off
a hook and put them on Nicolette's ears. The foam in them was hard and
crumbly, left black dandruff all over Nicolette's shoulders.

I said, "Houston, I don't want her wearing them."

He hooked his finger at me. Pointed back towards the kitchen, back where
Nicolette couldn't see me. I went in there, Houston right behind me. We about
bumped noses when I turned around.

Houston said, "Tell Cora I had a dream."

His breath was shine and menthol, his nose a skin-covered beak.

I said, "Do what?"

He said, "Tell Cora I had a dream about her. Tell her I dreamed she was
down inside a pumpkin. Stuck to the bottom. She was the candle down in the
jack-o-lantern."

I said, "Houston, stop."

He said, "The face on the jack-o-lantern was mine, Dawn. Her light shone
through my face." Houston grabbed me by the shoulders and shook me.
"Somebody was shaking the pumpkin. They was wind trying to blow out the
light." Houston stopped shaking me. "Do you mind telling her for me?"

I said, "Kind of."

He asked why.

I said, "Cause it sounds crazy."

He said, "Dawn, tell her I'm worried something is going to happen to her.
Tell her I'm willing to come back and look after her. Tell her I'm willing to let
bygones be bygones."

I said, "Houston, she caught you in the backseat of her car in the church
parking lot during Sunday morning services with a girl my age."

"Dawn," Houston said, "that wasn't what it seemed. Cora don't even go to church."

I said,

MAYBE SHE THOUGHT THE SEEMING WAS BAD ENOUGH.

He said, "Dawn, I'm worried about her. That's the truth. The fire was coming out of the top of her head."

I said, "I aint leaving Nicolette here. You lost your mind."

Nicolette hollered from the other room, "Yeah, you are."

He said, "Dawn. Fire. Out the top of her head. I dreamed it clear as day."

I said, "Listen to your music, Nicolette," and to Houston, "Well, what is Mamaw spose to do about what you dream?"

Houston's eyes got runny. His chin quivered. He pulled his jaw in and it got clear his teeth were out. He pecked the edge of a bill against the kitchen counter. He said, "Her hair was so black. Black as coal."

I said, "What are you talking about?"

He said, "Black is the color of my true love's hair."

I said, "Houston, I got to go.'

Houston's shoulders trembled, like a dog after a bath. He said, "There was always fire in her, Misty Dawn."

I said, "Houston, you got to settle down."

He said, "That's why she loved me. I aint scared of womanfire."

I said, "You sure you don't want me to take Nicolette?"

He said, "Promise me, Misty Dawn. Promise me you'll tell her."

"All right," I said. "I promise." Didn't make no difference to me.

Houston pecked the bill envelope against the back of my hand, said, "Hey." I looked up into his watering eyes. He face cracked a smile. He said, "That'd be good."

~~~~~~~~~

JUNE WAITED till she got out of the parking lot before she asked.

"What did he want?"

I said, "Trying to worm back in with Mamaw."

June crossed the new road that went up Drop Creek and into the old middle of Canard. Coal truck blew his horn at us. A city police leaning on his cruiser stared at us. I give him the stinkeye. Another coal truck downshifted, rolled through the stop sign at the corner.

June said, "I wish she would take him back. She just idles up there."

Mamaw used to be good to get up in the face of the coal companies, challenging their mining permits, taking up for people who were getting blasted out of their houses, writing letters for people whose water got turned orange and poison, taking people to see the thousands of acres left bare and unstable— and back around the turn of the century, she and some others won a couple fights. But between the pills and the president, coal had knocked down most of the people willing to say something. People seemed tired out on fighting something big as coal, and though they still talked and had their meetings, it was mostly talk. That summer, Mamaw and this statewide treehugger outfit were lining up movie stars and such to come see what was going on. They'd had a dude in one of those boy bands and an actress who'd been about legalizing dope to come on flyovers. Mamaw paid for them flyovers with money she'd inherited from her sister, who made a bunch of money on coal.

I was proud of what Mamaw did. Houston had backed up Mamaw, when people would talk bad about her, soothing it over, so people would still come to their photo studio. So they could have money to live. It couldn't have been easy. That was what he was talking about at the apartment. Loving Mamaw's fire. When Mamaw got in a scrap, she was a woman on fire. As for that pumpkin shit, I don't know what that was about.

I looked at my phone. I had a missed call from Willett.

I said, "Pull over, Aunt June."

June stopped her car beside the railroad track at the only place for miles my cell phone worked. A bald man sitting on a four-wheeler cried into his cell phone behind us. A woman up ahead hollered into hers about the bad price she got for a bunch of mine batteries.

I called Willett about when we'd be getting to Kingsport. Willett wanted details. His mind don't work right unless it's full of stuff he don't need to know. I told him, "We'll be there when we get there, Willett. I got to help Momma."

I must've sounded cross, cause Aunt June said, "Dawn."

"Willett," I said, "Why don't you take care of yourself, stop worrying about us?"

Willett was at his mother's. She was fixing 4th of July food. Willett's nosiness always got worse when he was at his mother's.

"Dawn," Aunt June said.

"Why you got to take on everybody else?" I said. "Everybody else aint your problem."

Albert said he'd heard people say my mother wore a recorder when she went to buy pills.

"Honey," Aunt June said.

There was a strip of dirt twenty feet wide between the road and the railroad grade. Somebody'd planted four rows of corn in it. The stalks ran sixty yards down the tracks. The corn was tall as Nicolette. I told myself Nicolette wasn't why I got married, but I guess she was.

I was getting heavy, couldn't sit down without fat rolling over my middle, pinching me, making me grouchy. Only people skinny around here are on pills. My mom was skinny as a supermodel, a supermodel needed a good night's sleep.

I got out of June's vehicle, walked down the railroad track. I wished Nicolette was with me. She'd find things on the ground I never would. I turned to look at Aunt June. She stood outside the car, her elbows on the roof. Her head rested on her arms looking down the track at me. The wind turned the leaves upside down and the air looked like grape pop. It was fixing to rain.

"Willett," I said into the phone, "I gotta go. I'm fixing to get hit by lightning. Hunh? Nicolette's with Houston. At his apartment. In the High-Rise. Yes. We'll be there before dark, yes."

The raindrops came in stinging gobs, tiny jellyfish pelting me by the thousand.

I said, "I got to go, Willett."

I hit the red button on the phone and my husband was gone. Thank you Jesus. A trailer set across the road from the train track cornfield. Car wheels filled up with cement all in a row down the edge of the yard kept people from driving in the grass. Outside toys, red yellow and blue, giant dollhouse, purple pink and white, a brokedown trampoline, a rabbit-wire pop-can silo messed with my seeing till I almost missed the woman on the porch, woman way bigger than me, sitting across a kitchen chair in the gloom, chin tipped up, peering over top of the paint-peeling porch rail. I didn't wave at her, and she didn't wave at me.

June came to Canard to try and straighten us all out. She'd been living in Tennessee, but she grew up here.

I DON'T THINK ANY OF US KNEW WHAT **STRAIGHTENED OUT** WOULD LOOK LIKE.

The woman on the trailer porch stood and turned around, her massive shorts thin and pale yellow, spotted and hanging wide around her knees. She swayed as she made her way to the door, a storm door without no glass in it, just a frame. She went in the house without closing the door, and I could see right through her house out a window on the other side, into the summer light, the rain light, dull and serious, the serious business of rain filling the river behind the trailer. Her house was too close to the river, the corn too close to the train track, her too close to me, everything one bad day away from crashing into everything else, one bad day away from getting washed away and ruined.

I was twenty-two years old. It was all ridiculous. I couldn't see no point to it. I looked up into the sky, gray like line-dried bedsheets, tiny jellyfish pouring out of it into my eyes. All I did was think. How could I get rid of Willett? How could I get Nicolette somewhere easier? How was I ever going to lose any weight? Why did this woman have to live so close to the river? Why aint they figured out time travel yet? It never stopped.

I didn't have no more business doing as much thinking as I was doing than a dog did doing the dishes. I had too much to do. But I couldn't stop thinking cause it seemed the world was a blank, a bottle of pills without no directions for use on it. Somebody was asleep at the switch. Somebody was falling down on the job. I wish I knew who it was. I'd go where they work and beat their ass.

June come to my side like I knew she would. She had a raincoat on. I don't think I ever had a raincoat. I'd just stand there dripping and Momma say, "She'll be fine. She aint made of sugar."

"Come on, sweetie," Aunt June said.

My Aunt June's face beneath the bright yellow hood of her raincoat was like the center of a flower, the place where bees go to get what they need, a place made to be touched, but I couldn't touch it.

"Let's go, honey," Aunt June said.

I went with her, back to the car, out of the rain, and the dry beige inside of her clean red Honda car wadn't no solace, nor were the cool turquoise lights of the dash. They were the same no solace as other people laughing when you got cramps. Same no solace as a sunny day on television when you're cold and soaking wet and can't remember your nose not running, your bones not aching, can't remember sleeping through the night.

Twenty-two years old.

I said, "What the fuck, Aunt June?"

She looked at me for a second, stared out the windshield a lot longer. "It's a good question," she said, and started the car. June said, "Is Willett's mother having a bunch of people over for the 4th?"

I said, "Just us I guess. You want to come?"

"No," June said. "I need to get this class figured out."

I said, "Well."

Willett's mother's house was his father's too, but his father was so sick and his mother was such a force that it was easy to say it that way—Willett's mother's house. The fall before, I finally got Willett to move out of his mother's house. I did all right in town, but it was good to get out, get a place of our own, a place where things weren't so fixed up, a place where you could walk down the road without worrying about being accused of doing something, of taking somebody's something, of tearing up somebody's something.

Willett's mother would fix too much. There would be enough meat for twenty people and she would just cram whatever was left in the refrigerator or the freezer and it would stay there until it was no good.

June turned off the highway and headed up on Long Trail, where Mamaw lived, about a mile past where my daddy's people lived in a gob of jacked-up houses against two hillsides and down in a bottom, close enough for constant spying and tormenting of one another. Mamaw lived off by herself, above everything.

We pulled in the carport next to Mamaw's Escort. She came out on the patio, which she did more and more. Ever since I'd gone to Tennessee, Mamaw swore off housekeeping. She ate at the sink, let everything pile up where it fell.

"Have you got Tricia straightened out yet?" Mamaw thought my aunt June too ambitious in her plans to get my mother off dope.

"Mom, you want to come into town and eat, or go to the store?" June said. "You won't have a vehicle until Dawn gets back."

"I don't need it," Mamaw said.

June looked at Mamaw like she was a page of math problems. "Are you sure?" she said.

Mamaw put the key in my hand. "Be careful," she said. "I love you."

I said, "I love you too, Mamaw."

"June," Mamaw said, "You might as well be careful, too."

"I love you, Mom," June said.

Then me and June each got in our vehicles. I went and got Nicolette from the High-Rise and went to Kingsport. June went back to the house in town. And Mamaw went back inside her Mama Bear Wallow.

GENE

Next morning, me and Brother knocked at That Woman's about eight. It was a minute before she come down. When she did, she was pulling a shirt on over another shirt.

I said, "I think we found your door."

"Oh," That Woman said, looking at the big door Brother held in front of him. "Do you think it will fit?"

"Well," I said, "We're thinking it's your door."

The door was the same color as the frame, but the glass knocked out.

"Oh," That Woman said. "Where did you find it?"

Brother said, "At the river."

That Woman said, "What was it doing at the river?"

I said, "Just laying there."

That Woman didn't have no shoes on, said, "Well, Let's take it out in the yard," pointed out towards the side of the house. Then she went back in.

Brother said, "She's a odd one."

Me and Brother took the door out in the side yard. That Woman went down to her vehicle and got out a hose and packed it up the steps. I run to help her, causing the door to slip out of Brother's hands and go sliding down the hill, but me and That Woman and Brother was able to catch it before it run out in the street. We got the door washed and dried off mostly, and it didn't take long to hang since it hadn't been out there by the river but a little while. A little hammering and banging, and we was done.

That Woman said, "What do I owe you?"

Brother just stood there. That Woman looked at me. I said, "Whatever you think."

She got her billfold out and give us eighty dollars, said, "Is that enough?"

We'd of been tickled with half that. Brother started down the steps. We'd told a man we'd help him tear the roof off his mother's house, and I knew Brother was wanting me to help him get it done so he could go to wrestling at the Armory that evening, but That Woman stood there, her hand on that door, looking at the holes where the glass had been. The bugs was flying over the high grass in her yard and I said to Brother, "You go on. I'm gonna finish this yard."

Brother give me a look, but he went on, so it must not have bothered him too bad.

I went to mowing. I was about finished, out in the side yard that evening when Belinda Coates pulled up in front of That Woman's house in her pink Camaro. I was hoping maybe when I got done, me and That Woman would get a chance to talk—talk about how hot it was or how I got one of my injuries. Just whatever she wanted to talk about.

She had the quietest ways, That Woman did. She only wore colors you'd see in the woods, and when she moved her hands, it was like watching birds settle on a phone wire. I liked how there wadn't no ruckus to her, so I was hoping Belinda Coates would leave her alone.

Belinda Coates was short and solid and would have been nice-looking if she wadn't such a terror. You'd probably recognize her from the paper or the detention center website. She didn't have no mother nor father, not that I ever heard of, and she mostly stayed with her uncle Sidney, who kept his name out of the paper fairly well, but we all knew was pretty much behind everything bad they ever put in the paper. And a fair amount of other bad as well.

Belinda sat in that gaudy mess of a car she drove, drumming her fingers on the steering wheel and checking her mirrors. I knew That Woman was in the house, but they wadn't no way I would tell Belinda Coates that. I thought about mowing so the grass would throw on Belinda Coates's vehicle. I thought that might make her leave, but more likely she'd start something up with me, which I didn't have no interest in. I'd done my share of arguing and making a horse's behind of myself, and I was trying my level best to steer clear of such.

I was weedeating under a weeping cherry tree. Belinda Coates started blowing her car horn and That Woman and her yellow dog come out on the screened-in porch to see what was going on.

I knew That Woman thought highly of me because when I stopped to drink a pop she had asked me would I be interested in feeding that dog and taking it for walks when she was gone. That Woman didn't have no man nor kids, not that I could see, and it seemed that dog was near everything to her. I guess somebody who'd had it before had beat on it and tied it up and left it when they moved away and That Woman had saved it, and so she prized it even though it looked like every other yellow dog you'd ever seen.

Belinda Coates took a break from blowing her car horn when she seen That Woman on the porch. Belinda Coates started hollering, "Tricia Jewell, if you know what's good for you, you'll get your ass down here."

That Woman did a lot of cleaning up on her sister Tricia's house. I know because I helped her do it. We packed clothes soaked in toilet water and broken glass and just plain filth down them steps for days. And when That Woman had them haul up some of her furniture from Tennessee to put in that place, I helped pack that stuff up them steps too.

That Woman come out from the screened-in porch and started down the steps, and when she did, Belinda Coates yelled up at her, "Who the hell are you?"

When Belinda Coates did that, the yellow dog stood up on its hind legs so it could see out the porch screen and started barking hard as it could go, rared up like a person, barks booming out over town like the tornado siren. That Woman tried to hush the yellow dog, but she couldn't. She came down a few more steps and said, "I'm June. I'm Tricia's sister. What's your name?"

I had stopped weedeating by then and was standing sideways on the hill facing them, one leg higher up the hill than the other. Hard to stand like that, steep as it was.

"Don't you worry who I am," Belinda Coates said. "Where's Tricia?"

That Woman come down some more, about twelve steps between her and Belinda Coates. That Woman sat down collected and calm, said, "She aint here, honey. I don't know where she is. I wish I did."

Belinda Coates come around the front of her car. She put her hand on the wall at the base of the steps. "I don't believe you," Belinda Coates said. "You're lying. You're just another lying Jewell."

I stepped closer, still packing my weedeater.

"I aint a Jewell," That Woman said, "but I do wish I was lying."

"Tricia Jewell got my daddy throwed in jail," Belinda Coates said.

Belinda Coates was talking about her uncle Sidney Coates.

"She got him throwed in jail and got his money confiscated cause she's a rat snitch and when I find her she's a dead rat snitch. Said my daddy sold her pills and he never did. Never sold her pill one."

That Woman started punching buttons on her cordless phone. That's when Belinda Coates come on up the steps and slapped the phone out of That Woman's hand. That phone went flying, and Belinda Coates busted That Woman right in the side of her face and That Woman tried to stand up but Belinda Coates pushed her back down.

I was still a ways away and they was an unruly hedge between me and them, but I didn't care, because Belinda Coates smacked That Woman in the face again, this time with her other hand on the other side of That Woman's face, and I said, "Hey! You wait right there," and I headed over there, because see,

I HAD A NOTION
I WOULD MAKE A
GOOD HERO
FOR THAT WOMAN.

So I said, "Hey!" again and then when Belinda Coates got a handful of That Woman's hair and started yanking That Woman down the steps, I said, "You stop that now," and stepped right into my weedeater and went chin first into them steps and when I tried to get up, my feet went out from under me and I went tumbling down That Woman's hill and That Woman shouted and I imagined it was because of me, but more likely it was where Belinda Coates was flailing her, but whichever it was, I went over the edge of that wall, which was about a four-foot drop, and landed right on my forehead on the sidewalk in front of That Woman's house.

My forehead split open like one of them TV wrestler's and I sat up and wiped the blood out of my eyes and seen a man from the waterworks grab ahold of Belinda Coates and it surprised me how the bald of his head looked like the head of the lawyer lived next door to where my sister did before she shot herself the morning of Easter past, me trying to get in her locked kitchen door, my arm all bloody through the broken glass of the deadbolt, her all tore up because her husband was gone on pills and had took up with this girl they had known in high school who was also gone on pills. I begged my sister not to do it, her with the gun in her mouth, her who had fixed my meals my whole life, had got me little jobs and made Brother take me on, who read my stuff for me, who begged me to stay out of them payday loan places. I told Sister I couldn't do without her and she shot herself anyway and when she did I had gone to that bald lawyer's house and his wife looked at me through the locked storm door glass and said, "Gene, what's the matter?" and I said, "I need some help with Sister."

As it was, that waterworks man held Belinda Coates by one arm while he got the police on That Woman's cordless, That Woman saying, "No, no, no, we don't need the police, no, no, no," and my head light as dried grass and that dog barking like if it didn't, That Woman would tie her up and move off, and That Woman's beautiful bathtub eyes telling me she didn't need me to be her hero, and that I wadn't never going to be no more to her than the man who mowed the yard. But that didn't mean she didn't need me.

3

AIRPLANE GIRL

DAWN

Friday night, Nicolette slept in her car seat all the way to Kingsport, so I had the sundown light on the dragon-green ridges to myself. When we got out of Canard County, we were in Virginia, and stayed in Virginia for a hour till we got to Kingsport, which is in Tennessee.

Kingsport smelled like something dead you'd left in the car trunk and forgot. The last sun lit the white vapor plumes coming off the paper plant, the shiny new supermarket where the book press had been, the old stone bank on the corner in the middle of town. The chemical plant smokestacks where Willett's dad worked glowed like the lightsticks they throw out to mark the corners of wrecks on the highway at night.

My husband's hometown seemed like more of nothing than anything I'd ever known. People with nothing to talk about but going to work, going to ballgames, eating ice cream, and going to the beach. Nothing.

Willett's mother lived on a broad street in town with big flat front yards, grass like carpet, and trees grown on purpose tall as trees get. The houses were big as schools. His mother's, the smallest on her street, was still plenty big.

It was dark when we got to the house. My nerves were raw and my bones sore. I packed Nicolette to the front door. Her concrete head on my shoulder drove pain into my chest. Willett come to the door keyed up, hair shooting this way and that like shavings off a drunk man's whittling. He smiled with his mouth open, made me want to throw a little fish in it, like they do dolphins in them aquarium shows.

I said, "Hidy." I didn't have any reason to be sore at my husband.

HE WAS LIKE
HE ALWAYS WAS.

But for whatever reason, I was sore at him anyway. Willett hugged me and I let him. It felt OK. He kept it up till I got annoyed. I pushed him off with the hand not holding Nicolette. I set Nicolette down.

Nicolette stood there with her eyes closed. When her father hugged her, she said, "Did you get fireworks?"

Willett looked at me, said, "We got some sparklers."

Nicolette wobbled, eyes still shut, said, "Light them all at once. Be like your hand on fire."

Willett shook Nicolette by her shoulders.

I said, "Don't wake her up, dumbass."

Willett said, "Guess what," his eyebrows bobbing up and down.

I said, "I don't know, Willett. You found a quarter in the sofa?"

"Good guess," Willett said, "but no."

"I'm putting her to bed," I said. "I can't fool with you both at once."

Willett's mother had Nicolette a pallet on the floor in the room where we slept. I flopped her on the bed, and she lay on her belly, claiming as much bed as her stubby arms could.

I found Willett in the kitchen on a hard chair amongst his mother's catalogs and gadgets, sucked into a hippy movie with men on motorcycles and giant moustaches and women with bikinis and flower necklaces on the television set next to her dish drainer.

He said, "Here, look at this," and before I could say, "Here, look at *me*," Willett's mother come in, honeyed up. She said I looked tired and asked if I was getting enough rest.

I said, "I think so."

The phone rang and she answered it "hel-looo," and began telling the person about Willett's father's bowel movements and vomiting, the smoking habits of the nurses at the hospital, how long she spent on the phone with the insurance company. I told Willett I was going to bed.

He said, "You sure you don't want to watch this with me?," his face like a dog in a cage on an animal shelter ad.

I left him there, aggravated at my own meanness. Nicolette was dead asleep. I set on the far edge of the bed and waited for the world to fall. When it didn't, I got in bed and turned to the wall.

I woke to Willett and Nicolette both in the bed with me, to morning light and the sound of Willett's mother coming to get them to go to the 4th of July parade.

Willett's mother asked him did I want to go. I said I didn't and went back to sleep. And so it was me eating the Cocoa Puffs Willett's mother got for Nicolette, me who heard my mother's slurry voice on the answering machine saying she was coming over to spend the afternoon with us.

~~~~~~~~~~

SATURDAY AFTERNOON, me and Willett stood looking out his mother's front room picture window. Willett put his dry hand in mine. Out the picture window, Momma got out of a Jeep with Evie and two guys I didn't know. One was muscle-huge, wore black leather, oily Fu Manchu, faded Def Leppard T-shirt with the sleeves cut out. The other was fat-huge, balding with stringy brown hair trailing off his shoulders, a man-sized pillhead groundhog. Willett turned from the window.

I said, "Where are you going?"

He said, "To check on the fire."

When I opened the door Momma was smiling, gray in the teeth and dark red around the eyes. The other three stood behind her looking at Willett's mother's fancy flowers and yard ornaments. Nicolette came to the door. Momma crouched and wrapped Nicolette in her broomstick arms.

Momma said, "Yall look," over her shoulder. "Beautifuler than I said, aint she?"

Fu Manchu nodded.

"No such a word," Groundhog said, "as 'beautifuler.'"

EVIE LOOKED AT ME LIKE I WAS POISON.

She climbed back in the Jeep. Her knee bobbed.

Willett's mother came down the hall. "Hello," she said. "Welcome. I'm Dorothy, Willett's mother."

No one said anything.

Willett said, "You ready to start cooking?," putting his hands on my shoulders. I shrugged him off.

Fu Manchu said, "We got to go," and got in the Jeep.

Groundhog waddled to the Jeep, started it. Off they went. Willett's mother gave Momma a big hug. Momma hugged her back and come in the house looking high and low at all the old furniture and silver stuff Willett's mother had.

Willett and his mother grilled hamburgers and hot dogs. We ate them on a glassed-in porch in heavy metal lawn furniture painted black with bamboo-printed seat cushions. When we got done, Willett's mom said, "Let's sit and talk," which is what we'd been doing, but she took us in another room to do it some more.

Momma sat on a flying carpet–looking rug on the floor and played with Nicolette with toy soldiers and cars that Mrs. Bilson saved from when Willett was a little boy. Willett come in the kitchen with me. He said things would be all right, but he couldn't know that.

Willett's mom's questions were popcorn popping with nobody watching the microwave. She asked about Hubert and my grandparents and other different ones that had been at the wedding. She asked if anything new was going on in Canard County. Momma didn't answer much, and nothing bad happened, but it was all jangly nerves and dead air.

Willett's mother told him to see if his daddy would eat a hamburger. Willett slipped down the hall, took his daddy a plate in his room. I followed him, but at a distance, watched from around the corner where they couldn't see me. Arthur, Willett's father, turned his head on the pillow, said, "There he is" when he seen Willett.

Willett walked to the bedside and put his hand on the pillow above his father's head. He said, "You want anything to eat?"

Arthur said no. Willett sat down on the edge of his father's bed with the tray on his lap. The window blinds were closed. The light from the reading lamp clipped to the headboard made Willett's dad look turtle-headed. His upper lip came to a point beneath his nose. The remote control for the television lay beneath his hand on the layers of cotton blankets.

Willett asked did he want him to straighten his covers.

Willett's dad said "No, they're OK," and squinted and swallowed slow, like he was hurting. "Maybe when Dawn gets her nursing degree," he said and then stopped, wincing.

"Yeah," Willett said, his voice trailing. "I don't think her heart is in that."

"So what then?" Arthur said in a hoarse whisper. "What does she want to do?"

"Tattoos maybe."

Arthur asked was I any good and Willett said I could be.

Arthur said, "What about . . ." and lifted his hand off the remote and pointed at Willett.

Willett looked at his own pink hands and said, "I like being with Nicolette. Watching out for her."

"That's important," Arthur said. "Kids."

Willett said, "I reckon I'm going to work at the plant. Driving a forklift. In the pellet building."

Arthur asked what shift and Willett said, "Screech's, right now."

Willett's father nodded.

There was a commotion in the living room and Nicolette let out a squeal. Willett turned his head to the door and then back to his father.

Arthur said, "Go on."

Getting a job at the plant. That was Willett's guess-what.

～～～～～～

MOMMA SAID, "Come on, little airplane girl," and took Nicolette's hands and started to spin. Nicolette laughed and her feet lifted into the air. Momma coughed and let go of one of her hands. Nicolette squealed as her other hand slipped free. She crashed into a big cupboard thing of old toys and antiques Willett's mother had set up. Old, old Santa Clauses went flying everywhere. Corner of the cupboard caught Nicolette above the eye, and blood ran in her brow. Nicolette stood herself up and ran straight back to Momma.

I said, "Nicolette, come over here."

Willett put his arm around Momma. Momma put her head on Willett's shoulder, fake shocked. Willett's mom went to Nicolette, pushed her hair back, took her and put a Band-Aid on her brow. Momma went behind her, asking Mrs. Bilson did she have some kind of ointment nobody ever heard of.

Momma's carrying on scared us like when a truck goes too close by you walking at night. No time for fear till it was over. We were so shook when Momma asked to come with us back to the trailer, we didn't have the wits to make up a reason to say no.

～～～～～～

MOMMA had never asked where we live before and we never told her. On
the way there, she stared out the backseat window of Willett's hand-me-down
Buick, fluttered her eyes at Nicolette's trying to get her time.

Nicolette grabbed hold of her shirtsleeve, wanting to know Momma's
favorite cartoon, wanting to know had she been in an airplane. "Say, Momma
Trish. Say."

An edge come on Momma's voice could've cut a pop can in half. Said, "I
don't know, goddammit. God Amighty, Dawn."

I said, "Nicolette, leave her alone." What I wanted to say is,

But I didn't.

"Tricia," Willett said, "you need me to stop?"

"Need you to stop talking," she said. Momma stayed grim and tight, but she
didn't lose it. Then about a mile later, Momma said, "Stop there."

She went in the bathroom at a filling station. She was gone a good fifteen
minutes.

Willett said, "I'm worried about her."

I said, "I'm worried about her and those guys knowing where we live."

"She aint doing too good, is she?" Willett whispered, "She looks like she
might jump out of her skin."

"How would she do that?" Nicolette said, looking scared the first time all
day. "How would she jump out of her skin?"

I said, "She aint gonna jump out of her skin," pounding Willett hard on the ball
of his shoulder. I said, "Don't say stupid shit like that in front of her. It don't help."

Momma came back to the car, wiping her mouth, and we went on to
the trailer.

OUR TRAILER set in a quiet park with a creek run through it outside Kingsport. Willow trees stood waiting for kids to chase in and out amongst the whips of their branches. There were trees stout enough for tire swings and plenty of room between the trailers, like you wouldn't see nobody do now. Now everything is stacked tight, cracker boxes crammed on a shelf in a jammed-up dollar store.

We walked in the trailer to Groundhog lying on his side, barely on the sofa he was so huge, his shirt off and sweating, sucking his thumb, eyes opening and closing slow. The TV blared the bells and screams of a game show. Slobber ran down Groundhog's wrist.

I said, "Get off my sofa, you nasty fuck."

Momma said, "Where's the bathroom?"

I said, "Take her, Willett. Watch her."

Momma said, "God Amighty, Dawn."

I said to the couch, "Get your fatshit ass out of my house." Groundhog rolled over away from me. I slapped both hands on his arm to drag him off, but he was so sweatslick, I lost hold. I gouged my fingernails into him, rolled him off onto the carpet. Shook the whole trailer when he hit. Fu Manchu laughed from my kitchen. Everything in the refrigerator was out on the counter. Mustard splattered like paintball on the floor. Bread stacked up outside the bag seven slices high.

I said, "God Almighty." So as not to cry I started kicking Groundhog. Fu Manchu laughed and shoved his mouth full of potato chips. I started stomping Groundhog. I said, "Get up." He curled up like a ball.

"Get him out of here," I said to Fu Manchu. When he didn't do nothing, I said, "Don't bother me to call the law, motherfucker. Get him up."

Fu Manchu said, "Evie let us in. She had a key."

I said, "What?"

Fu Manchu said, "We're invited guests."

I said, "I didn't give Evie no key."

Evie come up the hall. "Yeah you did," she said. "You sure as hell did."

"Get the fuck out of here," I said. "Before I blow the hell out of all of you."

Groundhog said, "I'd like you to blow the hell out of me."

I pulled a piece of old shower curtain rod out from under Willett's chair. I rared back to bust Groundhog over the head with it. Fu Manchu come up behind me and snatched the rod from my hand. He shoved me over top of Groundhog. I fell headfirst onto the sofa. I turned to get up but Fu Manchu shoved me back down. Groundhog got up. They stood over me, a stone wall of suck. Cool air come off Fu Manchu, like an open icebox. He drew the shower curtain rod back like he was gonna backhand me.

I started crying. I wasn't scared of getting hit. I was grieving. Grieving for my lost house, my lost safe spot. I cried cause my baby's private place, my quiet place, the peace place where me and Willett might be able to work things out was gone.

You don't know, do you? You don't know what it's like to never want anything cause you don't have a way to keep it safe.

EVERY SINGLE THING IN MY LIFE GOT BROKE.

Or stole. Or lost. Every chair in pieces. Every rug pissed on. Every glass and plate and toy and pretty little thing on every shelf shattered. You don't put your hand down in the cushion of your burnhole sofa cause you'll come back with your finger cut on bottle glass or a needle or tin can lid. Blood beading like a superball cause can't nobody give a shit.

But our house hadn't been like that. It wadn't perfect like Willett's mother's, but it was ours and it was nice cause none of my family knew where I lived.

Fu Manchu went back to the kitchen, lay that curtain rod on the counter. He took out his hog-sticker lock blade. He cut summer sausage into little pieces and he raked them off the counter into his hand. He threw them in his mouth like they were my baby's teeth. He stared at me.

I said, "GET OUT."

Fu Manchu said, "I heard you before." He was bigger than the refrigerator. I felt like one sweep of his arm might knock my house down.

Groundhog crashed to the floor, set with his back against the sofa. Willett come back down the hall, Nicolette hanging on his leg. She went to Groundhog and put her hand on his face. She said, "Momma said leave, Slobberface."

Groundhog raked his arm and caught Nicolette in the side of the knee, knocked her down, which was enough for Willett and he set into kicking Groundhog, saying "Don't you ever, EVER touch her." Which we all stood and watched till Momma come out of the bathroom, bolting down the hall like a wiener dog shot out of a cannon, and Evie said, "This is stupid" and grabbed the Jeep keys off the counter and left out.

The rest, Momma included, filed out after Evie. Nicolette dragged a chair to the sink and filled up a squirt gun I'd been using to train the cat to stay off the counter and out of my spider plants. I didn't make a move to stop her, nor did I when she went running out the door straight as a string, pointing the squirt gun dead ahead of her. Willett grabbed the squirt gun as she turned sideways and slipped past, and I finally did stand up.

"Here, girl," Momma called from the front seat of the Jeep.

Nicolette ran to her grandmother. Willett stood there, pointing Nicolette's squirt gun at Momma, his finger on the trigger. Momma hugged Nicolette and the Jeep started moving before she set her down. But she did get her set down before they took off, and then Momma was gone in a cloud of gravel dust.

I WOKE up that night alone in bed. Willett's snoring came through the closed bedroom door. I got up and went down the hall. Willett's legs curled on the sofa. The streetlight on the corner lit up the room. On the table next to him was the blue folder holding his new hire papers.

I sat down on the edge of the couch and opened the folder and held the direct deposit form to the light, did the same with the medical plan papers. The credit union papers. The paper explaining how Willett gets time and a half for all hours over eight worked in a shift, double time for all hours over twelve. The employee newspaper. The sign-up form for the employee softball league. The menu from the employee cafeteria. The membership card for the employee recreation center. After all this time. My husband. An employee. I stacked the papers and my heart hammered like somebody beating on the wall when you're making too much noise in your motel room. I put the papers in the blue folder, took them out and held them to the light again. I closed the folder and moved to the chair facing Willett. He lay on his side with his eyes open.

"Permanent," Willett said.

I said, "That's good, right?"

"Right," Willett said.

I said, "Come to the bedroom," and went and checked on Nicolette. Then I got in bed. Time I fell to sleep, I was still alone.

TUESDAY MORNING, I lay in the bed staring into a pile of clothes and a pencil drawing I did right after high school of six lady astronauts. Light filtered through the pink sheet covering the window. Willett's arm draped across my stomach. I took his hand in mine. He snored like a little baby cow.

I moved out from under Willett and sat up on the side of the bed and began to fold clothes. Willett's band T-shirts. His boxer shorts. A wet pair of my jeans. I got two wire hangers out of the closet, hung the jeans on them, and hung the hangers on the new shower rod. Willett stirred as I come back in the bedroom.

He said he loved me and I said I loved him. I went to Nicolette's room and closed one eye, held the drawing of the lady astronauts up to a blank wall, wondered would Nicolette like me to paint her a mural of the lady astronauts.

I got my navy-blue pants out of the laundry bag, dressed standing in the kitchen. I pulled a powder-blue button down shirt out of the bag, smoothed it out best as I could. I worked at a copy shop. Had been for a while. It might be that when Willett's pay from the plant started piling up I'd be able to quit.

I opened one of my schoolbooks for nursing. Two hundred dollars for a book. Now Willett had a job like the ones his father and his grandfather and uncles and some of his aunts and a lot of his cousins had kept their whole working lives. I'd seen the pins on their lapels, on their blouses, in the pictures in the halls of their brick houses. Twenty-year pins. Thirty-year pins. Forty-year pins. He could be there forever. I could be whatever. I could be new. I could be not a nurse.

Willett rose and stretched. When he did, he knocked the lamp beside the bed off into a pile of towels on the floor.

"Goddamn, Willett," I said, but I couldn't be mad at him. I set the lamp back up, got the towels and shirts and stuff, and put them in a basket.

Willett moved the lamp aside looking for his work pants, which lay hanging over an aquarium had three pitiful guppies left floating around in it. Willett whistled and bobbed his head in his own little going-to-work world.

~~~~~~~~~

WORK THAT day at the copy shop was church bus slow. They sold office supplies at that copy place, so I went and opened a thing of scissors and got a bunch of magazines and cut pictures out of them. I cut out a movie star pushing a baby stroller, acting like she didn't want nobody to know it was her, when obviously she did, or she wouldn't have on the hiding-out-movie-star costume. Black sunglasses and a tight, showing-off-fake-boobs T-shirt and a hundred-dollar baseball hat like you see rich women wearing when they run out on the bypass, ponytails bouncing, trying to act like they're in Lexington. Then I found a big old picture of a pit bull, its mouth full open, looking like a shotgun wound with teeth, its head filling up both pages of a magazine spread. I cut that out and lay it next to fake hiding movie star, and it looked just like that dog was going eat both her and her baby clean up. That made me feel better, and I was fixing to go get a glue stick and glue them to a big piece of paper and then draw some stuff around it for Nicolette, leaving her space to make up a story about them or whatever, when this bunch of women with helmets of hair, all in yellow and pink and flowerdy print dresses with sunglasses big as Big Mac boxes, their bare arms like those long skinny loaves of bread French guys carry around on the back of their bicycles, their teeth white as mall toilets.

They was fixing to have a church bazaar which I don't even know what that is and they wanted a flyer to hand out to their friends and they wanted to know what kind of paper I thought they ought to put their church bazaar flyer on and so I got out fifty million different paper samples for them, and one of them said, "That lime's too hot," and another one said, "That pink looks tacky," and they finally said, "Honey, what do you think?" like they were doing me some big favor to ask and I said I didn't have no idea, and then I wondered to myself how many chomps it would take a pit bull to bite one of their heads off and I thought if you took their hair off first, a dog might could do it one chomp, and I was thinking such not because I cared one way or the other, but because they kept debating and debating about their paper color, and wouldn't never stop, and so I thought, you know, their heads are actually pretty small if you take the hair out of consideration, and so I was looking at my pit bull picture and then back at the small-headedest one of them, when the biggest one said they'd decided. I took out my order pad and she fished out a piece of paper from the fifty million samples all over the counter and she said, "We'll take this one. What do you call this one?"

And I said,

Which was like the most boring, obvious thing they could have possibly chosen. I didn't say nothing. Or maybe I did, but if I did it wasn't anything real bad, just like "I'll be damned" or something like that, and probably said it under my breath, but they give me a funny look and said, "If you don't want

our business, you can tell your manager we took our business elsewhere," and
I said, "I am the manager," because the stupid boy who was the manager was
with his stupid friends staring out the front window of the shop, not paying a
speck of attention to what was going on, and so them women left and I just
said, "Bow-wow-wow-yippy-yo-yippy-yay" to the back of their helmets of hair,
and went back to thinking about Willett's blue folder and all his employee-ness
and how the world was my goddam oyster.

$$\sim\!\sim\!\sim\!\sim\!\sim\!\sim$$

WHEN THEM women left, it got quiet and everything was fine till I had
to change the toner on one of the big main copiers. I spilled that toner
everywhere—on the carpet, down in the copier, all over the job I was copying,
all over myself. The manager and the two other boys working my shift blew
snot laughing. They all went to the state university in town. They made fun of
me, how I talked, the way I drug out my words.

"Fuuuuuck," I said, when the toner got on my face and hair.

They had a time laughing at my dustyass face, but after a minute they went
back to wishing for cars they seen in the parking lot. I went back to cleaning up
after myself and wishing them dead. The lights in that place were gray as the
carpet on the floor and the paint on the walls, and didn't none of it ever change,
morning noon or night. The boys laughed and talked about vomiting in public,
and the fat funny-looking country kids in their classes. I got out the big vacuum
cleaner that place had—it was big and gray too—and went to sucking up that
toner powder. They were laughing louder than the vacuum. Laugh it up, boys, I
thought. Cause it wouldn't be much longer. In a minute here, I'd be working for
extra money, not bill money. And maybe I wouldn't be working at all.

When I finally got that mess cleaned up and the clunky-ass vacuum cleaner
put up, I went back to copying. I was copying some book I knew was copyright
violation but the boys had give me ten of the forty the guy needed it copied
give to them. So I had the copier going top up. The light went straight to the
back of my eyes, and hurt.

The copier was going ca-chunk ca-chunk ca-chunk ca-chunk. The bell on
the door rang. The toner had got up my nose. That toner powder was like
coal dust. But it wasn't. It was clean. Even though it messed everything up, it
was clean, an indoor mess. It made me miss everything home, home like it was
before Daddy died. Made me miss a genuine mess. Made me miss Momma
making Daddy change clothes at work, making him shower at work, when his
mines had a shower, so he didn't come home covered in mine mud and dust.
He'd have his work clothes in garbage bags. I'd see how dirty that work was

when she'd do the wash. But he didn't track it through Momma's house, not when we all lived in the trailer out on Long Ridge.

That toner powder added to how I felt that day. I didn't want to go home, I didn't at all want to live at home, didn't want to live in Kentucky. But in that moment, on that day, I sure did want to *be* home.

All the sudden I was tired of being inside, tired of being in town, tired of being swallowed up in gray. Despite all my family's crazy shit, I wanted to be back there.

I couldn't help it. I wished someone would come in smelling of moss. Smelling of woodsmoke. I wished someone would come in smelling of game and grease and cigarettes and gasoline. Paint. Even if somebody would come in smelling of paint, that'd be enough. Not likely here. People come in the copy shop were people living on paper, on presentations, on handouts, on printing for eight cents a page, on Internet access two dollars for ten minutes. I stood over the copier, light strobing my face. I could feel the customer behind me, but I didn't turn around, cause if I did, the customer would be my customer. Let one of them chatty boys do the talking with the customers. But this customer come in with a smell I couldn't figure out.

Ca-chunk ca-chunk ca-chunk.

B.O. and wet dogs was part of it.

Ca-chunk ca-chunk ca-chunk.

There was chewing tobacco in it.

Dawn, I said to myself, don't turn around.

Ca-chunk ca-chunk ca-chunk.

"Hey girl," the customer said.

Ca-chunk ca-chunk ca-chunk.

"Turn around here."

Ca-chunk ca-chunk ca-chunk.

Orange juice and honey.

Ca-chunk.

"Say," the voice said.

Ca-chunk.

"Can't you hear no more?" I knew who it was.

Ca-chunk.

I smelled my granny Jewell's moonshine recipe.

"Say."

Ca-chunk.

"Turn around here, you big tall thing."

Beep beep beep.

It was my brother Albert.

Beep beep beep. Something was wrong with the copier.

Albert said, "You need help with that thing?"

Beep beep beep.

I turned to the counter. There stood Albert, stringy and brown, a big blue slushee in his hand.

I said, "What are you doing here, Albert? How'd you know where I was at?" I stacked and restacked the papers on the counter without taking my eyes off Albert.

Albert's rat eyes twinkled like gas in a mower can. He said, "Hug?"

I come around the counter, motioned for Albert to follow me. He spread his arms wide as I went out the door into the parking lot.

He said, "No hug?" with a grin like a tent zipper.

Albert's bird-yellow pickup set in a handicapped spot with its "Army of One" bumper stickers in the back window under the two-foot-tall stickers spelling out "REDDNEKK" in gothic letters. Silver flames run back from the front wheel wells. Under lights. Tail lights blacked out. Pins holding the trunk down. Extra gauges ran up from the dashboard, which was spraypainted a lime green. Albert could waste money like nobody's business.

He said, "Where's your queerbait husband?" His head filled the truck's opposite window. Albert backed up and grinned.

I walked back towards the copy shop.

"What's the matter? Aint you gonna hug me?"

I said, "You got a woman. Go hug her."

Albert laughed with his arms wide open.

My dark face in the glass of the copy shop door could have told me. There is no way to make your family disappear. Nor was I ever going to know peace with mine. Hubert's face filled the glass next to my face.

Hubert said, "Where's your momma?"

I said, "Yall get out of here. This is my work."

"Your mother needs to call me," Hubert said.

I didn't even have the urge to say how pissed off I was, to tell Hubert to leave her alone, leave me alone, leave Tennessee alone. Hubert got me by the arm and jerked me around. I said, "Get your fucking hands off me, Hubert."

He said, "I need your help, Dawn." Hubert's eyes was like the front end of bullets. "She's gonna get herself killed."

I said, "What am I supposed to do? Blink three times and make her appear?"

I could feel them asshole drips watching me from inside. Sweat was running in Hubert's eyes. He looked like a bottle of orange pop just come out of a cooler in some old store.

"Just hold her," Hubert said. "If you see her, hold her."

I met Hubert's bullet eyes with my own.

IF I SEE HER

I SAID.

Albert put a *Canard County Bugle*, our newspaper, in my hand. As usual, there was a big drug bust on the front page. And there in big color pictures above the fold was Groundhog and Fu Manchu, cuffed and not even trying to hide their faces. Hubert and Albert got back in the truck.

I said, "Hey," and Albert started the truck. I ran up to Hubert's window. He rolled it down. I said, "Did Momma rat on them two?" and pointed at the paper.

Hubert said, "I don't know. Why don't you blink three times and ask her?"

Then they were gone. I went back in the copy shop. The boys were behind a row of shelves, but I heard them.

"Her boyfriend," one of them said.

"I thought it was her brother," another said.

"Probably both," said the third, and then come the laughing.

I run as hard as I could, put my shoulder into them shelves. There was twelve foot of them hooked together. They went over easy and I caught all three of them dicks under it. They were rocking the shelves trying to get out, but I stood up on the flipped shelves, like a surfer, them hollering, hurt, while the desk calendars and candy bars went flying. I stomped till one of them cried and then I walked out of the store.

4

~~~~~~~

DRY IT UP

DAWN

I didn't answer the phone when work called Wednesday morning. I was done copying.

"Well," Aunt June said when I told her, "why don't you come take my summer class?"

I was sitting up in bed when she asked me. I put the phone in my lap. Cause I don't want to, I didn't say. I also didn't say this:

Aunt June was wanting to make a difference teaching them classes at the community college, and I'm sorry, Aunt June, but I'm afraid what you're doing don't. There were photographs by the thousands mounted on the walls in the building where Aunt June taught—photos she and her students put there the summer before, photos taken with throwaway cameras by kids and church people, by everybody in Canard County, pictures of endless mamaws standing at stoves stirring skillet bottoms skimmed with gravy, people standing out front of trucks with their fighting chickens balanced on their arm, feathers pluming down, grandfathers and grandchildren with guns, endless trailer underpinning backdrops, endless four-wheelers, photos of baptism hot tubs, children holding hot dogs and plastic tigers, plastic cups, plastic motorcycles, little plastic men with flowing plastic hair wearing plastic wrestling tights, pictures of people in the dollar store, children sitting in tires, children looking bored in school, looking bored behind cyclone fences in the yards of coal camp houses, children wallering in piles on brokedown trampolines, old men on couches with their eyes closed and their forearms resting on the top of their heads, a hillbilly parade, and it did give you something—I won't deny it gave you something—but I don't know. I don't know, Aunt June.

I DON'T THINK IT DOES ANYTHING.

So I sat in Kingsport Wednesday. Sat in Kingsport and wondered had my mother scored. Had she found her pills? Had she really snitched like June said Belinda Coates said she had? Was she really about to get killed like Hubert said? Momma might deserve killing. She might. I don't know. So I sat at the trailer.

The only thing cheered me up was the thought of Willett tooling around the factory floor in a forklift hauling plastic pellets to and fro. Corporal of industry. My plastic man. That blue folder full of employment papers sparked up my why-I-like-Willett. I was feeling good and warm, about that anyway, when Willett showed up in the back doorway, sawed off at the waist where we didn't have no back steps.

I said, "What are you doing home?"

He said, "I have to train before I can work. The trainer got sick. They sent me home. Go back Friday, they said."

I asked if they were still paying him.

"Yeah," Willett said, climbing into the house. "Can you believe it?"

A pretty song came on the radio. A woman sang high and content in a voice had a cup of tea waiting when the song was over. I took the cap off a Pepsi. Willett opened a packet of instant oatmeal lying on the counter. He sang along with the cup-of-tea woman.

I said, "You're in a good mood."

Willett said, "I am," and stuck his head in the refrigerator. He come out with the milk. "The baby still at Mom's?" he said.

I said she was.

Willett said, "Maybe she could stay over there tonight."

I said, "She could."

Willett said, "Maybe after while we can get out the baby pool."

I took the cap off my Pepsi, said, "Maybe so."

A car raced by, loud. Somebody doesn't have a job, I thought. Not like us. Not like Willett. Willett put his oatmeal in the microwave, went to the bedroom and changed into his favorite shorts, came back, and lay down on his belly in the TV room and ate his oatmeal. Willett's shorts were shiny and baby blue and hung below his knees. There on our dingy gray carpet, his butt looked like the sky clearing after a snowstorm.

Willett got up and sat down at the computer. He downloaded an mp3. Music pumped from the speakers. Willett turned the volume down and the speaker fell behind the computer. Willett got off the chair and the chair fell over. Willett kneeled, stuck his head under the particle-board computer desk.

Willett's butt crack rose up out of his shorts like a sea serpent coming up out of the ocean of his behind. The song on the computer wailed on. I fingered the flash drive hanging around my neck held the emails Willett sent me when we were courting. I kept that hanging around my neck because Willett was liable at any moment to bring that computer crashing to the ground,

Me and Willett met cause Willett played music on a radio station I listened to. His family ran the station. It was on the mountain named for his daddy's family on the back end of Scott County, Virginia, and it broadcast into Canard. Bilson Mountain Radio was pretty much all volunteers. They played what they wanted. Mamaw and Houston listened to the old music they played. Mountain music. And Mamaw liked the hippie meditation shows from California and troublemaker news shows from New York City they ran.

Willett's half-brother Kenny, the one June fooled around with, played lots of punk rock and weird music shows. I listened to them. I liked music my friend Decent Ferguson called "murder music," old stuff like Bikini Kill, Sonic Youth, Malignant Growth. And because Willett had to do just what Kenny did, he played murder music. And so I listened to Willett on the radio too.

Willett's voice is terrible. He sounds like a clothes dryer needs greasing. He made a lot more sense as somebody to be with when he started writing me. He wrote humongous letters. I still have them. I wont tell anybody where. Pretty soon after we started writing, email started. I have all my emails from him gathered up on a Xena the Warrior Princess flash drive he brought me back from a comic book thing he went to in Chattanooga. I wore that flash drive around my neck for a long time, strung on a shoestring I got off one of Daddy's mining boots.

Those emails had stories about Willett traveling to see bands with his friends from college, stories about him being in New York City and Atlanta and Nashville and Massachusetts. There were stories about him being in Italy and London, all the time seeing bands and sleeping in parks and dumpsters. After while he got a scanner and he'd scan pictures of himself in all those places, and the more stuff he sent, the more I could see myself a part of all that.

Also, he wore me down. When I first met him, I didn't much care for him. He was sweaty and sticky, still is, even though he doesn't do much with his body. But he just kept liking me, kept remembering what I told him, kept bringing me things couldn't help but please me. Like, somehow or other, he was the best at getting me makeup, and good at putting it on me. He'd do my eyes better than I could, which was weird cause in most things had to do with using your hands, he was a total clod. One time it took him an hour and a half to change the wiper blades on the car, and even then he tore them up and Albert had to steal some off another car at the Kingsport mall parking lot and put them on for him. Willett's dad said Willett could tear up an anvil.

Anyway, he could do eye makeup. Our best date ever was one Halloween he made me up to be a hot Frankenstein woman, green but hot, and I really was hot. Boys that always made fun of me and call me Lurch and stuff just stood and looked at me all night long at that party and would try and talk and couldn't think of a thing to say, just ask if they could feel of the bolts on my neck.

So stories of all that and memories of all that was in Willett's emails. That's why I kept them on a flash drive around my neck. So they wouldn't get messed up. And they didn't for a long time.

Willett banged his head on the underside of the computer desk. I said, "Willett, get up out of there."

Willett said, "It's good to be back in shorts. I treasure their satiny comfort." Willett stayed on the floor. He pulled his bowl of oatmeal to him. He reached me a pizza coupon he'd found behind the desk. "Two for one," he said. "Still valid," he said.

Willett called the pizza place lying there in the mess. I went and got the pizza, never said a thing about quitting my job. Two for one.

~~~~~~~~~

THE FISH on the bottom of the plastic kiddie pool were blue and purple and blended with the blue of the pool. Their eyes matched the bubbles that came from their lips. Me and Willett lay in the pool, packed shoulder to shoulder. I put my arm around him.

I said, "What are you thinking, boy?"

He said, "If you have to work, I might go to Virginia in the morning."

Willett loved to hang out at the radio station his half-brother Kenny and his papaw started back in the eighties. It was about an hour from Kingsport, between there and Canard.

I looked at the side of Willett's head. "Is that right?"

He said, "Mm-hm. Maybe I'll take Nicolette."

A butterfly shadow passed over us.

Willett's eyes run over my legs. "You want to go?"

I said, "I got to work." I was feeling softer towards Willett, but when the chance for a day alone kisses you on the lips, you kiss it back.

Willett looked at me like I was doing him a favor. He said, "You care if I go?"

I said, "I don't guess." I stood up and the water run down my legs. I picked up the empty pizza boxes, put on my flip-flops, and turned to Willett, said,

DURING THE summer, Willett's mother would get up early on Saturday morning and go down to the parking lot next to the library in downtown Kingsport to where farmers brought stuff to sell. Tomatoes and corn and beans. Watermelons. Peppers. Willett's mother came by and brought us stuff. She brought us beans she'd cooked. Real buttery. They made me miss when I was little and Daddy's mother was around or when we'd go see her in North

Carolina when she left Green, Daddy's dad. She cooked garden stuff. I liked it but never got it enough to get used to it.

Willett's mother left and I got the vegetables ready. And I made chicken tenders with Grippo's powder on them. I made a Cool-Whip-and-crushed-up-Oreo dessert. It was nice. We sat at a picnic table under a willow tree behind our trailer and ate. We stayed until the mosquitoes ate us up. Bit us through the Off! We went in the trailer front room and talked about getting a real house but also about how it was nice at this trailer park, quiet.

It got dark, and the booger lights came on in the park. I pulled back the curtains and let the pale orange light into the trailer front room. Willett took off his shirt and flung it over by the television. He flopped out on his belly. His back was a wad of meat, eggshell skin specked with moles and pimples. He spread his legs and I got down on my knees between them. I had me a felt tip, and with little jabby strokes I drew a giant dandelion exploding across his back.

I liked to draw on Willett's back. I'd always done it. I'd draw a picture on his back, and then a day or two later I'd get in the shower with him and scrub it off. One time I drew a whole field of dandelions on him. Another time a penny, gigantic Lincoln staring into Willett's underarm. Once a cuckoo bird, its wings spread from one edge of his back to the other. The Radio City Music Hall Rockettes. Daniel Boone, large. Different dogs from the trailer park, large. The local dairy bar. I drew trees remembered from home. Paintings from my Art 100 book. Icebergs when I wanted to move to Antarctica. I was constantly looking for something to draw on Willett's back. A microscope slide of gonorrhea. Whatever.

While I was drawing the big dandelion, Willett clicked around the Internet, the monitor and keyboard on the floor in front of him. We didn't talk much. The light faded, and Willett stretched his hand back towards mine. With his other he kept clicking, played a song by the Dead Kennedys. I stopped drawing to take Willett's hand. Then I let go and drew the seeds blown from the dandelion. And that's how we did when we got along.

〜〜〜〜〜〜〜〜

THURSDAY MORNING Willett left early to go to Virginia. A short man with a long beard across the way had a pile of bicycles behind his trailer. A black pickup pulled up full of more bicycles. Longbeard got in the bed of the truck and threw bicycles onto the pile. I was still in my pajamas. I walked out and asked Longbeard if he had a bicycle that worked. He said he did. He went to a shed beside the trailer and took out a black-and-red trick bike. I asked could I borrow it. He said I could. I rolled up my pajamas so they wouldn't get caught in the chain. I pedaled around the trailer park. I got out on the side road and went deeper into the hillside, past small little houses with lots of flowers in cut-up tires with their flared-out rubber petals.

Going up the holler behind our trailer park, my knees banged against the bicycle handlebars. Dogs barked at me. Little black ones. Big white ones. Long-haired ones three and four colors apiece. One little rooster dog ran up and down the cyclone fence marking his yard, barked crazy like he hated me, like I was going to kill his family and burn their house. That rooster dog made me nervous for what might happen to Momma, because maybe somebody was about to kill her, and maybe I should be barking. Maybe I should be a barking dog running up and down a fence line making a racket to warn somebody, to show I cared, to show I deserved feeding. With Momma, nobody mentioned calling the law. Momma was already a snitch, already working for the law, so they were probably mad at her as anybody else for running off. All her family and friends were either doped up and confused or ignorant and sober and couldn't do anything.

On top of the dogs barking, there were bugs buzzing and humming everywhere. By the million. The mist burned off fast. The sun came burning through the gaps in the trees the way it never would in a holler at home. Always some way in Tennessee for the sun to get in, even in the morning.

The houses were brick, or had nice siding on them. They had floweredy bushes and concrete deer and iron porch rails. The trailers had shingle roofs on them, and carports built to them, so as not to look like trailers. There was more money here. Even the people who didn't have much had some. How does that happen?

On up in the holler, houses got smaller and the road began to wind up. Houses started having little wood shed buildings and vehicles with shredded blue tarps over them out in their yards. The vehicles were green with mold and orange with rust, because the sun stopped getting in that part of the holler.

At the last house I saw before the blacktop gave out, before the road turned steep and grown up in weeds and garbage, there was a doghouse with a flat shingled roof. Moss grew at the shingles' edge. A white dog with a brown spot like a saddle on its back lay on the mossy roof. The dog was chained, and watched me, its chin across its folded paws, paws hanging off the front edge of the house. The dog eyed me, but it didn't bark. Skin hung off its eyeballs, showing the white part of its eyes, and its saggy red socketskin. The peoples' house was dark, the screens in its windows and doors full of holes and peeling. All the vehicles in the yard were being used for storage. The dog rolled over, showed its belly to me. It was a momma dog, but there was no sign of its pups. No sign of the people supposed to be at the house. The dog lay her head back away from me, left her titted up belly facing me. She sighed. I wished she could talk.

I was about back to the trailer when Hubert met me in a Lincoln Continental had been the color of a winter night sky new but had turned the color of dirty miners' coveralls. Albert was in the front seat beside him. Evie was in between them.

He said, "Where you going?"

I said, "Leave me be, Hubert."

He said, "They gonna kill your mother."

I said, "No they aint."

He said, "Come with me."

I said, "Come where?"

Hubert said, "Out to the lake."

Albert leaned up, said, "Going to water."

~~~~~~~~~~

HUBERT DIDN'T hang out much with anybody, except when he needed to decide something. And then he would have a party. Or if it was summer, a picnic. The word would go around. A place would get named, and where Momma was the closest thing to a wife Hubert had, she'd get told and would go early and Hubert would start a fire on his big grill and me and Momma would make hamburgers and keep making hamburgers and Hubert's brother Filbert who was a biker would bring all the other stuff and there would be food and yelling and screaming and throwing of garbage cans. I never would see Hubert talk to anybody, just wander around, lipping beer off his moustaches, watching people get wild. Finally Hubert would figure out what he was trying to figure out and sometimes he would leave and sometimes he would make everybody else leave. Sometimes the law would come and break it all up for Hubert.

So that's what me and Evie and Albert thought was happening when Hubert said we was going to the lake. The other thing was, Hubert went to water when there was trouble. He liked to float. He liked to lay his head back in the water and let it bob. And you didn't talk to him. Really, you tried not to be near him when he was doing like that. Just let him bob.

~~~~~~~~~

GOD DIDN'T give us no lakes in Canard County. Too much downhill, too much push to the water. So when the government decided we could use some help, they dammed up our rivers and they made us lakes. Had us make them. The people I come from were good enough to push the dirt around, to make piles where a man in a white shirt and a government sedan said make piles.

But what do I know about all that? What I know is like scratches on rocks, shards of tales.

I BARELY KNOW WHO I COME FROM.

But I know this: the lakes in Tennessee are bigger. Way bigger. Big shots have houses around them. I know our lakes barely got enough to put a picnic shelter around. A ragged boat dock with a shack at its end where men spit in the same sawed-off two-liter bottle, listen to Bill Monroe, and talk about bodies found on the bottom of the lake and bodies never found. The company owned around our lakes, cause they still might be something worth taking from the mountains thereabouts. I'm sure there is. Orange water feeds our lakes. They are poor affairs.

I know this too: my uncle Hubert went to water when he was worried. He put on short pants and he went to water. Hubert had never given up on my mother. He remembered her the way I did, the way she was before my father died. I seen more love in Hubert over the years. He still kept to himself in that building his father built to hang out with his rusty gang of thieves and petty officials. All them gone now, and now Hubert had only me and sometimes Evie and Albert.

When the law took Sidney Coates's money and everybody said my mother informed on him, we figured Hubert would plan a picnic, have us all go to the lake. Cause it was picnic season, plus that is what Hubert did.

"I could use a picnic," Evie said. "Things is too tight around here."

Hubert grumbled something none of us caught, ended on the words "ice cream." So we figured a picnic was what was fixing to happen. But it wasn't.

We were sitting in that building Thursday afternoon, all of us on stumpy chunks of oak save Albert, who sat on the backseat of a LTD. The rest of the LTD set burned up in the yard.

Evie and Albert argued as usual, about something stupid like whether fish or birds was smarter. Hubert stood up, said, "Let's go," and headed towards the barn door. We give him a head start. Hubert opened the passenger door of the Continental, told Albert to drive. Me and Evie got in back and Hubert told Albert to head out towards the lake, but when we got to the picnic shelters by the hauled-in beach, Hubert told Albert to keep going. Albert did, on up into what Evie called Yesterdayland, where folks kept bees, everybody played music, and nobody counted on the law to settle things.

Hubert's daddy was Green Jewell, and Green's mother was from up that way. Her people still had a place, still had land up there. But it was way far away from the Trail so hadn't none of us been out there much, so we leaned on Hubert to tell us where to go, show us how to be.

Hubert said, "Turn in here."

We crossed a wood bridge. An old woman walked towards us with a dead snake hung over the blade of her hoe. Albert stopped the vehicle and she stood at Hubert's window.

Hubert said, "That's a nice one."

The woman said, "Never cared for snakes."

Hubert said, "How you doing, Peck?"

The woman said, "Hubert, I been worse."

Hubert said, "How's your garden?"

"Pitiful." Peck leaned down and looked at us. Stood back up, said "Who you got?"

Hubert pointed at me and Albert. "Him and her is Delbert's." He jerked his thumb at Evie. "She's a Bright."

Peck leaned down again, looked at Evie, said "My daddy courted a Bright. She run off with a gravel man in here building the dam."

Albert said, "Your daddy's better off."

Evie popped Albert on back of the head.

Hubert said, "We're going up to the falls, Peck. Why don't you come with us?"

Peck looked out over the place like an Indian in one of those paintings by a white man, one of them ones where the Indian looks all noble peering out over a canyon full of buffalo, noble even though he's in the middle of getting assfucked by a bunch of cowboys.

"Can't," she said. "Waiting on Shasta to bring me them babies. Untelling when she'll get here."

Hubert said, "Good to see you, Peck."

Peck said, "Good to see you too, Hubert." She probably would have said tell so-and-so hello, but Hubert didn't have nobody around him anymore and so Peck just stood there.

We drove past the place where I reckon Peck stayed given they was a garden on the side big as a grocery store parking lot with string-run beans and corn thigh-high and tomatoes already ganging on the vine. Then we went by a long house with white siding and storm windows and a two-vehicle carport. It was a nice house, a good liver's house, built solid, but it didn't look like nobody lived in it, nor had in a while—shingles blown off the roof, downspout come loose, sheets against the front windows.

Evie said, "Whose is that?"

Hubert said, "That's where my papaw lived."

Albert said, "Snatch?"

Hubert said, "What they called him."

Me and Albert had heard about Snatch, our father's grandfather. He was a union man. We grew up on tales of him shooting gun thugs from the woods above the road to mines on strike, tales of him tying scabs to the railroad track. The scabs' screams when the train cut them to pieces woke me many a night, even though the killings were long before I was born, back in the thirties. Hubert and Daddy had showed us the road where the company drug Snatch by a chain behind a truck to the state line, threw him over a hill into a den of snakes, left him for dead.

I remember Snatch in a hospital bed in the front room of Green's house, hooked up to oxygen cause of black lung, face gray as pipe. I come in crying one time when I was five. Albert'd run over one of my frogs on his Big Wheel and there was nobody home to cry to, only Snatch. Snatch opened his dinosaur eyes, raised up on his bed, tubes in his nose, stuck the broke-off stump of his right first finger at me, said,

Said it to me like I was grown. It stayed with me from that day on. I was grown. Got that from Snatch.

"They called him Snatch cause it was what he loved the best," Albert grinned, his teeth like hominy. "Aint that right, Hubert?"

"Pull off here," Hubert said, pointing at a wide spot off the road. We was back in the woods by then, Highhead Mountain rising up above us like a preacher had the goods on us and fixing to lay us low. The pull-off spot was robed around with laurel and when we got out we had to duck and dodge through it.

Hubert got a red canvas bag out of the trunk of the Continental. Bag had a strap where you could sling it over your shoulder. Hubert headed up through a gap in the laurel, which closed up behind him. Albert scrambled after Hubert, fell, and then he was gone through the laurel.

Evie said, "What's he doing?"

I said nothing to Evie, who once had been dear to me, now just part of my problem, part of everybody's problem. I didn't have a friend now and that was Evie's fault.

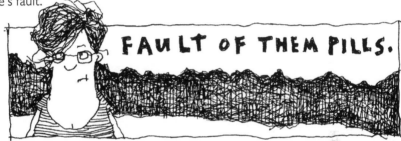

It was near-dark in the laurel. I could barely see the horned ghost of Albert's white wifebeater floating up the path, but I saw enough to follow, grabbing hold of roots and tree trunks, rocks and mud, till the path leveled off, skirted the hillside, and hooked right beside a creek running flat, past overhangs and rock towers, hiding places and lookouts enough for a hundred Indians and outlaws.

Hubert got going good once he got out in the woods, and I never did catch him and Albert, but little goat Evie caught me. She had trouble keeping pace, so she didn't say much, and we moved huffing and puffing through that church of woods till we got to where the trail swung up in our faces and we could hear the sound of the falls.

When we caught up to Hubert and Albert, Hubert's shorts dropped from his waist and naked Hubert stepped down into a pool eddying off the creek seventy feet below where the water crashed from a rock ledge. The waterfall landed in a rainbow spray and made the ferns and bushes and tree limbs in its sway shiver. Hubert's mouth made a little O as he slipped into the chill water up to his chest. Albert crouched above him on the trunk of a fallen tree, a monkey henchman floating in the summer sparkle.

Evie said, "What are you doing?"

Hubert's eyes were closed. He said, "I need yall to pass through the water."

Evie said, "Do what?"

Hubert lay his arms out flat on the surface of the pool. "I need you to go through the falls and bring me back something."

Albert said, "All of us?"

Evie said, "Why we gonna do that?"

Hubert's eyes opened. He lay back in the pool, wetting the back of his head. "It's money," he said. Hubert floated and turned. "Lots and lots of money."

Albert come off his perch and rockscrambled towards the fall. Evie caught him before he reached the spray.

Hubert said, "You go too, Dawn," his eyes closed again. "Don't leave it to them two."

At the top of the waterfall, drops of water jumped free of the rest of the fall, but by the time the drops hit the rocks below, they were all in the same place. I followed Evie and Albert behind the sheet of water.

<center>~~~~~~~~~~</center>

THE MONEY we found in the darkness behind the falls was duct-taped inside two garbage bags. We followed Hubert down the creek to a wide place where the water flowed slow and the creek bed looked smooth shiny and hard as the floor in the courthouse lobby. We took the money out of the garbage bags. It had mold on it. Some of it you couldn't tell what it was.

Evie said, "This money is nasty."

Albert said, "I think something shit on it."

"Money's money," Hubert said. "It don't go bad."

We'd all asked Hubert over and over where it come from, and every time he acted like he hadn't heard us. I stopped asking him.

Evie said, "Do we have to wash every bill?"

Hubert said, "You don't have to wash none of it."

Evie said, "Shoo."

Hubert nodded.

Evie and Albert settled into cussing and picking at each other. They dipped the bills into the creek, their hands flat under the water, rubbing the presidents' faces back to life. Hubert moved from one tree to another, his hand against the trunks, bad leg dragging, grimacing.

Hubert leaned into my ear, grumbled, "So much racket."

I said, "That creek is so clean."

Hubert looked at the creek. His throat rattled like a stick drug across a metal grate. "Your mother," he said, walking away from the creek into the boulders, talking where I couldn't hear him.

Evie said to Albert, "You splash me one more time and I drown you. I aint even kidding."

I said to Hubert library low, "Do what?" and followed him into the boulders, followed him back where it could be just me and him. I came around one boulder and he was sitting on another, his hands in moss, breathing hard.

I said, "You're hurting, aren't you?"

He drew his lips tight, said, "I don't know your mother's worth the investment."

I sat down beside him. I wanted to lean on him. I didn't.

I said, "Does old money stay good?"

"It does," Hubert said. "Legal tender."

The tops of the trees rustled. The light sprinkled down like sugar.

"If Momma wasn't in trouble," I said, "what would you do with that money?"

Hubert sniffed. He wasn't crying, but his eyes were watery. "Nothing," he said. "It aint out here for using."

I didn't ask no more.

I said, "You don't smell like you're taking care of yourself."

Hubert coughed but nothing come up.

I said, "You getting enough to drink?"

Hubert said, "I reckon."

I said, "Smells like it."

Hubert looked at me sideways, said, "Why don't you go help your brother?"

I said, "Who else knows about this?"

Hubert didn't look up, said, "I don't know. Too many lost years. Too many nights."

I leaned forward, my elbows on my knees. I stayed talking low, said, "What are you talking about?"

Hubert said, "Too many years in the wilderness."

"Hubert," I said. "You need to think about getting married."

Hubert turned his head to me, said, "You proposing?"

I said,

"I don't know who all I told," Hubert said. "They was years when I didn't care who knew what." Hubert stood up.

"Well," I said, "you couldn't of told too many. It's still here."

Hubert turned in his spot like a dog with arthritis winding up to sit down. "Don't care who knows," he said.

I wished Hubert would sit back down, but he went back and watched Evie and Albert wash money, and before long Hubert told them to forget it, and we stuffed the money in the red canvas bag, and we trooped back down the creek.

When we got back to Hubert's place, June's little red Honda car was there.

When June seen Evie she said, "Missed you in class this week."

Evie said, "I know what we're supposed to do. I found out. We're supposed to write a paper. And I got me a topic now."

Hubert said, "I want you to take this back with you, June."

June looked at the red bag. We all did.

Story Hubert told was this: Cinderella had called Hubert said Sidney Coates hired a man in Stickerbush to make my mother disappear. Hubert called Sidney said what if Hubert put back the money Sidney had lost. Sidney said it'd be a start. People was scared of Hubert, but it don't pay to have that much money in the house, not when you had a June who could take it and make it safe.

"All right," she said.

We followed June in the Continental to the Virginia line. When June's car slipped down the hill, Albert pulled in behind a coal truck idling at the top of the hill. Hubert got out of the Continental and smoked a cigarette. And then we went back to the Trail.

GENE

That Woman had a notion for what might happen that summer. She had a
bunch of younguns taking a class at the college and somewhere she'd got
money to pay them to take it. She'd got money for them to—I don't know
what you'd call it—make displays they put out where people could see them.
Summer before she'd had money, give everbody who wanted one one of them
throwaway cameras and then took the pictures they took and printed them big
and put them all over the county and I guess it was popular and she showed
people she could get people together to do something that wadn't fussing and
fighting and wadn't just waiting in line to get something free and it seemed to
make That Woman real happy to do it.

So that summer of oh-four when me and her met, she had another
bunch of students and had a project lined out for them. The guys down at the
courthouse, the fiscal court, or whatever you'd want to call them, they had this
idea what Canard needed was a big old sign on the ridge looked down over
town, and that sign would be like that big Hollywood sign they got out there
in Hollywood, except our sign instead of saying "HOLLYWOOD" would say
"COALTOWN!" with an esclamation point at the end of it, which would show
everybody how proud we was to be a town pretty much made out of coal.
And That Woman, she said her and her students would do it. And so she asked
me could I come down to Kingsport, down in Tennessee, to haul back some
stuff she needed to make this sign.

I said sure, but that I didn't have much way to haul stuff. I didn't have a
truck or nothing, but if she didn't mind helping with the gas, I'd make as many
trips in that little Nissan I pack my mower in as she needed me to make. And
she said, "No, I got somebody with a truck," and I said, "Are you sure, because

that Nissan is real good on gas." And she said, "Gene, honey, this is stuff like telephone poles and big sheets of plywood. I don't think you could haul them in your Nissan if you wanted to." She said she had a man with a truck, and that's how I come to know Kenny Bilson, the other man loved That Woman.

~~~~~~~~~~

IT WAS muggy the morning I rode with That Woman down to Kingsport. Where I'd been such a mess the first time I rode with her, I'd found me some washed stuff, white canvas pants and white T-shirt. They was paint-spattered, but they was clean and so was I. I slicked my hair down and put a little vanilla extract behind each of my ears to kind of top it off. That Woman noticed it right off when we got in the car, before she rolled the windows down.

She said, "Gene, you been drinking?"

I said, "No, that's that vanilla extract to help with my scent."

She said that was nice. She said, "Thank you."

I said, "Granny used to put a drop of that on when she had men come over."

"Well," That Woman said, "that's good."

Then she asked was Granny dead and I said she was and she said she was sorry and I said wadn't no need to be sorry cause Granny was old when she died and real Christian so it was just as well.

That Woman said, "That's right."

I showed That Woman where I had a BB stuck under the skin of my elbow since I was little and I talked about how Brother and me lived with all kinds of people before we settled in with Granny, and I run through all the bird calls I know and generally the time passed pretty quick down to Kingsport.

When we hit Kingsport, we went to That Woman's house. It wadn't nothing special on the outside, just one of many on a street looked like a coal camp, but That Woman said there had used to be a textile mill at the end of the

street, on the other side of a big woody park, and that must have been nice, I
said, to be able to walk to work through a pretty bunch of trees like that, and
she said, "Yes, I'm sure it was, in many ways."

When we got inside That Woman's house, it was like walking into a cake,
a cake with caramel-colored icing, everything clean and unstepped on as fresh
snow. There was flowers in vases, and the vases was pretty as naked bodies, and
the flowers went good with the colors that was in the curtains, and the blossoms
flowed with the patterns that stretched out everwhere in the front room of That
Woman's house. I felt like I had entered into a chamber of earthly delights, and my
breath got a little short, and I began to cough. I thought maybe something had flown
down my throat and got caught, cause I'm sure my mouth was hanging wide open.

That Woman got me a glass of water and asked did I want to sit down on the
sofa and when I did I seen a portly man out in the kitchen watching something in
the backyard. He had on short pants that come down to his knees had a bunch
of pockets in them and he rubbed a beard looked like a wad of orange moss on
his chin and he had kind of loose curly hair piled up on his head and he wore a
T-shirt said The Psychedelic Furs, which I thought was maybe where he worked.

That was Kenny Bilson. He come in there in the front room where me and
That Woman was at, and he sat down in a arm chair facing us on the sofa, said,
"What do you say, partner?"

I nodded at him. Didn't see no reason not to.

That Woman said, "Where's your truck, Kenny?"

"Still at the house," he said. "I figured I'd take Gene and we'd go from there."

"So," That Woman said, "this is Kenny, Gene. He's a good friend to me and
he knows where all the stuff is yall got to load up, OK?"

And I was actually pretty cheerful about things at that time and I said,
"Why, sure. Pleasure to meet you."

That Woman told Kenny how as long as we got that stuff to Canard and
unloaded by Sunday that that was fine. She didn't have to teach again till Monday.

And so we stood there a while and it was OK this, and all right that, and then
when we got ready to go, Kenny took his hand and put it in the small of That
Woman's back, like to pull her to him. Then he caught himself, and That Woman
didn't have to put both hands into his chest to stop him, like she was fixing to do.

They come apart, them two, like none of that hadn't never happened, and
I knew right then that he wasn't moving in on her unwanted, he had just moved
in on her at not the right time. And when that sunk in on me I got a headache,
and my heart shattered like if you'd froze it and then beat it with the claw side
of a clawhammer.

I don't need to tell you that day went slow and hard. Kenny had him a nice house sitting up on a hill with a bunch of other houses next to it on the same hill, joined by a curvy little road, one of many such roads in a maze of houses, confusing to navigate where all the roads and the houses looked just the same. And I knew right when I walked in Kenny's house he had him a wife. You could tell by how much useless stuff was sitting on the furniture. Candles, fake ivy, fake fruit.

IT ALL TURNED ME SOUR AS A LEMON.

Then it got worse. Cause once we got keys to the truck which was a twenty-six footer looked like it had been a rental, we went over and got Kenny's friend Calvin. And Calvin, he didn't do nothing for me at all. He looked like he ought to live at the beach, like he went to discos all the time. His teeth was real white, his hair black and shiny and straight as a poker, and his skin was a fake brown. Kind of orange, really.

Kenny had hired him to help us work, but he didn't have on what looked to me like work clothes. He had on real skinny-legged jeans and a shirt with pictures of palm trees all over it, and the worst was he had on flip-flops—to load a truck. Kenny didn't say nothing about it neither, but he give Calvin a long look.

Calvin finally said, "Well. Your old lady has that party tonight, don't she?"

Kenny looked pained, and I don't know cause didn't nobody tell me, but I bet neither Kenny nor his wife had asked Calvin to go to whatever party it was they was having.

~~~~~~~~~~

WE ALL piled in the cab of that truck and Kenny took us out on the four-lane to a warehouse set back behind a farmhouse and we went in there and that thing was stacked floor-to-ceiling with candy—them Dum-Dum suckers like they used to give out at the bank and them Smarties Sister would eat a pack at a time, but mostly it was Christmas candy, and most of that was candy canes. Then behind that was all kind of toys—not big stuff, but rubber balls and plastic dolls and lots of stuffed animals. They must have been a thousand blue kangaroos in there.

We drove right through that warehouse, past all that Christmas stuff, and then in the back was the stuff June needed, the plywood and the poles and a whole big scaffold. Kenny pulled in so the back of the truck was right where all of it was, and let a ramp down and we went to loading, and I'll have to admit, Calvin worked pretty good, but they sure wadn't no dead air when he was on the job.

"If I was ranking my wives' titties," Calvin said at one point, "I'd put Desiree first, and then Aster and then Felicia. Though Felicia got a boob job after we got divorced. But that can't figure in the rankings, since I aint directly experienced the new situation. But you know, if she's at your wife's party, Kenny, I think maybe she might still have a little love in the tank for old Calvin."

Since I don't much care for such coarse talk, I was well pleased when Kenny said, "Shut the fuck up, Calvin," at which point Calvin started talking about how him and his bingo buddies beat a bunch of boys in basketball the night before.

"Schooled em in my flip-flops, John," Calvin said to me.

Kenny said, "His name is Gene, dumbass."

Before long we got the truck loaded and ate some lunch. Kenny's wife called him on his cell phone and told him she needed some something from the store for that party they was having. Kenny and Calvin decided to go get Calvin's Bonneville, which was parked at his mother's, where Calvin lived.

While we was on the way over there, Calvin asked Kenny what was all that stuff in that warehouse.

Kenny said, "That's the stuff they throw off that train."

Calvin said, "What train?"

Kenny said, "That one they take up in Virginia and Kentucky at Christmas time and throw candy and toys off in them coal camps and them kids scramble around and pick it up, make everybody feel good about themselves."

"If I wadn't so lean," Calvin said, "I'd make a badass Santa."

"If only," Kenny said, squinting like a wore-out man just got four hours added to his shift.

One time, it was at the end of the first day of school, me twelve or so, and me and Brother and this boy Brother run around with, they called him Dog Turd, or Turd, cause if they was a dog turd anywhere around he'd step in it sure as you was born, we three got in between the gons of a unit train down in

Canard we thought was going to Bowtie, where Turd lived. And the train, it did go to Bowtie, but it didn't stop in Bowtie. Turd, he was scared to death of his daddy and so he decided he was gonna jump off that train and get back home.

We begged him not to do it, but he said he was gonna do it anyway. He jumped, but his foot caught, and he went face first into the track. Didn't nobody know what had happened but me and Brother and we didn't know what to do cause we was way back in the middle of that train, and you might could guess, we was pretty scared to move after what we seen happen to Turd.

So we just stayed on the train, and it didn't stop till it got to Kingsport, and when it did, me and Brother climbed off and started hitchhiking back to Canard, but we got our direction wrong, and was almost to North Carolina before we got turned around, and we ended up sleeping in some man's corn crib, and didn't get home till the middle of the next day.

We walked all up and down where we thought Turd would be, but by the time we got back to them people's we was staying with, they told us how a stickweed gang from the jail had found Turd's body. He was dead. I always hoped he died when he hit, but nobody never told us.

I do know this: we went to live with Granny not long after that, and she whipped us ever day for two weeks, ever time she thought about us jumping that train. We just let her beat us, cause we knew she loved us, and was whipping us out of love, which cut the sting a little.

That was Turd's real name. Elston Corner, Junior.

But we called him Turd, and I got him on my mind, and I got on my mind how I'd hated trains ever since, and so I couldn't think too well of them kids scrambling after that train for rubber balls and suckers and blue kangaroos. I couldn't hardly think at all, and so it was that when I come to my senses, I was in the backseat of that Bonneville of Calvin's, waiting on Kenny to come out of the store, listening to Calvin run his mouth.

5

ONE GOOD REASON

GENE

Calvin said, "See, Kenny's problem is he don't know hisself. He don't know who he is."

IS THAT RIGHT? I SAID.

Calvin said, "I was telling Momma this morning, 'Kenny don't know where's he at. Don't know where he come from. He's like a fart on a Ferris wheel.'"

I didn't say nothing, just looked out the car window. I didn't understand Tennessee. Things was different. People didn't know you talked to you like they did and they taxed you too hard. I was only there cause That Woman asked me to come. That Woman. She grew up where I did. Same county, but out on the ridge, breathing lighter air. I stayed afraid she would float off on a cloud of her own ungodly beauty.

Calvin said, "But you know what, dude? Kenny's got his eye on a new woman. I know he does."

Kenny got back in the Bonneville packing a blue plastic bag. Kenny had a big old gut and his hair was unruly. I don't know what That Woman seen in him.

"Did you get the right stuff?" Calvin said.

Kenny nodded. They was in the front seat. I was in back. The upholstery was falling in from the Bonneville's ceiling and when Calvin got rolling, it flapped like ocean waves. Calvin tore through curves and I had no idea where we was. It was old two-story farmhouses and real windy roads and cows standing around everwhere. It was July and didn't seem the sun would ever go down. I was wanting to see what Kenny and Calvin would do, hoping it would be bad so I could tell That Woman and she wouldn't think Kenny so bright. Maybe she'd see him for what he was, which I was hoping was bad.

We got back on a main highway lined up with furniture stores and bright shiny restaurants and we pulled up in front of the least bright and shiny one they was—The Straightaway Grill.

Kenny said, "Calvin, don't go in there."

Calvin already had the Bonneville door open and one foot on the gravel. Calvin said, "I got to have me some of that casserole." One of Calvin's ex-wives worked in the restaurant. They had a hash-brown casserole Calvin said haunted his dreams.

Kenny said, "She aint going to give you no casserole."

Calvin said, "She still loves me."

Kenny said, "She's got an EPO on you."

"That's her mother's idea," Calvin said.

"Don't go in there, Calvin," Kenny said.

The door slammed on the Pontiac and the mirror fell out of the rearview. A police car pulled in next to us and two police went in the restaurant. Kenny put his hand over his face like he was wiping something off of it. He looked back over the car seat at me.

He said, "You doing all right, Gene?"

I said I was.

"I don't mean to get too personal," Kenny said, "but you aint got no warrants on you or nothing, do you?"

I said,

The restaurant door flew open and Calvin come to the door. He hollered back in the restaurant, "I can't believe you called the cops. You're a goddam heartbreaker, aint you?" The cops came to the door. Calvin stepped out towards us, but he kept hollering back inside. "You get more like your mother everday, Desiree. You know that? Everday. People aint going to be able to tell you apart if you aint careful."

Kenny leaned over and pushed Calvin's door open. Calvin got in, beat on the steering wheel with both hands. He put the car in reverse and blew the car horn one long blow. Them cops stepped towards us and Calvin backed out, blowing the car horn all the way, like he was in a victory parade.

When he finally stopped blowing, Kenny said, "Did you get your casserole?"

We was back on the four-lane, the restaurant far behind, but Calvin give the car horn one more long blow.

~~~~~~~~~~~

KENNY'S WIFE said, "Why did you bring Calvin here?" They was talking back in the little closet room where the food was stacked. "And where did you get that other one?" I reckon the other one was me.

Kenny said something low and mumbly I didn't catch and Kenny's wife said, "Kenny, these are my friends," and Kenny said, "Well, they're *my* friends," and then I heard Kenny's wife say, "Jesus, Kenny," and they stepped back towards me and I backed down the hall into where all these blonde women was talking, sitting on high stools in a real clean kitchen, big bright color bowls filled with chopped-up salady stuff and piles of corn on the cob and fat red and green watermelon slices and raw hamburgers and hot dogs piled up on plates, and it was about as nervous-making a room as I'd ever been in and so I went out on the patio where they was a big old yard mostly fenced in and mostly mowed. Big boat in the back corner floated on high grass. There was kids running around, jumping in and out of an aboveground swimming pool, bunch of men standing around looking like bosses in clean shirts and tight haircuts, looking like they didn't really know each other, kind of awkward talking about nothing and taking a keener interest in the doings of their kids than they might otherwise would've.

Calvin was standing next to a gas grill looked like it was a whole kitchen with a stove eye built in and places to set stuff and towels and tools hanging off it, full of meat. The smoke rolling off smelled good and Calvin was waving his arms telling some big tale, talking like he was best friends with everybody there, like he'd known them forever. Against my better judgment, I sidled up next to Calvin.

"So we was locked in the bathroom," Calvin said. "Couldn't none of them Tarheel North Carolina Republican assholes get at us." I don't know how Calvin could've got drunk no longer than we had been there, but he sure seemed so. "And after while they was banging on the door. And finally Kenny opened the door and grabbed one of them by the lapels, set him on the commode, locked the door back, and said, 'You give us one good reason why we shouldn't kick your ass right now,' and you know what?"

Didn't none of the men listening to Calvin's story say what, so I said, "What?"

Calvin said, "He didn't have one. He couldn't think of one good reason why we shouldn't kick his ass."

I said, "What did you do?"

"Aw," Calvin said, "we turned him loose. We was guests at the wedding. We didn't want to cause no trouble for our buddy getting married."

Them other fellers went back to staring into the gas fire. Calvin started in on a tale about Kenny's bachelor party and then Kenny come up, said, "Come on Calvin, let's go," and Calvin said, "Where we going?" and Kenny said, "She needs something else."

"You got the wrong thing, didn't you?" Calvin said.

"That's right," Kenny said. "I did."

"Told you," Calvin said.

I left out with them, trying to think what my reason would be for somebody not kicking my ass.

WHEN WE got out to the Bonneville, Kenny told us what it was. Kenny's wife had wanted us out of there. Which I didn't blame her. Me and Calvin stuck out in there like two used rubbers in a bowl of peanuts. I was glad to be gone, but Calvin pitched a fit, said this was exactly what he was talking about, said this is why Kenny needed to get shed of April. He said it standing on Kenny's concrete driveway, and didn't stop when Kenny's two little whiteheaded boys walked up, twins about five years old. The thicker one said, "Daddy, where you going?"

Kenny said, "Gonna make sure these sure these gentlemen get home all right."

The other twin said, "Daddy, aint they old enough they don't need a daddy?"

Kenny squatted down, said, "Honey, I got to go with them so I can pick up my truck." They looked at him big-eyed and Kenny said, "Aint yall been swimming?"

The thick one said, "We was waiting on you."

And Kenny said, "Well. Yall go back in there and get ready. I'll be back before you get your waterwings on." They stood there and Kenny said, "Do what I tell you."

And they went in the house.

Calvin said, "April is undermining you with them boys."

"Shut up, Calvin," Kenny said, and we got in the Pontiac and backed out of Kenny's driveway.

We drove about a minute and Calvin said, "Kenny, you reckon you could loan me five hundred till payday?"

Kenny said, "You aint working, Calvin. You aint got a payday."

"Kenny," Calvin said, "the damned old IRS got me hemmed up. It aint me. It's federal."

"Jesus, Calvin," Kenny said. "When you going to lend me some money?"

That shut Calvin up, and we rode past the chemical plant on the edge of Kingsport, forests of smokestacks, coal piles big as mountains, and Calvin said to me, "John, now where are you staying?"

"His name is Gene, dumbass," Kenny said, "and just take me to the truck. I'll take him."

I was staying at That Woman's house. I said, "Right over there by the train tracks on Mill Street." I pointed, said, "Right over there."

Calvin whipped around, cut under the train tracks, and in a minute we was sitting out front of That Woman's crackerbox house. Calvin jumped out, said, "I gotta take a whiz."

I said to Kenny, "Don't look like she's here."

Kenny said, "You got a key?"

I said, "Hunh-unh."

Kenny said, "Shoo," and got out of the Pontiac.

Calvin tried the door and peeked in the windows. Kenny waved me up on the porch and took a key out of his pocket, opened the storm door, and unlocked the house. Him having the key to That Woman's house took something out of me, but I couldn't keep from going in there to take in the misty flowerdy smell I knew would be inside, that come-hither smell like cinnamon and soap and your grandmother's tea. I closed my eyes to take in the smell a hundred per cent. When Calvin went, "Jesus Christ," my eyes opened to the sight of paper money laid edge to edge everwhere in the front room of that house—tens and twenties and fifties and hundreds laid all over the chairs and sofa and tables. Money was stretched down the little hall back towards That Woman's bedroom. The money was wet and set on paper towels drying out. It was hot in there, baking hot, and the three of us stood there piled up, our eyes big as eggs.

Calvin said "Jesus Christ" again and Kenny set down in the easy chair facing the kitchen and he said "Jesus Christ" too.

<hr />

CALVIN COULDN'T help himself. He went to counting it, walking up and down the rows of bills laid out plumb as dots on a domino. I stood in the doorway on a plastic runner and Calvin lost track of his counting any number of times. I would've helped him but I aint no good at counting neither and finally Calvin said, "They must be a hundred thousand dollars here."

Kenny finally said, "Where is she?" to the house itself and then he turned to me, said, "Gene, you know what this is?"

I said, "No sir, I don't. Except that it's a lot of money."

We noticed a lot of the bills was old, like from the 1960s, and a lot was from the 1970s, and this, see, was the summer of 2004, and it was odd, very odd, odd on top of all that money being spread out there in the first place.

Calvin said, "I don't know about you boys, but that's money enough to solve all my problems."

Me and Kenny took a good long look at one another and the storm door creaked behind me and That Woman said, "Kenny," with the breath going out of her and she stepped past me to him and they didn't touch but you could tell they was wanting to and Calvin looked past me and I turned to see what he was looking at, and there stood Tricia, That Woman's pillhead sister, and she had a suitcase you could've put her in twice and she had makeup over all the trouble she'd been in, and makeup over all the trouble she'd caused, and when I looked back, Calvin's mouth was hanging open and I didn't know if I was there. It was a strange feeling and I just sat down, my head light and gassy, and I heard That Woman say,

When That Woman come back with my glass of water and sat down, we was all sitting down.

"June," Kenny said, "what is all this?"

That Woman sat with her knees together. She wore a white shirt looked like it could have been a man's, shirt like a lawyer would wear, or an undertaker. Her hair come down across one eye and she brushed it back with a hand light as a turkey feather. When she went to talking, sound of her voice was like the whisper of rain, made you quiet, made you want to lie still in a bed and not turn on a light when dark come through the window, filled the room before it come to the window itself, and she said:

"I don't know what to tell you."

We all set there looking at each other and looking at that money, and Tricia, the sister, sparked her lighter, lit a cigarette.

"Honey," That Woman said to her sister, "go out on the porch."

Tricia said tense as a screen door spring, "My pleasure," and when she got up to go, I figured Calvin would too, and sure as his eyes followed her out, his behind stayed right there on the sofa next to me.

"Honey," Kenny said to That Woman, "whose money is this?"

That Woman said, "Hubert's."

Which is what I figured, cause Hubert is That Woman's outlaw brother-in-law, and actually, he wasn't That Woman's brother-in-law. He was Tricia's dead husband's brother, and he was sweet on Tricia, always had been. See, that whole bunch was piled up on one another like a box of puppies. Whatever one was into, they was all into.

"What's it doing here?" Kenny said. "And why's it all wet?"

"And why's it old?" Calvin said. "Will it still spend?"

"Are you Calvin?" That Woman said.

"He's been talking about me," Calvin said. "I knew he would."

"June," Kenny said, "why's there money all over the house?"

"You know Sidney Coates got arrested," That Woman said. Sidney Coates was our county's biggest drug dealer.

"I'd heard," Kenny said. "And I heard they found a bunch of money at his house."

"Thirty thousand," I said.

"And you heard they think Tricia informed on them," That Woman said.

"I hadn't heard that," Kenny said. "Did she?"

Tricia come back in the house, said, "Don't matter if I did or didn't if they think I did."

"So this is to pay them back," Kenny said.

"So they don't kill her," That Woman said.

Calvin leaned back on the sofa, said, "Daggone."

IT WAS ALWAYS SOMETHING WITH THAT WOMAN'S SISTER.

"Help me gather this up," That Woman said.

We couldn't help watching her when she got down on her knees started stacking that money up in little piles. Her shirt rode up her back and you could see them muscles either side of her spine. Lord, they was easy to look at.

Calvin, he looked at That Woman too, but mostly looked at Tricia. He give her a little wink, but she just looked at him like he was her own reflection in a mud puddle. Kenny kneeled down beside That Woman, and I kneeled down beside her on the other side.

"So," Kenny said, "when yall taking Sidney this money?"

"Tomorrow night, I reckon," That Woman said.

"You going by yourself?" Kenny said.

That Woman raised up on her knees. "You asking to go with me?"

Kenny said, "Yeah, I'll go with you. If I can."

I said, "I'll go with you."

That Woman said, "I reckon Hubert'll take me. Somebody will."

Tricia huffed, said, "I got to go." She bounced up, rubbed her hands on her thighs. "All this money," she said, "making me nervous."

Tricia had been sitting on the edge of a chair flipping through a clothes magazine while we was stacking money.

Calvin jumped up too. "Where you wanting to go, darling?"

"I got my own vehicle," Tricia said.

That Woman said, "You don't need to be driving nowhere."

Tricia said, "I got to go to the drugstore. I need tampons."

Calvin said, "I don't mind taking her."

That Woman said, "Kenny, take my car and run her down to Mack's."

Kenny said, "You sure?"

"Yeah," That Woman said. "Hurry."

Kenny left and That Woman went in the kitchen, come back with a ziplock bag full of rubber bands. We put the cash in five-hundred-dollar bundles, them rubber bands snapping around that money. Calvin scooted the bundles over to where I could reach them, but mostly it was me and That Woman doing the work. I could imagine me and her putting up pickles and tomatoes, canning all kinds of good, old-timey stuff. I smiled at That Woman and she smiled at me and then she went in the other room, come back with a red duffel bag, started piling that money up in it.

It's a funny thing to be around that much money. You don't think it's going to be weird because, you know, you been around money before. But that much of it gives off a smell kind of gives you a buzz—like homemade liquor or a good clean dog. I felt it myself, and I didn't have no interest in none of it, none of it but doing right by That Woman.

All the money just barely fit in the bag, and right as That Woman zipped up the bag, the phone rang. That Woman went in the other room to get it, and Calvin looked at me, opened his eyes wider and raised his eyebrows like they was a thought we was sharing, but if there was, I didn't know what it was.

"You go to church, John?" Calvin said.

"I know where one's at," I said.

Calvin nodded. That Woman went down the hall, put something up in the closet.

WHEN I come to, I was in the trunk of Calvin's Bonneville. The Bonneville needed shocks. Other than that, it wasn't too bad. There was a bed of pop cans and I could rest my head on the jumper cables. Hardest part was not knowing what happened, and in particular what had become of That Woman. I knew me being in the trunk of Calvin's Bonneville was part of him taking That Woman's money, twenty-eight thousand dollars she'd packed up in a red bag to get her pillhead sister out of trouble, not so Calvin could run off with it soon as he got the chance.

I wondered why Calvin hadn't left me in That Woman's house. I was glad he hadn't, cause it made it possible I might end up the hero. I might get back That Woman's money, or even better, save her from certain death or some such.

These thoughts were a comfort, even after Calvin stopped and it started getting uncomfortable hot. I tried to think of winter growing up in my granny's house when me and Brother would stay under the quilts and covers and argue who was going to get up and stoke the fire after Granny got too sick to do it. But I couldn't make my mind work on the ice in our pee bottle or our breath blown out in clouds above our heads. Seems all would come was the toasty feeling me and Brother give each other under all them quilts and covers, a toasty feeling which turned double super hot in that car trunk. My sweat was like butter. I was a turkey in a oven. I shucked off my clothes, but couldn't get no relief. Them pop cans started gouging me.

I tried to sleep, but when I went to quiet out, it made me hotter. I pretended I was in a tanning bed. I thought about people paying to sleep in a hot box and how the trunk was better in a way, cause I didn't have all them bright lights shining on me. That line of thinking eased my mind and I slid off to sleep.

~~~~~~~~~~

WHEN THE trunk flew open, Kenny said, "I'll be damned."

The light was bright after that trunk dark. My vision was all stars and sparkles. I stuck my arms out to block the sun. Cool air washed over me. Kenny turned away from my naked shininess. He walked a circle around the Bonneville, peered off into the woods. Kenny come back and stood over me. "What are you doing in there?" he said.

"Sweating, mostly," I said.

Above the creek bank where the Bonneville was parked was the back side of a bunch of big stores.

I said, "Is she all right?"

Kenny said, "June?"

I said, "Yeah."

And Kenny said Calvin had locked her in a closet, then knocked me in the head and run off with the money. Kenny said he'd got her out and she was OK.

Kenny walked off down the creek. I put my britches on and walked up to the store buildings. Back of a dumpster out behind one of them stores, I heard a man crying. I wasn't going where it was, because generally a man don't want another man to see him crying, but I thought, well, maybe this man's got his foot caught in something. I'd hate to of just walked by and a man lose a foot.

So I went to the crying.

CALVIN WAS jammed back in a wedge a dumpster made with the rough block of the back wall of one of them store buildings. He'd put himself together a hidey-hole out of cardboard and long log-looking pieces of foam. I had to squat to see him through a square little open spot.

Calvin wiped his eyes with the heel of his hands, said, "What are you doing here?"

I said, "Calvin, I come in the trunk of your car."

"But how'd you get out?"

"Kenny let me out."

Calvin said, "I thought I killed you."

I said, "It wadn't that bad, Calvin."

Calvin stood up, knocked his little fort over. He took off walking over the gravel and grass between the store and the Bonneville.

I said, "Calvin, where you going?"

He didn't say anything, which I didn't think he would.

I seen the red bag of money amongst the cardboard and foam. "Hey, Calvin," I hollered, and picked up the bag and started back to the Bonneville. I got to the car about the time Kenny did. Calvin was in the driver's seat rooting around on the floorboard and up in the sun visor and down in the seat cushions.

"Kenny," he hollered. "Where's the keys?"

Me and Kenny was standing on either side of the car. Calvin kept hunting the keys till he give up and put his head against the steering wheel and went back to blubbering.

I put my hand on his shoulder, said, "Honey, what's the matter?"

When I done that, he threw the door open, which like to break my arm. He jumped out and took off running through the woods beside the creek. Where there was so many roots and so much brush, he didn't get fifty yards before he tripped and went chin first into a big old rock and knocked himself down into the creek, which was topped by a nasty brown foam and had sawdusty stuff swirling in it.

I was afraid Calvin had knocked himself unconscious, face down in the creek like he was. Kenny jumped in, waded waist-deep and got Calvin up under his arms and wrenched him out of there. Between the two of us we got him on his back, far enough up the bank to where we wadn't too worried he'd slide back in. Calvin had a gash run with the ridge of his chin took nine stitches to close. Kenny took his shirt off and wadded it up for Calvin to press against his chin.

Calvin sat up, dazed like a baby woke to a new world. Kenny said, "Calvin, do you know us?"

He said, "Not as well as I'd like."

Kenny said, "What's the capital of Tennessee?"

Calvin said, "Kingsport."

Kenny said, "I think he's all right."

I said, "I didn't know Kingsport was the capital of Tennessee."

"It aint," Kenny said, "but Calvin thinks it should be." Kenny stood up. "Always has."

Calvin said, "Yall want to smoke a joint?"

Kenny said, "You got a joint?"

Calvin said, "No," said, "I thought you might."

Kenny looked at me and I shook my head and Kenny said, "Calvin, why did you put Gene in your car trunk?"

Calvin said, "I thought he was dead."

Which made sense to me, cause I breathe real slow. Especially when I get hit in the head.

Kenny said, "Calvin, what are we doing here?"

Calvin looked up at the sky and squinted his eyes and let his mouth fall open like he was waiting on the words he needed to drop onto his tongue.

I swear I aint never seen a face so full of hope. I mean, it was impressive. I looked up at the sky too.

"I just needed that money," Calvin said. "Needed it sitting next to me." Kenny turned his back to Calvin. "But then when I got it," Calvin said, "I didn't want to do right with it. Didn't want to give it to the taxman. Didn't want to pay back Desiree or Felicia or Aster. Didn't want to give it to my children. Just wanted to go with it. Just wanted to go."

Calvin leaned up on his hip and pulled a map out of his back pocket. Mud smeared the map as it come loose, and Calvin lay back on the creek bank and unfolded it. He held the map out in the air above him. It was worn in its folds and Calvin studied it for a good little bit and then let it float down over him like a picnic blanket.

He said out from under it, "Why don't yall just bury me right here?"

Kenny said, "Calvin, I aint never seen you like this."

Calvin said, "I been like this. Forever."

Kenny said, "Gene, help me get him in the truck."

Calvin said, "Boys, let's us just stay here a minute longer. Let's us just stay here and be still a minute."

And that's what we did. We heard the creek meandering and the minivans in the parking lot and me and Kenny seen a creek turtle stick his head up and then go back under. Calvin said from under his map, "Boys, I believe I'd of been better off born a dog."

Kenny looked at me and said, "Calvin, honey, we've all felt like that."

When Calvin looked at me over the edge of that map, I nodded it was true.

The blood off Calvin's chin was filling up Kenny's T-shirt and Calvin, he looked kind of woozy and squeezed the T-shirt and blood welled out of it and got in the lines of his fingers. Calvin smiled and pointed the T-shirt at me and said, "Give me one good reason why I shouldn't kick your ass."

"None of us do," Calvin said.

"Calvin, you want to go to the hospital?" Kenny said.

~~~~~~~

THE HOSPITAL sewed Calvin up. Calvin sang "Long Black Veil" to the woman who cleaned his wounds. He said to her when he was done, "You know, I like a woman with meat on her bones."

~~~~~~~

WHEN WE took Calvin back to his mother's house, she was sitting on the porch with a pan of broke-up beans in her lap. She stood when she seen us in the failing light. Calvin limped up the walk and then come back and leaned in Kenny's window and said, "You boys don't mind bringing the Bonneville back over here?"

We said we didn't.

Calvin said, "Boys, if I got to be in it, I'm glad to be in it with you."

Kenny said, "Get you some sleep, Calvin."

Calvin nodded and patted the base of Kenny's window frame. Then he went in the house with his arm over his mother's shoulder, said something caused her to gouge him.

~~~~~~~

WHEN WE came back with the Bonneville, Calvin's mother's house was all lit up. I got out of the car and got in Kenny's truck. We went back to That Woman's house and I can't tell you how glad she was to see that red bag of money. It didn't seem to occur to none of them to speak to the law about it, which suited me fine.

We set in That Woman's kitchen a little while and drank sweet tea and then we went out and sat on her porch. On the porch, Kenny and That Woman drank whiskey and me and That Woman's pillhead sister drank Pepsi, and I felt better about things, about Kenny being with That Woman. It was peaceful in That Woman's yellow bug light, felt like there was room enough for all of us.

Room enough for all of us was an easy feeling to sleep on, especially when Kenny followed That Woman into her room. That easy feeling served me in good stead again about four in the morning when That Woman's pillhead sister snuck past me on the front room couch, slipped past with the red bag of money out to the Bonneville idling rough at the curb. If it hadn't been for that easy feeling, I don't know how I'd of felt when the Bonneville and Calvin and That

Woman's pillhead sister slid off into the mist and stink of another Kingsport July morning. Don't guess I ever will know, cause despite the best efforts of so many good people,

6

RUNNING COAL

DAWN

Monday me and Nicolette set on the top row of aluminum bleachers next to the ball courts where the river used to be in downtown Canard. Ten donkeys stomped up and down the court with grown men dressed like circus clowns on their backs playing basketball. Frost-headed mothers and sweaty kids with cheez doodle lips surrounded us. Cinderella Stewart come up on the bleachers' backside and stuck his cat-scratched pimplehead between my feet and said, "Your mommy's in trouble, Dawn."

I said, "You aint supposed to be around kids, Cinderella. You forgot what the judge said?"

I tried to talk low when I said, "Fuck you, Cinderella. Come get me when she aint," but two frosty heads turned to look at me. I told Nicolette not to move and slipped over the back of the bleachers. Cinderella was a mouth breather and where he'd been out in the sun his face looked like a gas station pizza. He leaned his head forward, neck stretched out like the hitch on the back of a pickup truck.

He said, "She stole a bunch of money. Run off with some dude."

I said, "This is so not news, Cinderella."

The truth is, I already knew what I was going to wear to Momma's funeral. It had got to where every time I seen her alive it was an interruption of my grief.

Cinderella said, "I tell you what else. Belinda Coates killed June's dog."

I said, "Shut up, Cinderella."

Cinderella said, "Poisoned it. Said she'd do the same to Tricia when she found her."

I said, "I love that dog." Which made me mad I said it, because I love the dog, but I didn't need to tell Cinderella.

Cinderella said, "It was a whole bunch of money she took."

Nicolette come up beside me and I said, "Let's go, Nicolette."

She said, "Mommy, that horse stomped that man."

I said, "It's a donkey."

Nicolette said, "Why'd he do that?"

I said, "Come on, Nicolette." I told Cinderella to leave us alone, told him to go back to wherever he goes when he aint telling me stupid stuff I already know.

Cinderella raised his hands like he was getting robbed. His palms were lined with dirt. Grease streaked and spotted his Canard Crazee Daze 10K T-shirt and you couldn't tell did the grease come from food or machinery. Nicolette took a picture of Cinderella with her throwaway camera she got off June. We walked up in town where June and them were working.

Nicolette said, "What happened to that man's face, Mommy?"

"Nothing," I said.

GENE

That Woman told me and Brother to come to the old Progress Building downtown. Told us to be there at 7:30 in the morning. Said we'd be cutting the plywood to make her COALTOWN! letters. At seven, me and Brother was sitting down there smoking at the coal memorial. The students started showing up, and by the time the late ones got there, That Woman still wasn't there. That hateful Evie Bright, piled up with nightmare Belinda Coates, told me to go up to That Woman's house to see where she's at. I did, went up them steps, and That Woman was sitting there on her porch, rocked forward, ankles together, elbows on her knees, and she had canvas bags full of stuff piled up at her feet, like she was waiting for a ride.

I said, "Ma'am, you ready to go?"

That Woman stood up, gathered up them bags had tools and tape in them, and she grabbed a four-foot-tall roll of butcher paper and I put my hands out and she give me a couple of the bags, and I got hold of the roll of butcher paper and we started down the stairs. She went in front of me with a heavy step. We put the stuff in her car and she asked did I want to ride down there with her and I said I didn't mind to do that. She pulled out from the bank to let me in and when I got in, she said, "Where do you reckon my sister is?"

And I said, "Untelling."

She said, "Did you know that man? Do you know Calvin?"

I said, "Just met him that day."

She said, "Do you know where he lives?"

I said, "Kenny does."

She said, "Kenny said he would find Calvin. But they're good friends. Friends for a long time. I don't think Kenny cares for my sister. He says she needs to fix herself. Says I'm letting myself in for heartbreak trying to help her."

I said, "Hard to know about something like that."

She said, "Other day I found myself thinking how good it would feel for my sister to die. I can't believe I thought that. I can't believe I'm telling you."

"Well," I said,

SHE DOES SEEM A TRIAL.

That Woman said, "But she's my sister."

I didn't know what to tell That Woman. Personally, I don't think you can give up on people. Not ever. But I couldn't speak for her. I said, "Them younguns are waiting on you to come tell them what to do. And they're wanting to know when they're going to see a payday."

That Woman said, "Is your brother there?"

I said he was when I left. That Woman nodded. We went on down there and started working. Didn't say no more about That Woman's sister.

DAWN

June and them were putting together plywood letters forty feet tall on the ground floor of an old three-story brick building. Somebody said it was the first building built after the railroad come, after they knew for sure there was money in coal. When it was new, they sold furniture out of it, then stoves and radios, then other stuff of increasing uselessness, but wadn't nothing in it the summer June was there but dead pigeons, piled-up junk from a dozen bad ideas, and the racket made by the saws and drills and hammers of June's crew.

There'd been copper around the upstairs windows and under the eaves of the building till it got stolen in broad daylight with people watching from the restaurant across the street and in offices in the old courthouse. Why weren't they being nosy like they are every other time in the history of Earth? Cause they aint got the nerve, not when it comes down to it.

I come up beside Aunt June from behind. She was standing inside the doors on the corner of the building closest to the post office. A box fan in the store window blew on her hair, which was sweaty and stuck to her head.

I said, "So what are yall doing exactly?"

June said, "Well, we're making a big old sign. Like the one in Hollywood. It's gonna go on the hillside behind the floodwall and say, "THIS IS A COALTOWN!""

I said, "Why?"

June said, "Cause they're paying us. Cause it will build our capacity to do community art projects."

I said, "Who's paying you?"

She said, "The county. They say they want it up by the time Bush gets here."

I said, "Bush who?"

She said, "Bush the president. He's coming end of the month."

I said, "I thought you was against coal."

June said it ain't that simple. I knew Mamaw didn't agree with this COALTOWN! sign. Traitor to the land, Mamaw had called her.

June said, "We'll do this and then we can do something else, something that asks a harder question."

I said, "Whatever, Aunt June," and thought to myself, you start with this here and that's as badass as you'll ever be. I said, "This is stupid. It makes coal company sucks out of everbody works on it."

Aunt June picked up a chunk of two-by-four and swung it up over her head and brought it down across a turned-up milk crate, made a pop like a firecracker. Everybody in there, probably twenty of them, jumped. June's eyes was like coals in a grill ready to cook when she turned on me. She said, "Why don't you just go on then, Dawn. We're trying to do something."

Evie Bright and Belinda Coates sat in the store window on the pondwater-green carpet. They sat bumping their legs on the wallboard behind their feet, passing a slushee back and forth, laughing behind their hands at me. A table saw sang high and mean. People went back to screwing two by fours to the plywood, cutting their eyes at me. How could Evie sit with an evil skag like Belinda Coates? How could she stop being my friend and start being that dog-killing heifer's? Cause pillheads go where pills are.

I didn't want to stay there, not in that store, not in that town, not in none of it. The room spun around me like a backwards merry-go-round, me sitting still on a psycho-looking painted horse, its teeth painted pink and its gums painted blue, and the world ripping a big circle. I squeezed down on Nicolette's hand, and the thought came on my mind like a hot doughnut on a china plate: it would be easy to let go of Kentucky. It would be easy to let go of living in a coal-mining place. But I couldn't go. Nowhere to go. I didn't belong in Tennessee. I was cut from cloth too rough. I'd die of boredom there. I was stuck, a crow nailed to a cross in a crazy man's garden.

Out the window at the courthouse, there was a man with a mullet and no sleeves to his shirt, big hammy shoulders, sitting next to a man in a Korea War veteran ball cap and Members Only jacket. Another man had silver sideburns and a plaid short-sleeve shirt with a white T-shirt underneath it, shaving off a chunk of poplar with his hawkbill. Everywhere you look, men sitting around, breathing out judgment, weighing things down.

It come on me how bad I wanted brown liquor and ginger ale. I hadn't drunk much since Nicolette'd been born. But right then, standing in that stupid store building, I wanted somebody to sit on the porch and drink liquor with. Somebody new. Somebody perfect. I said, "Come on, Nicolette," and we went and sat on the courthouse lawn, with our back to a memorial naming everybody ever got killed in a coal mine in Canard County. Take you all day to read the names. Hundreds of them. I felt bad for every one of them, every husband, every mother's son. But them being dead didn't make smaller the all-day puke feeling in my stomach.

Weedeater was working for June, standing on the sidewalk holding an empty woven plastic bag, kind fifty pounds of cement powder come in. His brother was in a third-story window dropping bricks and chunks of block down on him, and Weedeater caught the bricks in the bag, or let them crash on the sidewalk if they was too big, and everyone walking down the street crossed over to the courthouse side so they didn't have to walk through Weedeater's dumbass ground zero.

The air got dead hot and me and Nicolette moved under a oak tree. I set there watching the stupid roll off Weedeater and his brother. June was inside, supervising her students fiddlefarting around. Weedeater caught a chunk of block in the sack, like the sack was a hammock and the block was jumping in it to take a nap. It was pretty to watch, the way he'd bend his knees and slack the bag to catch the weight, pretty like lightning is right up until the second it strikes something belongs to you and fries the shit out of it.

When June looked out the window and seen Weedeater catching that block, she went, "OH!" so big you could see it through the plate glass. She come running out and hollered at Weedeater to stop. When she hollered, he looked up, and a brick hit him right between the shoulder blades and doubled him over. His face twisted up and then the second brick busted him in the small of the back and he went to his hands and knees, sidewalk tearing the skin off the heel of his hands.

I smacked a mosquito on Nicolette's thigh, made her a tiny insect blood tattoo. I flicked the dead mosquito and he went flying through the air leg over leg. Weedeater rolled over on his back, his legs churning like he was dreaming about riding a bicycle. June got down on her knees beside him, head going back and forth like she didn't know what to do. Weedeater's brother set in the third-story window frame and lit a cigarette. The skank Belinda Coates and Evie and the rest of the people taking June's class come out to see what happened. Belinda and Evie lit cigarettes.

Belinda said, "Did it kill him?"

Evie kicked Weedeater in the foot.

Weedeater groaned: "Uhhhhh."

Evie said, "Don't reckon."

"Gene," June said, "can you hear me?"

Weedeater's eyes fluttered open. "I can work," he said, and raised up on his elbows.

"No, he can't," Evie said. "Watch them eyes roll. That's what they do before they go in a coma."

"Gene," Aunt June said, "can you stand up?"

Gene rolled over, got on his hands and knees.

Evie said, "I bet he can't."

Weedeater stood up, and then wobbled. June got him around the waist.

June said, "Help me, Evie."

Evie looked at Belinda, then got ahold of Weedeater under his arm. Weedeater lurched forward and about took June and Evie down with him. June got under him and held him up, kept him from crashing to the sidewalk. June and Evie walked him over to the curb and set him down.

Evie said, "This means we don't have to work no more, right?"

By that time me and Nicolette was standing over there with them. I didn't much care for Weedeater, but if he was going to die, I wanted to see it. But when I got close enough to see in his face, that he wasn't going to die was obvious.

Weedeater said, "Where's Brother?"

Evie squatted between the truck and motorcycle parked against the curb where Weedeater sat and looked him dead in the eye.

She said, "He's up there," and pointed to where his brother perched.

Weedeater pushed his head back until he could see what was behind and above him and said, "Brother, don't fall." Then he lowered his head back down, his eyes all buggy.

"June," Evie said, "you better send him on home. Fore he sues you."

June said, "Hush, Evie."

I said to Evie, "You can't quit till you gone too far, can you?"

Belinda Coates said, "Well, it's true, aint it?"

I looked Belinda Coates dead in her eye in case it was possible to kill a person with pure hate. Kill my dog. You must've lost your mind when you done that, Belinda Coates.

"Hey!" Evie hollered up at Weedeater's brother. "You need to take him home."

Weedeater's brother set there with his arms crossed, smoke rising out from between his fingers.

"Say!" Evie said.

Weedeater's brother tapped the ash off his cigarette.

Evie said, "You better hope don't none of that get on me. I'll come up there and beat your ass myself."

Weedeater's brother didn't say nothing. I doubt he was scared of Evie, but he didn't much look like one to fight.

Belinda Coates said, "What are you doing here?," looking at me.

I heard they was having a pillhead bitch contest and I come to put my money on you, I wanted to say, but since Nicolette was there I didn't say a thing.

Nicolette took hold of my hand and said to Belinda Coates, "You're not nice," and then she looked at me and said, "What's wrong with her?"

I said, "Hush, baby. Or she'll take you to court."

Weedeater stood up and said, "Where's my bag?" And he started to spin like an airplane in a war movie that's had its wing shot off.

Evie said, "June, you better get him out of here."

June said, "Maybe we should take him to the hospital," and when the word "hospital" come out of her mouth, Weedeater's brother went, "Now hold on there," and he come flying down the stairs out to us, said, "This here's a family matter. You aint sticking him with no big hospital bill."

Belinda said, "It's the college ought to pay, itn't it? He was doing work for the college. They got insurance. They got to." Then she got over in Weedeater's face, who was by then leaning on the front of the truck there at the curb, and said, "I bet that smarts, don't it, Gene? I bet your organs are bruised and busted from that, aint they?"

Evie said, "He could be drowning in his own juices and not know it."

"Here," Belinda said, "you ride in my car."

It had got confusing fast for Weedeater's brother. You could see it on his face.

June said, "I guess we should get you checked out, Gene. If the college won't pay, I will. It'll be OK."

June had got soft living in Tennessee. You don't say you're going to pay people's doctor's bills, even if you are.

Her saying that made me not want to stay in Tennessee.

GENE

That Woman took me to the hospital in her little red car. Brother rode up front. They didn't talk much, Brother and That Woman. I did hear That Woman say she was sorry for hollering at me, getting me distracted, getting me hit in the back with a hunk of concrete.

"That's all right," I heard Brother say. "He's easy distracted."

That's good, I thought. I didn't want That Woman feeling bad.

When we got down there to that hospital, the one in Canard, I was hearing little birds sing. I asked Brother were there really birds singing, and he said he didn't know, maybe, somewhere they was birds singing.

DAWN

June took Weedeater and his brother to the emergency room, and did get the college to pay for it, but I reckon she got in some hot water for it, cause they was waivers she didn't get everybody to sign, but the college did pay for Weedeater's hospital. I reckon they took their time on it, and Weedeater's brother was sore about it, still sore about it, always will be sore about it, I reckon.

Weedeater was all right, nothing broken, but the college told June Weedeater couldn't work no more for them, not on June's projects, cause he didn't have sense enough. When June told him, he started crying, which gave me the creeps cause a man cry over a piddly little job like June was giving him, aint no telling what all else he'd do. I mean, she was still letting him mow her yard. Wasn't like she put him on a train out of town.

Also, it turned out Pharoah, the dog I got for June that I always wished for my own, wasn't killed after all. She was hemmed up in the house all day while June was doing her Hollywood sign, but after the college fired Weedeater, many days Pharoah went to stay with Weedeater. Which was fine, cause June kept her flea medicine up to date.

GENE

Before light the morning after That Woman sent me home from her sign-making job, Sister's old man come banging at the front door window to the little house out behind Sister's. I was dead asleep in the chair. Pharoah come up off her front feet, barking in a fright. Sister's old man wore khaki work clothes, partying-like-a-younger-man lines around his eyes.

He said, "Gene, you want to work?" They was already sweat on his lip and forehead.

I asked him where at.

"Running coal," he said. "Up Dogsplint."

I went with him in my day-before clothes and he didn't stop talking the whole way up Drop Creek.

"This is your chance," he said. "Change your life."

He talked like he didn't have no part in Sister killing herself.

"You do a good job here," he said, "and you could be working a good long while. The work is lined out." Said it like I didn't know he was into them pills, like I didn't come in there and find him wasted, popcorn all over the floor, scrawny blond head in his lap strung to a bag-of-bones body.

"I'm counting on you not to screw this up," he said, like I didn't know. "You think you can do that?"

I just let him drive, looked out the window, tried to think of something else. We drove by a gang of men in jail orange weedeating, hanging off the sides of a gulley, chewing tobacco and not looking up. Their T-shirts was dirty and yellow.

~~~~~~~~~~

THEY'S A lot of training you go through before they let you work in a coal mine. Training on the equipment, safety training, training on all the laws, training on what to do if something goes wrong. I done all that back in the spring, got my miner's card, and Sister's old man tried to get me to work then, but after Sister shot herself, I couldn't do it. Couldn't do nothing, really. They's a couple days couldn't nobody find me. I run up on the mountain behind Granny's, out where me and Brother played when we was boys. I stayed up there in the spring woods, little sprigs of green and purple, pretty yellow sprouts poking up through the dead leaves, for most of a week.

I piled brush and heaped up rocks, tried to tidy the woods best I could. I don't know why. Wadn't no point to it. Just piling stuff up. Sleeping in the wet, listening to the rain.

Ever since that time, when I see something human-made out in the woods, like a little run of rock wall, or rocks set in a square—most times, I expect I'm like you, I think, well, they must've been a house here, or some cow pasture or cornfield, and generally, I expect that's right, that's what it was. But now I think too maybe that was some other person's life flown all to pieces and they come out here to set something in order where nobody but the birds and squirrels would bear witness. We just don't know what all's happened, do we?

As we pulled up to the mine, a memory come to me. At that training for coal miners I went to, one of them running it asked me to carry a tray of danishes with frosting striped across them, each wrapped up by itself, into the room where the coffee was. One man grabbed one off as I went by, but ever time I got to a door, one of them men would open it for me, or push them fellers piled up in the hall out of the way. Somebody was always watching out, making sure I got on my way, and I got it in my head that meant something about coal miners, about how they pay attention to each other, pay attention to how to keep things moving forward.

When I got to the mine, they give me stripes to wear, said I'd pay em back out of my first check. Same for the rubber boots with a steel toe. They give me a respirator in case I got into bad air. They give me a battery for my light, which hitched to the front of my hard plastic cap.

I was sitting there with my stuff on, my back against the strand-board wall of the locker room, when a man decked out same as me come smiling my way. He was clean and red-bearded and you look in his eyes and they was calm, like Sunday morning, like That Woman's eyes, and you could tell he'd be a good one to work with, that he'd work safe and not let you get in trouble. He stuck his hand out.

He said, "Denny Stack."

I told him my name and he asked was I ready to go. I said I was. We stepped out into the hot damp of the July morning and into the cool dark of the mine, like stepping into the mouth of a giant fish just come out of the water. There were fans big as Granny's dinner table pushing air in one tunnel, pushing it out another. Cables snaked in and out of there, cable thick as a child's arm, carrying juice to run the equipment. The walls of the mine, called ribs, were solid coal. Cutting machines ran loud as locomotives, steel toothbrushes with drill-bit bristles scrubbing the coal from the wall onto a belt. The belts rumbled and rattled on their supports, carrying the coal out of the mine. The coal seam would rise and fall in height and so then would the top, which was rock, not coal.

"Don't pay to move rock," Denny said.

We kept walking in. It didn't seem real to me. Seemed like I was in a movie come on after you went to sleep in your chair.

"You get used to it," Denny said.

I barely seen Denny behind the light on his cap. He was glare and shadow. My cap was green, cause I was green. Green cap showed everybody to watch out for you. That you was new. This mine was the one Dawn's daddy died in, Hubert's brother. A coal-cutting machine had pinned him to the rib, cut him in half. Denny told me about that as the seam got lower, squatting as he caught his breath.

We had been walking twenty minutes I guess. The top was four feet off the floor, and it kept sloping down till it was like crawling around under a house that didn't never end.

"You get used to it," Denny said again.

Denny told me about a man who got into juice, got fried like a squirrel. He told me about big round rocks that fell out of the ceiling, looked like the big kettles the old people used to render their lard and make their soap.

"Kettle rock drop right out of the top," Denny said. "Mash you flat as a flitter."

We got to the place where I was going to be working, the seam barely a yard high. Denny shone his light down on the ground beside where the big conveyor belt was carrying out coal. He said, "See that coal's fell off the belt?"

I said I did. We was both on our knees by then. Mostly over on our elbows, too.

"Well," Denny said, "that's your coal. Shovel it back on the belt."

"Then what?" I said.

"Aint no then what," Denny said. "You just move on down the line and do it again. Till somebody come and get you."

I threw my light down the tunnel. The light just run out of gas in the darkness, stopped shining, and the darkness went right on.

"Here's how," Denny said, and he lay over on his side, started shoveling coal back on the belt.

Looked to me like about the most uncomfortable, unnatural act I'd ever seen.

"You got it?" Denny said over the rumble of the belt.

I said I did. Denny nodded, handed me the shovel, said he'd be back after while. Said he'd come get me around dinner time. I went to shoveling, on my back in the gray mud, my shoulder mashed into the ground, my side getting wet, throwing the shovelsful of coal across my front onto the belt. The grind of the cutting machine came to me through the dark up the belt, ungodly loud. I kept scooting down the beltline, kept shoveling, but after I guess thirty shovel loads I tried to sit up, but the top wasn't hardly high enough for me to do it, so I lay back down and kept shoveling. It was hard to get my light on what I was shoveling, but I kept at it. Kept at it. It wasn't twenty minutes I wanted out of there so bad I thought I might cry. But I kept on. Move, arms, move, I said to my arms.

It was cool in the mine, so I didn't really notice when I started sweating. When I did, I took me a drink out of the milk jug of water Denny'd give me. Since I couldn't hardly raise up I had to kind of lean sideways and tip that jug into my mouth. I lost a fair amount of what come out. Then I went back to scooting and shoveling. I tried counting the shovel loads. Got up to five hundred and I had to go to the bathroom. Sister's old man had got me a big coffee which I don't normally drink. I crawled down the tunnel got into a side spot, worked my pants down, and cut loose right there on the ground. Heard something squeak like an old car trunk hinge when that poop of mine hit, a rat most likely. I went back to shoveling.

While I was working, I tried to think of something else—birds flying through the sky, the sky so big and white. Leaves floating down off trees in the fall of the year, swirling in the sky, headed ever which way like people coming out of a ballgame. But I couldn't think of anything for long, because my shovel would stop.

And Denny'd told me: don't let that shovel stop.

I loaded the shovel blade again. Turned it out on the belt. Again. Again. Again. I kept thinking any second they was going to come and tell me it was time for a dinner break, and they didn't come and didn't come. Then come out of my throat a baby noise, and then tears, and I cried. I aint going to lie to you. The tears come out of me like I was a busted main.

DAWN

Me and Nicolette ate bubble-gum ice cream for breakfast. Hubert had potatoes. The July sun come early, made it hot in the booth closest to the front window in the old drugstore. Nicolette wore orange, purple, and white striped tights, her favorites. I told her she was going to burn up, but she said she didn't care. Said she wanted to play I-Spy.

"I spy with my little eye something black," Nicolette said. "Something black, Momma."

I said, "Hush, baby."

Hubert said, "You shouldn't give her ice cream for breakfast."

Hubert rolled his bottom lip between his teeth. He had ketchup in his beard hairs. I asked Hubert did Sidney Coates know Momma stole his thirty thousand dollars. Hubert drank coffee, stared at nothing.

Nicolette said, "Can I go to the bathroom?"

I said, "I'll take you in a minute."

Nicolette said she could go by herself.

I said, "No, you can't."

She said, "Yes, I can."

I said, "Listen, if you're not back in two minutes, I'm coming to get you."

Nicolette took off running and I ate some of her ice cream, asked Hubert how he was going to find Momma.

Hubert said, "I'll find her."

I said, "I want to go with you when you hunt her."

I said, "I'm going."

Hubert said, "What are you going to do with her?" and pointed towards the bathroom.

I said, "Leave her with Houston."

Hubert blew across his coffee.

I said, "She'll be all right."

Hubert said, "It's been two minutes."

I said, "Do what?"

Hubert said, "Since she went to the bathroom."

"So?" I said. "She's slow."

Hubert said, "You told her you'd come get her."

My mind crowded up like a teenager's funeral visitation. Momma pilled up. Momma snitching on Sidney Coates for selling pills and cocaine and everything else. Sidney Coates getting busted and the cash in his house seized. Hubert trying to pay back Sidney the money he lost so Sidney don't kill Momma. Momma stealing the money Hubert was going to give Sidney to keep him from killing her and then her run off with it with a tanning-bed addict from Tennessee. And the thing was, it wasn't just us. Everybody in the county had some crazy like that. Idiots fanning out from Drop Creek to Feist, like locusts in the Bible, stealing anything the pawn shop would take, passed out and pissing on decent people's sofas, staggering through the dollar store like zombies. The whole thing weighed you down. Made you feel like you were packing cinder blocks everywhere you went.

I turned to see Nicolette put her foot on the bottom row of the birthday card rack next to the table, wanting a higher-up card. I caught the rack right as it was about to tip.

Nicolette said, "Momma Trish needs a card," the stripes over her serious pudgy thighs knocking together at the knees. "She could be scared. She could be getting robbed on the road or stabbed with a knife or throwed in the river."

Nicolette had been listening to murder ballads with her papaw Houston.

I put her back in the booth, said, "What good's a card gonna do if she's stabbed or throwed in the river?"

Nicolette said, "I don't know."

I asked her which one she picked. She showed me one with a dog on it, said some dopey thing about birthdays and dog years.

Sidney Coates come in the diner, his lips shiny and fish-thick. His eyes darted around like unruly children. Smell of blood filled my nose. You could always smell blood on Sidney Coates, but you never could see it. He slid into a booth on the other side of the store.

All of them were going to jail. Hubert. Sidney Coates. Albert. Evie. They were going to get rounded up like everybody else, get their picture put in the paper in V-neck T-shirt and tank-top sleeping clothes, khaki pants and housedresses pulled on right before they got cuffed, parading in front of cameras, not even covering their faces, sit in jail a while, come out meaner and tireder and looking less like they thought they could ever win. You felt sorry for them.

Sidney Coates sat drinking coffee with one hand and pop with the other. The waitress brought him a dish of ice cream, and he spooned it in his coffee. He spooned it in his pop, too. Hubert sat looking at Sidney Coates. Sidney Coates raised up like his back hurt. Hubert got up and went over to Sidney Coates's booth.

They sat there like they were old farmers talking about hay and husbands lost their way. They sat with their hands on the table, their backs straight, like standup citizens. Their lips barely moved when they spoke. Their heads didn't move at all. I figured Hubert was trying to get Sidney to go easy on Momma even though he didn't have the money to pay back what Momma cost Sidney. Whatever Sidney was saying was mostly no, because Hubert's neck started stretching. His head moved towards Sidney Coates. Hubert's mouth opened wider and his jaw hinged open and closed faster.

Sidney Coates took a pen out of his shirt pocket and started drawing on a napkin. Nicolette sat jammed up next to the window glass, me between her and them men.

Nicolette slipped under the table and ran up the drugstore aisle before I could grab her.

I said, "Nicolette, come here," and she didn't do nothing but keep on dashing up and down. I got up and she ran over to the booth where Sidney and Hubert sat. I scooped her up in my arms.

She said, "That's me," and pointed at the napkin Sidney Coates was drawing on. He was drawing a picture had to be Nicolette cause the stripes on the tights Sidney was drawing were just like hers. When Nicolette said, "That's me," Sidney didn't do nothing, just kept on drawing.

I turned to go, and Sidney Coates cleared his throat. Then he took the picture of Nicolette and tore it in half, stacked the pieces and tore them in half again. When they got small as he could tear, Sidney Coates cleared his throat and emptied his hand of the napkin pieces into his red plastic pop cup. He held his butter knife by the blade and used the handle to push that paper past the ice cream down to the bottom of the cup.

Then Sidney turned his stuffed deer eyes on me, eyelids riding over the glass balls like a shirt not covering a fat man's belly. He cleared his throat again. His eyes popped open and he stared at me like I was what he ate, like I was bleeding and he wouldn't have no trouble catching me,

He just kept staring like I was supposed to melt so he could eat me with a spoon instead of having to tear me into chunks he could fit in his mouth.

I set Nicolette down, said to Sidney Coates,

Sidney Coates smiled.

I said, "Hubert, I'll talk to you tomorrow," and I walked out of there.

When I got outside, the summer light blinded me, light clear as children crying in the night, bright as welder sparks, the sky full of pressure, mashing me down inside myself.

I said, "Where you at, Nicolette?" even though her hand was right there in mine.

She said, "What are you doing, Momma?"

We went and got in the car, the seats already hot in Mamaw's Escort. I headed back up the mountain, out to Mamaw's house where didn't nobody ever go and if they did, we could see them coming.

I didn't put Nicolette in the backseat, didn't put her in the car seat. I kept her in the front seat with me, kept my hand on her except when I shifted gears, and we went back to Mamaw's. On the way, I didn't mind the rock trucks slowing us down, didn't mind the sun blinding me.

When we got out at Mamaw's, Nicolette asked me why I was breathing so hard and I said I wasn't. She knew better but it didn't matter she knew better because she was just a little girl and I was a grown woman, her mother, and mothers know best, except when their husbands die in coal mine accidents and they grieve themselves down in a pill bottle and get in trouble with the law and start wearing tape recorders when they go buy Oxy and get other people arrested and get their lives threatened and the lives of the people close to them threatened and then them not even care cause they're so far gone, but other than that, other than when that kind of stuff happens, mothers always always know best.

GENE

I got through that first day in the coal mine. I come home and slept in the chair. Didn't eat nothing. Woke up the next day, walked down to the store, bought a biscuit with sausage and bacon and egg, some pop and crackers and snowball cakes and Vienna sausages, and Sister's old man took me back up there again and I started in again and cried a little the first hour, and a little less the second, and by the third day I didn't cry the whole shift. But I kept getting more and more give out.

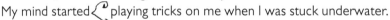

THE DAY the pump pumping water out of the mine failed and the water backed up, it was third shift, the wee hours of Sunday morning, no repairman on the site, us running coal.

Denny come by to check on me. Things was running good. It was my fourth day. I'd worn my stripes all once, washing them in Sister's washing machine, and even though I still had the green cap on, I didn't feel quite so new. I had my thermos of coffee and my gallon of water. I had me a couple of pork chops in my dinner bucket and my dinner bucket hid. Denny give me a pat on the shoulder before he went back to work, and I was feeling all right.

Little while after Denny left, I fell asleep laying on my side shoveling belt, deader than a hammer, dreaming of That Woman, my shovel curled up to me like That Woman in my dreams. That cold wet of that mine water backing up come crawling on me and I woke up and kept shoveling, but the water kept getting higher till it was a foot deep and rising in a space barely a yard high and still didn't nobody come and the water rising rising rising. I wondered was I still in my dream, but I was awake as you, and when that water had filled my little pass halfway up, I started on out and I reckon I had took too long to leave because I couldn't keep my head out of the water, and had to hold my breath. It wasn't for long, maybe a minute or two, but that's a long time to have your head underwater.

My mind started playing tricks on me when I was stuck underwater.

I seen big lizards with fins like fish around their necks. They come swimming through green and orange and yellow hula hoops, lightning flashing in the water. They was oil in the water catching that lightning like thick soap bubbles. Them round fossils you found in the top spun in front of me, looked like seashells, like poker chips. I heard singing like mermaids, high-pitched and squealy, like Holiness women when the music lifts you up on your toes. I seen That Woman all dressed up in ferns and seaweed. Her head bobbed backwards and forwards unconscious.

I wondered did I look like a sea monster. Was my face all scaly? Did people dread the sight of me when they heard me walking, stealing along on my big paddle feet? The water went down my throat and nose at the same time and it felt like water went in my eye sockets. In that instant, when I felt like my head was about to crush, I didn't want to be covered up no more with water. I wanted out of that.

My hand was flat against the top and there not room enough for me to get my head up out of the water. I figured out I could lay back and get my nose out for a little bit. But to breathe not water you had to focus real hard on not panicking.

I was making a fair job of it. I wadn't flailing too hard. But I was flailing, where I never was good at swimming and generally avoided water. After a while it got to me, got me panicked. I stopped thrashing and goodbye come on my mind. Goodbye to Brother. Goodbye to Pharaoh. It has hard to settle in on my goodbyes thrashing around like that. The water pushed me. You'd've thought it would have pushed me to where it was going, but it didn't. I stopped saying goodbye. Stopped flapping my arms trying to get to air that wadn't there. I took a minute to feel of myself. Felt my belt hung on the conveyor. I reached right quick and unbuckled my belt. When it come loose, I come loose. I flowed headfirst with the water. I put my arms out over my head, out front of me, so I wouldn't bust my head on nothing, and before I knew it that water was pushing harder, and I was going faster, faster than I really wanted to go. And where I still wasn't getting any air, I went back to saying my goodbyes, in particular to That Woman.

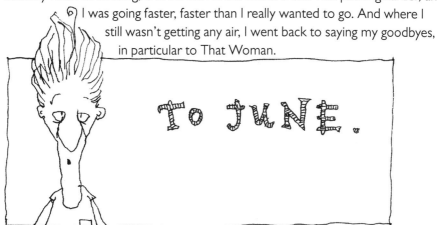

Told her I'd enjoyed taking care of her yard and her dog and that I was sorry if I'd paid her attention unwanted. About that time there was a kind of upswoosh and the water kept flowing but I could get up on my hands and knees and I was sucking air. Sucking that good sweet air.

DAWN

June's little red Honda car sat under the carport when me and Nicolette pulled up at Mamaw's. A leather bag color of a caramel cream, nicer than any bag I knew, sat on the backseat next to a purple-and-red duffel bag June had ever since I'd known her. There were pieces of posterboard and a set of magic markers showing through a Megamart bag back there too.

June came out of Mamaw's house the same time Hubert pulled up in his dark green pickup with the blue-tint windows. June came up to her car, put her key in the lock, acted like she couldn't see me.

I said, "Where you going, June? Going to hunt for Momma?"

June said she was going to West Virginia.

I said, "What for?"

Hubert came up and stood beside me. June called the name of some hippie stoner actress who had been coming around telling everyone she didn't like mountaintop removal and using her famousness to get people stirred up about how bad it was. June said she was going to West Virginia to get arrested with this actress up on a strip job somewhere.

I said, "How long you going to be gone?"

She said she didn't know.

I said, "What about your class?"

She said, "I got that covered."

I said, "What about Momma? Your sister? Your sister you said you come here to help," and here I kind of mocked June, "find her way through the darkness."

June said, "Dawn."

I said,

June said, "Dawn, honey."

I said, "Cause if you are, I wish you'd tell me where that light is, cause I don't have no idea, and I'd sure like to know."

June opened the car door and I slammed it back. Nicolette said, "Mommy," and looked like she was fixing to cry, and I said, "Don't you dare cry," and Nicolette cried anyway, but quiet, and Hubert picked Nicolette up and held her in his arms. June stood there stiff and straight, her eyes watering up behind her turtleshell driving glasses.

June said, "I was wrong about your mother." She put her hand on the door, said, "I was wrong about myself. I can't do nothing for her."

I said, "You're just scared. You're scared because Belinda Coates slapped you one time. You going to give up on your own sister because of that. That sucks, June. That sucks so hard."

June's eyes flashed fire. She was finally mad. She said, "Well where should I go, Dawn? Where should I go to hunt her? Hunh? I'm as likely to find her on the road to West Virginia as anywhere."

I said, "Not if you aint looking for her."

June stomped her foot on the concrete pad. She dropped her keys. "Dawn," she said, "Who do you think I am? What kind of person do you think I am?"

I said, "A quitter."

Hubert asked June who this man Momma went with was. He asked her about Calvin.

"He's some friend of Kenny's," June said.

Hubert said, "The radio station guy?"

"Mm-hmm," June said.

"Don't reckon Kenny's got no part in it," Hubert said.

June said she didn't think so.

"Mm-hmm," Hubert said.

Two four-wheelers went by on the Trail below. Each four-wheeler had a boy and a girl doubleheading. They were laughing and talking back and forth, speeding up and slowing down, so the four-wheelers were right next to each other, rolling along being all carefree together.

Hubert said, "So you seen her last when?"

"Early that morning," June said.

"Driving what?" Hubert said.

"Some kind of old car," June said. "Big Buick or Pontiac or something. Had a bumper sticker said 'The Power of Pride' on it."

"Right," Hubert said.

June said, "Well. I'm going."

Mamaw walked out of the house. She walked towards us and waved, said, "Hubert." Then she went around the side of the house and out of sight. June got in the car. I was done hollering at her. I felt heavier than a truck motor. June's window rolled down. She put her elbow on the door.

"Bye, Dawn," June said. "I'm sorry."

DON'T MATTER I SAID.

"Bye, sweetheart," June said to Nicolette.

"Bye, Aunt June," Nicolette said. "Be careful."

Aunt June looked at Hubert and tightened her lips. She backed the car out of the carport, out the driveway, and drove off down the Trail. Nicolette went the way Mamaw went.

Hubert said, "You all right?"

"Might as well be," I said.

Hubert said, "I'll find her."

"No, you won't," I said. "Something'll go wrong and wash her right back here. She won't be able to hide."

"Well," Hubert said. "Might as well hunt her while I'm waiting. Be something."

I said, "You reckon?"

Hubert asked what I was going to do. I told him I was going to stay there till something else made sense.

"Well," Hubert said, "you got my number."

I said I did.

Hubert said, "Keep your head up."

When I didn't answer, Hubert climbed in his truck and left.

GENE

I walked out of the coal mine and didn't go back. Walked past Sister's husband without saying a word. He said something to me, but I didn't hear it. I got a ride home from Denny Stack, the miner'd been nice to me my first day. Turns out Denny Stack is kin to That Woman. He's Cora's brother's boy. He told me that in the truck on the way back to Sister's. He dropped me off, and I went in my place and took off my clothes. Fell asleep in my drawers on the chair in the front of the house. I come to to the sound of Pharaoh barking outside. That Woman was standing in the door. I pulled my pants on. My head spun like a washing machine.

That Woman looked like a ghost standing there, like she might wisp away. She pushed her hair out of her eyes. I opened the door. Pharaoh stopped barking, laid her ears down.

That Woman said, "Good morning, Gene. Did I wake you?"

I told her she didn't, told her I didn't sleep much. Said, "Bout every other day, I catch a few winks." I asked her did she want something to eat.

She said no thank you, asked would I take care of Pharaoh for a few days. Said she didn't know how long. She seemed agitated. I must've smiled cause she said, "Gene, did you lose a tooth?"

I told her I'd knocked one out in the mine water, told her about my adventure in that underground sea.

She handed me Pharaoh's leash, said, "You've had a rough time of it here lately, haven't you?"

I didn't say nothing. I just looked at her. Tried to listen to her the way Brother did a truck motor when he was trying to figure out what was keeping it from running right.

That Woman said, "Gene, are you OK?"

Because I reckon I was wobbling.

She said, "Gene, let's set you down."

She got me behind the elbow and took me to my chair. When I got there, I lay my head back, stared at the stucco on the ceiling. It swirled like outer space galaxies. Pharaoh licked my hand hanging over the armrest. I closed my eyes and traveled back in time to the day Calvin and Tricia run off.

I saw in my mind how Calvin come to the house early that morning. I heard him rattle up to the downstairs bedroom window, the one where That Woman's sister was. It was a big rattle, like it come from a giant snake, snake big as a phone pole. I saw his giant jar of Oxy Cottons, a jar big as a pickled baloney jars sitting on a store counter. Humongous bottle of pills. Which is why That Woman's sister run off with him.

I opened my eyes. That Woman was staring at me like I was a fish in a bowl. Said, "You all right, Gene?" and I said I was and she said maybe it don't make sense for her to leave Pharaoh with me. Said, "Maybe you're too busy to fool with her."

My head cleared. I about bumped her nose standing up, said, "You know what? I still have some food back there in the closet." I went back in the bedroom where there was a garbage bag half full of the fancy dog food That Woman fed Pharaoh. I dipped out a cupful, filled her bowl.

I said, "Where you going this time?"

She said, "I'm going to a sit-in, Gene. In West Virginia."

I said, "I thought you did that already."

She said, "This is a different one. At a different mine."

I filled Pharoah's water bowl, set it down. I hadn't had a chance to talk to That Woman about what happened in Tennessee, her being with Kenny and her sister running off with Calvin, me getting thrown in the car trunk and not getting to be her hero. Hadn't talked about that twenty-eight thousand dollars getting gone.

It was a lot for her to deal with, especially where it was family, and not always on the right side of the law, and I'd say quite stressful, and then on top of that all she was doing for that class, that big project with the letters, answering to all kinds of people, and it aggravating both her mother and niece, who sure let her know about it. Then her running off to West Virginia to get up in someone else's business. I don't know. I was thinking maybe she needed somebody to talk to.

So I said, "Is that Kenny going with you to West Virginia?"

She said no. Said, "He's got to stay here for the radio."

I leaned both hands on the kitchen counter and said, "Who's going to look after you?"

That Woman sat down in my chair and closed her eyes, leaned her head back. Pharaoh licked her hand like she had mine. I set down on one of the stools at the counter and waited for That Woman to say something. She didn't. So I reached my hand out towards her and I seen how brown my hand was compared to her white face and I come aware of how I smelled and I wondered could my hand being that close to her ever feel good to her. My chest closed up and I was breathing like I was back in that mine, back swallowed up by water. I got excited like a man does. Her eyes didn't open. I wanted to lay my hand on That Woman's cheek, on its whiteness and softness. I imagined it would be like laying your hand in the stainless-steel pan of sour cream on the potato bar at the steakhouse. But then I thought, "She don't need me touching her like that."

NOT RIGHT NOW.

That Woman opened her eyes and my hand was still hanging there in the air above her face. That Woman jumped up and knocked over the lamp and I stood up straight and my excited man business felt like it was about to break off and That Woman didn't say nothing, just ran out the door and left me there with the dog standing at the slammed shut door. That dog whined like a train hitting its brakes.

That Woman went halfway down the hill to her vehicle, down the flat rocks notched into the hill. She got into the shadow cast by Sister's house and turned back, came back up the hill, her head bowed. She raised her head as her hand hit the knob and looked right at me, eyes like fire pokers.

That Woman let go of the knob, turned and sat on the stoop. Her neck glistened like a water snake warming in on a rock in the eddy of a river.

I cracked the door, said, "You want your dog back?"

She turned her head toward me, her cheek down in her shoulder. Didn't look at me, just turned her head to the side. That Woman said, "What were you doing?"

I said, "Getting too close, I reckon."

She sat for a minute, then she nodded.

I said, "You seem wore out."

That Woman said, "My mother has done more good for more people than I ever will."

I said, "That's a hard thing to count."

That Woman smiled.

I said, "And you don't know. You might get in a place to do something for a whole bunch at once. Like find out about a bomb about to go off at a car race or something. Save hundreds and thousands at a whack. Get caught up that way."

That Woman said, "You never know, do you?"

I said, "No, ma'am. You don't."

That Woman said, "Why don't Kenny want me? Why don't he get rid of his wife?"

Pharoah whined.

She said, "He aint never going to leave her. Not with all them kids."

She put her head on her knees.

I said, "Well, we don't never know, do we?"

She raised her head up, said, "I don't need him. No point to a man, is there, Gene?"

THAT ONE STUMPED ME.

I wanted to agree with her, but I hadn't totally give up on being a man myself. I let the birds tweet a minute. Let the sun get hotter. Then I said, "Well. There's bound to be a point. To all this."

That Woman stood up, rubbed her hands down the thigh of her pants, said she had to go to West Virginia. She took two steps down the hill, stopped, said, "Thank you, Gene." Took sixty dollars out of her front pocket, said, "Here's for in case I don't get back before you need to mow." The money passed from her hand to mine, and That Woman said, "I appreciate you, Gene."

Then she walked off the hill and left the world yawning open like a sinkhole.

7

SPRAY PAINT & BURN

DAWN

My grandmother didn't much care for Bill Clinton, but the one come after? Lord.

"This little dickhead we got now," she said, "I wouldn't piss down his throat if he was dying of thirst."

Mamaw had on a long-sleeve denim shirt and leather garden gloves black and shiny in the fingertips. She had both hands full of poison ivy she'd cut down off a fence. The fence went around an aboveground swimming pool she got rid of when June went off to college. Foolishness, she'd said. Pool was Houston's idea, she'd said.

Nicolette ran in circles in the grassed-over gravel where the pool had been. Mamaw walked with her elbows locked, the poison ivy out away from her, and threw it onto the bank on the other side of the fence. Mamaw was slipping. Used to be, she would have bagged it, or taken it farther off, thrown it down a sinkhole. June said one time when she was little, Mamaw burned a pile of poison ivy, and Houston walked through the smoke and got poison ivy in his lungs. They had to put him in the hospital over it. Mamaw didn't burn poison ivy after that. Said she didn't need the doctor bills.

Mamaw spit, bent over, clipped another dozen strands of vine at the base of the fence, pulled it loose, and had a double fistful when she said, "We aint got no law. Nobody to stop them doing whatever they want. Stripping. No answer for it." She ground her jaws back and forth like millstones, dirt and flecks of leaf hanging in the lines of her shiny face, face the color of good fried potatoes. "And now these gas wells," she said, and spit again. "Beats anything I ever seen." She started back to the spot where she was pitching the vine. "Rip and tear," she said, "rip and tear." She chucked the vine over the fence.

116

She turned with her palms out to me and Nicolette. "I'm glad I aint gonna be around much longer to see it."

Nicolette stopped swatting the seeds off dandelions with a stick. She said, "Where you going, Granny? Florida?"

Mamaw stared at Nicolette, her arms out from her sides, said, "Who wants to go to Sand Cave?"

~~~~~~~~~

THAT DAY was Nicolette's first trip to Sand Cave. Mamaw put potato chips and Hershey bars in a backpack. She filled aluminum bottles with water. She made sandwiches out of thick-sliced baloney. Then we set out walking down the Trail.

Nicolette held my hand. I wondered why Mamaw was on about the coal mines. I reckoned her and June had been talking. They stirred each other up. Mamaw didn't act like she cared whether June got in on Mamaw's fixing-the-world projects. And when June did do something, like go to West Virginia to protest, Mamaw criticized the way she was doing it. They was like a pot about to boil over all the time, sizzling out on the stove eye, making you nervous.

My mother was steam floating above Mamaw and June's cookpot of world-fixing. She just floated away, disappeared, left everything sticky and greasy behind her. I wondered that day was Momma in sunshine like us. Was the wind blowing her hair? Was she driving fast in Calvin's Bonneville?

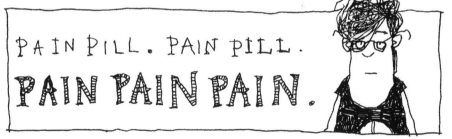

"Mommy," Nicolette said, "Somebody squashed that turtle." There in a dapple of sun a bright red crater opened in a yellow-black turtle back. I looked up at the sky. Two vultures circled like a waitress's rag on a dirty table.

"Cut down here," Mamaw said, and pointed with her ski-pole walking stick down a graveled path. "Nicolette," she said, "come away from there."

Nicolette come up from her squat at the turtle's side. The vultures came a level lower. That turtle wasn't sharp enough to stay out of the sunshine. Got your Vitamin D, didn't you, turtle? Should have got it from a pill, turtle.

Mamaw said, "It's a tortoise."

I said, "What's the difference?"

Mamaw said, "Look it up."

Mamaw didn't help me on stuff like that now I had a baby.

Sand Cave was a bigmouth cave lay below the Trail about a mile from Mamaw's house. Nicolette kicked her shoes off soon as she hit sand, went running right in its mouth.

I said, "Nicolette, come here."

Mamaw leaned over and picked up Nicolette's shoes. She kept her other hand on the ski pole. She put her fingers inside Nicolette's shoes and held them both in one hand. "Let her go," she said.

I said, "There's water in there."

"She won't find it," Mamaw said, "not till we show her."

It was Mamaw took me for swimming lessons when I was little. Her and Daddy. I didn't want to go. Nobody I knew had to take swimming lessons. Nobody on Daddy's side, which was about the only people I ever saw when I was little.

"That's stupid," my cousins said. "Who takes swimming lessons? You need to take not-being-stupid lessons." My cousins were crusty-eyed, Kool Aid–mouthed jackasses.

I took swimming lessons back when Mamaw and Houston had the photo studio. Mamaw traded this woman with a pool lived up Falstaff Acres her daughter's engagement pictures for them letting me swim in their pool and the mother teaching me how to swim—how to breathe right in water and do all them strokes. I hated it. Hated it because I hated Falstaff Acres, hated that woman's peppermint breath, hated her red fingernail polish on her hands holding me in the water while I had to churn my arms like an idiot. I hated why I had to go there, too.

I had to go cause I had bad dreams when I was little. Bad dreams about water—monsters in water, big storms of water, water black and green at once, water didn't have no top and me down in it—and I'd scream out, they'd say, scream out but I'd never hear it. I'd just wake up and there'd be Daddy sitting on the edge of the bed and when he'd see my eyes he'd hug me to him and his face'd be wet where he'd been crying, and his cheeks would be like a scrub brush.

I'VE ALWAYS HAD TROUBLE WITH WATER.

I said, "Mamaw, I don't want her running off. She don't need nobody's help to find water or nothing else."

Mamaw handed me the shoes and stepped back against the wall of the cave mouth and took her own shoes off and worked her toes down in the sand and said, "I know it. That child aint got a fearful bone in her body."

Nicolette come running up with something's skull. Said, "Look, Mommy," and I said, "Put that down. It's nasty." I knocked it out of her hand.

Mamaw poked at the skull with her ski pole.

"What is it, Mamaw?" Nicolette said.

Mamaw rolled it with her stick, said, "Fox."

Nicolette grabbed hold of my hand. "Let's go, Momma. It's dark. You need to go with me."

Mamaw put her shoes back on, gave Nicolette hers. Mamaw got down in her sack and pulled out two knocked-around flashlights. She give them to me, then pulled out an elastic strap had a light on it like a miner's light. The strap was rainbow-colored and the way it pinched her hair when she put it on made her look like she ought to be in a coal miner exercise video.

Nicolette said, "I want me one of them."

"Here," I said, and handed her a yellow flashlight.

Mamaw took a drink out of her water bottle and reached it to me. I shook my head. Nicolette took it and drank fast, spilled water all down her front.

Mamaw said, "Slow down there, girl."

Nicolette swallowed water hard, her throat pulsing like a vein. Mamaw shook the bottle when she got it back, put it in her bag, moved deeper into the cave. The path got narrow. The rock walls were covered with words written in spraypaint and burn. Mamaw clicked her light on and turned sideways and climbed up some rocks through a hole the size of a garbage can lid.

Nicolette turned towards the hole and looked back over her shoulder at me. "Shove her through," Mamaw said. Nicolette raised her arms and Mamaw's hand came out of the hole. I got my hands on Nicolette's hips and heaved her up.

When we all three got through the hole, the only light was our light. Our three flashlights filled up the narrow squeeze we passed through for the next fifty yards. When we got to the other end, we had to climb up on what felt like a platform, like an overhead compartment in some giant geologic Greyhound bus. We all three got up there. Nicolette had smudges down her temples, but a face-busting smile to go with it. Mamaw and me scuttled along best we could— Nicolette moved way easier.

On that rock platform with its low top, we were three girls hiding under some Big Momma's bed. First I giggled and then Mamaw and then Nicolette laughed a great flat laugh of her own. We moved deeper back under the mountain. We came on a slot through the rock. From inside came the sound of trickling water, like a leak.

Mamaw said, "Here we are now."

Through the slot was a flat spot, long and wide as a high school basketball court. It was water-surfaced, the ceiling high as in the old courthouse.

We were quiet in the face of that black water hole. The water burped and slid. Further out you could hear splashing, like water does off a eave without a gutter during a rainstorm. We got down in that pond room, which I reckon was a gathering spot for several streams. We sat down on flat stones piled to make a seat. When we set our feet in the water, you could feel it moving. I held my light out over Nicolette's feet like it was an operating room lamp. The dirt and sand flowed over her toes like smoke.

Nicolette got up and splashed and knocked around out into the middle of the pond, water up to her knees.

I said, "Come here."

"That's as deep as it gets," Mamaw said, "where she's at."

Nicolette dropped her flashlight in the water. I stood up. Mamaw said, "They're supposed to be waterproof." When I got to Nicolette, I saw the flashlight roll on the sandy bottom of the pond like a fish with a headlight. Then Nicolette's light went out. I felt all over my body like Nicolette might get taken from me. I might lose her to that flowing water or maybe to the dark itself.

Nicolette fell to her hands and knees, digging in the water for her flashlight. She stirred the bottom up, turned the water into clouds. She couldn't find the light. I could only hunt for it with one hand cause I had to hold my own. Mamaw came to us, a light moving where her head was supposed to be.

She'd first come to the cave with my grandfather, when he brought her to Long Ridge to live, after they'd been married a while, after she'd caught him catting around. He brought her out to the Ridge to try and fix things. The Ridge was where Momma met Daddy. Mamaw never could forgive Houston for that. She told me one time she got lost in her anger, lost for years over how Houston done.

Mamaw came and stood with her blue jeans rolled up, said, "Dawn, give me your light." I did. She said, "Help her hunt for it."

Mamaw turned off my light. There was only hers then. She said, "Did you find it?"

I said no. She said, "Well, come on then. Let's give the dust a chance to settle. She went back to where the rocks piled. Mamaw sat straight and solid, her hands on her knees, knees spread like a man's. She was lean and slight as a young cat. We sat beside her. Nicolette was wet and shivering.

Mamaw said to Nicolette, "You want your mother to take you out?"

Nicolette clung to Mamaw's leg, and then climbed into her lap. It surprised me Mamaw let Nicolette do that. But she did, and when she did, she wrapped her arms around Nicolette, moving her hand only to cut off her own light.

Then we were in total dark. Nicolette shifted in Mamaw's arms. Mamaw said, "What is your Aunt June doing?"

I said, "What do you mean?"

"What is she doing," Mamaw said, "there in that store building?"

"She's making a sign," I said.

For a minute, the only noise was water noise.

Mamaw said, "What kind of sign?"

I wondered would cave bugs run all over me in the dark. Cave rats. And over my baby too. I wondered would they run over us like we weren't people, like we was rocks, like I couldn't by moving my finger cause a light to come on and catch them.

"Say!" Mamaw said.

"A big sign for the hillside," I said. "One a person can read from down in town. Like that one says 'Hollywood' in Hollywood."

"Sign says what?" Mamaw said, her voice coming out of the dark like a radio show.

I said, "Mamaw, you know what she's doing. You know what her damn sign says."

"Why?" Mamaw set Nicolette down.

"Stay touching me, Nicolette," I said.

Mamaw stood and said, "Why's she doing it?" She sent a rock skipping across the cave pond in the dark. "What's it supposed to accomplish?"

I said, "I don't know, Mamaw."

Mamaw said, "She's just rubbing people's face in it." Mamaw spit. "Like they don't know."

The cave dripped and flowed. Nicolette picked up a handful of sand and small rock from the cave floor. She ran it through her fingers, from one hand to the other, like a medicine man's rattle, like a snake noise.

Mamaw said, "I don't know where your aunt come from. Want everybody to be happy. Don't have the first idea how to make one person happy."

Nicolette grabbed ahold of my hand and I thought, she's too young to be in here. This is a big scary place and there wadn't no point to bringing her here. Nicolette let the handful of stone and sand fall through my hand.

Nicolette said, "That feels cool, don't it?"

I wished I could see her face.

Mamaw said, "What about your mother?"

I let Nicolette run another handful of sand and gravel through my fingers. The darkness sparkled in my eyes like bad fireworks that don't go off right.

I said, "She's gone, Mamaw."

Nicolette put her hand in mine.

Mamaw turned her light on. She waded level as a crane out to where Nicolette dropped her flashlight. Mamaw's light went first this way then that. Then it moved with her in the direction the water flowed. I turned on my light and pointed it at Nicolette. She sat, her legs folded under her, running her hands through the sand and gravel, picking stones, laying them in her open hand.

She said, "Turn it off, Mommy."

"Why?" I said.

"Please," she said.

I snapped off the flashlight. Nicolette began to hum, to sing a song I didn't know. Mamaw's light moved farther from Nicolette's drop spot. Mamaw sputtered like a lawnmower about to need gas. She couldn't find the flashlight, but she kept looking, her the light,

Mamaw gave up hunting for the flashlight. She faced us from the far end of the pond, said, "That water got more push than you think." The light from her forehead went from white to yellow. Then it flickered. Mamaw put her hands to her head and shined her light onto the slot in the cave wall we'd come through.

"Step over there," she said. "Step over to that hole in the wall."

I pulled Nicolette up by her elbows, felt her shoulders stretch in their sockets. She got to her feet. We stumbled to the slot. I banged my knee. Mamaw splashed up behind us. She come past us and got below the slot just as her light died.

"Lord have mercy," she said, quiet, like she was really asking.

I turned my flashlight on. It came on yellow too.

"Let that rest," Mamaw said. She took my hand. I turned my light off. She said, "Give me your foot," and tapped me on the side of the knee. I raised my foot and she took me by the heel, guided my foot to her knee. "Now raise up," she said, and as I rose, I felt for the hole. I found it easy enough. The cave water rushed louder. "Go on, honey," Mamaw said.

I reached and found her shoulder, leaned forward and hit my forehead on the top of the slot. The flashes of bad fireworks come again. The pain shot straight back from my forehead.

I said, "Mamaw, how the three of us gonna find our way out of here in the pitch dark?"

She said, "It aint pitch dark yet. We got your light."

I got my head through the slot without banging it again. I found a spot to brace myself for when Mamaw reached Nicolette to me.

Mamaw gathered up Nicolette.

"Here she comes," Mamaw said.

Nicolette stuck her finger in my eye. "Hey, Mommy," she said like we was in her room, like I was lowering her down in the bed on any normal night.

"Hey, sweet baby," I said.

She come flying towards me. I went over backwards, hit my head again. Nicolette ended up so close I could smell her Hershey bar breath, the cave water on her cold little carp body.

Mamaw said, "Give me a hand."

I turned on my light, made sure Nicolette was in a good place. I took Mamaw's hand.

Nicolette said, "It's gonna be hot when we get outside. Let's stay here. Spend the night here."

I said, "God Amighty, Nicolette."

Mamaw lay breathing hard. I asked was she OK.

"Your mother," Mamaw said, "she'll be back, I reckon. Aint got no money, does she?"

I said, "She took some from June."

Mamaw said, "June give her money?"

I said, "Momma stole it out of her house."

"What money?" Mamaw said.

I said, "I don't mind to tell you, but I'd like to get out of here first."

Mamaw said, "Well."

I asked could I use my light and she said yes. I shined it on the path across the shelf and turned it off. When it went dark, Nicolette went, "WHOOOOOOP." I scuttled along, tortoise slow, hating caves, something always about to gouge a hole in you. I edged along. I went to turn on my light and check how close we were to the edge of the shelf, to the hole at the other end, and my light wouldn't cut on. I flicked the switch. Flicked it and flicked it.

"Gone?" Mamaw said.

"It won't turn on," I said.

"Probably gone then," Mamaw said.

"Dang, Mamaw," I said. "Why did you bring such sorry lights?"

She said, "Somebody's been using my lights."

"Do you remember the way?" I said.

"Yeah," she said. "Yeah." Her voice sounded lost, like the footsteps of a kid at a new school. I wished I could see her. I never much looked at my grandmother. I looked into the darkness where I thought she was. The water echoed faint and small.

"I got her, Momma," Nicolette said. "I got her around the waist."

The shelf was dry. It was tight and hard. I wanted out. I tried to think of the way out of the cave and couldn't remember when we went left and when we went right. I couldn't remember how long the shelf.

"UMMMMMMMMMMMM," Nicolette said loud. "UMMMMM." She laughed—"HA HA"—laughs like slaps. She said, "I can feel it, Mommy. I remember. I remember the song I was singing. It took me almost all of 'Red Rocking Chair' to get to where you lifted me up before—here." Her hand was in mine and she moved me.

"Slow down, baby," Mamaw said. "There aint no hurry."

Nicolette said, "We go exactly this fast." She sang a song she'd heard at Houston's. She said, "When we was here, I was singing this: 'Who'll rock the cradle, who'll sing the song? Who'll rock the cradle when I'm gone? Who'll rock the cradle when I'm gone?'" We moved with her. "Be careful," Nicolette said, "there's a big stickout rock near you, Momma."

That's how we found out about this thing Nicolette did. She sang all the time in her mind. My grandfather's old music went in her head whole. She'd sometimes sing out loud, sometimes not. And her song became how her memory worked. Everything was marked—places, things people said—by where she was in the song when a thing happened. She could play the songs backwards in her mind—"The railroad men they drink your blood like wine," Nicolette said—that's where you lifted me down."

Mamaw said, "Dawn, you be careful, but see if you can find where the dropdown is."

I scooted feet first, Nicolette humming now, hollow and spooky.

Nicolette said, "Careful, Mommy. You're close."

I found it.

Nicolette said, "Remember how there's kind of a place for your foot off to the side."

I did remember it. I found my way down into that narrow. "Come on, baby," I said. "It's not long now."

"Mommy," Nicolette said, "I can't get Mamaw to move."

Nicolette put her hand in mine. She led me to Mamaw's breathing. It sounded like the darkness was chocolate pudding Mamaw was choking on.

"Mamaw," I said, "are you all right?" She didn't say anything. I wanted for a light so bad. "Mamaw," I said again. "Are you all right?"

"She's all right, Momma," Nicolette said. "I think she is."

"Cora," Mamaw said.

"Yeah, Mamaw," I said. "That's right. That's your name."

"Cora," she said again.

"It's OK, Mamaw," I said. "It's OK."

"Say it," Mamaw said.

I leaned towards the sound of her voice. "Do what, honey?" I said. Rocks jabbed my knees.

Mamaw said, "Say my name."

"Cora," Nicolette said. "Granny Cora."

"That's right, darling," Mamaw rasped.

"Mamaw," I said. My hands hunted her. Not today, Mamaw.

"Cora," Mamaw said. My hands found her thighs. I lay a hand on each of her thighs. They trembled. I squeezed them.

I said, "What is it, Mamaw? What's going on?"

"Cora," she said. "Cora."

"Mamaw, please," I said. "Say something." My hands found the sides of Mamaw's face. Her face was still. I slapped her cheek. "Mamaw, please. You're scaring the baby. Stop playing, Mamaw."

A hum come out of Nicolette. She rubbed her hands in a way sounded like rain when the clouds roll towards Momma's house in town, up the steps, coming from the Stone Mountain, sound like sand spilling off a tailgate, sand through a child's hands. Nicolette's humming grew, like she had two throats. I put my face to Mamaw's. The cave water dripped harder. I heard thunder. Nicolette began to sing.

"Dig a hole, dig a hole in the meadow," she sang.

"What?" I said.

"Dig a hole, dig a hole in the ground."

"I don't know what you're saying," I said.

"Dig a hole, dig a hole in the meadow."

Mamaw's throat rattled.

"Mamaw, no," I said. "No. You can't."

Nicolette sang a song I had not heard my grandfather sing in forever, but had heard when I come to get Nicolette, when we were going to Willett's for 4th of July: "Dig a hole, dig a hole in the meadow, and lay Darlin' Cory down."

Mamaw's neck gave up. Her head lay loose in my hands, nothing to hold it up but me. I leaned forward, put my face on hers, glad not to see. The cave water tinkled like the bell on a cat's neck. "It wasn't supposed to be today, Mamaw." I held her like she was a doll, like she was mine, like she'd never let me in life. I held her tight as I wanted. I scared myself how tight I squeezed her, like I could squeeze her back to life. Tears came.

Nicolette set beside me, her shins pressed against my ribs. Her hand lay on my shoulder blade, which rose and fell like a sewing machine needle with my crying. Nicolette didn't say anything. She didn't sing. She didn't hum. She sat there. The sound of my crying bounced off the cave walls. I don't know how long I went on. A while.

Eventually I stopped crying. I set up, raised up from over Mamaw's body to my knees, which found a sandy spot there in the wedge, the last pass we had to get through before we would be back in the light of day, back on the outside of the mountain.

"You still know the way out?" I said to Nicolette.

She said, "What do we do about Granny?"

I said I didn't know. "Leave her here, I guess. Till we get some light. Till we get somebody to help us get her out of here."

Nicolette said, "You don't think we could do it ourselves?"

I sat there for a minute thinking about it. We didn't have that long to go. We weren't that far from getting out. She wasn't that heavy. I sat there a minute longer. "I don't reckon," I said. "We better get some help."

Nicolette put her hand on my shoulder.

"She'll be all right in here," I said. "I reckon." Nicolette moved her hand behind my neck. She rested her arm across my shoulders. She put her head down on me. I said, "We won't be long."

Nicolette said,

"No," I said. "I don't reckon."

"She aint afraid now?"

"No," I said. "I don't reckon."

I never saw anyone die before. And technically I didn't see Mamaw. I had to feel for her with my hands. Her head and shoulders were braced up on some broken rock. Her arms were spread palm down. Her legs were splayed. She was a starfish. I put my hands on her face. I said, "Where are you, Mamaw?" I put my head on her chest. I cried some more. Her chest was just there, not moving, not a person. Just something you would buy in a store. Something dead.

"Come on, Mommy," Nicolette said. She took my hand in hers. I stood. She got out front of me. I followed her sure as if she had a light. I stumbled a time or two, but we were soon back where we could see.

The spraypaint and burn on the walls made less sense than before. Scratches of words. Nobody with anything to say. Just trying to make a mark on the world. Wanting to mark it up, say they was here. They weren't there. Cause when they were, they didn't have no sense. If they did, they would have left the cave walls alone, wouldn't they? I mean, who packs spraypaint clean out here? Just so they can fuck some beautiful natural shit like a cave up?

Nicolette said, "I'm sorry I dropped my flashlight, Mommy."

It was raining hard out the cave mouth. It was a killing rain, beating things down. Raining so hard it blocked out the greenness of the world. That rain come down straight and hard, speeding up, slowing down, speeding up again. It turned everything a hissing gray.

"It's OK," I said. "It wasn't much of a flashlight anyway."

8

~~~~~~

WHAT WAS WHAT

DAWN

When somebody dies, 90 percent of what happens next is fake. Fake people acting sad. Fake people telling you how sorry they are. Some aren't fake. Some are real. The real ones aren't hard to deal with, but you got to treat them all like the ones that are really sorry. And that's what bites. Fake crying. Fake patting on you. Fake looks full of big fake eyes.

The rain was still pouring down when we left the cave where Mamaw died. I picked up Nicolette and started to run. After I'd had to have her lead me out of that cave, it was good to pack her, to help her do something she couldn't do. Nicolette made herself soft and small. Our weight pounded on my knees. I ran a little ways, then walked while I shifted Nicolette in my arms, caught my breath. Then I ran again.

We came to the path up to Houston's house, and by the time I come up on Houston's porch, the rain had let up. I set Nicolette down so she could walk up his block steps. Before I could knock on his door, I had to sit down a minute in the straight-back chair he kept by the porch rail. I saw in my mind Houston turned sideways with his elbow on the rail, his hand cupped to the air, listening. Listening. To God knows what.

A bird sang a trailing song. Same thing, same notes, starting loud and strong—tweet tweet tweet tweet tweet tweet tweet tweet tweet. Nine tweets, each less of a tweet than the one before. Over and over out of the bedsheet-white sky. Everything dripped with the rain. Everything sparkled. Other birds began to scree, doing the things they did to avoid getting killed, to make babies, to stay fed. Nothing fancy. Just being birds. My head was on my arm, and my arm was on Houston's porch rail. My grandfather's shadow fell on me.

"Bright morning star," he said. "The precious Misty Dawn."

His smile was fresh paint on a building better off torn down.

"Hey, Papaw," I said.

Nicolette told Houston Mamaw was dead. He sat down noisy, creaks and groans, his behind and the heels of his hands slapping the step as he landed beside me. He set there and the eave dripped. The birdsong, the insect drone covered him up. Nicolette came and leaned on me.

I said, "We got to get Mamaw out of Sand Cave."

Houston looked me in the eye. "All right," he said.

Houston had a Caprice that ran, especially in summertime. We drove back to where the path to the cave met the Trail. Our flashlights were good and strong. Houston told Nicolette to wait in the Caprice. I wondered what he thought she'd see worse than what she'd seen. But she didn't say a word. She lay down in the front seat.

When me and Houston got to Mamaw, Houston handed me his flashlight. He crouched and lifted her. He stood there in the light I shined on him, and for the first time it hit me. Houston didn't live no more in the house where we found him. He lived in a shitty one-room apartment in the High-Rise down in town. Houston held Mamaw's dead body in his arms. I had a flashlight in each hand trained on him. Like I was a gunfighter, like I was holding a jumprope of light.

Houston said, "We better go, sweetheart." He slid past me, went first, said,

I did. My grandfather and grandmother passed out of Sand Cave in the light I held, the picture their crossed bodies made broken behind a veil of tears.

~~~~~~~~~~~~

HOUSTON TOOK Mamaw's body back to her house. He lifted her out of the car and packed her inside. The house was piled with stacks of mail, stacks of magazines, stacks of things telling everything going wrong everywhere in the world. The sofa was stacked, the coffee table and the fireplace stacked. The only place clear was a spot on the kitchen table where Mamaw did her letter writing. Around the edges of the clear spot there was a coffee mug full of pens and xeroxed phone call lists, her pipe tobacco next to her pipe in a glass funeral home ashtray, her cordless phone base blinking red and green with calls, phone books out of date from Canard and Lexington and Frankfort, kept cause they had all kinds of numbers written on them with different ballpoint pens, numbers of lawyers and government offices and people getting screwed over. There were paper maps with place-names circled and creek names gone over in highlighter. It was all stuff that wouldn't get written on anymore, ashtrays and phone book covers that wouldn't get no fuller from Mamaw being busy trying to save the world.

Houston cried a little packing Mamaw upstairs to where she slept. He called for me when he got up there, and asked me to turn down the covers. Mamaw's bedroom was as put together and shipshape as the downstairs had been unruly.

I turned the covers back. I pulled the sheet and the velvet crazy quilt stitched with songbirds and chickens, flowers and stars, back down to the foot of the bed, and Houston laid her down, brushed the cave sand from her face, got it all over the bed, her jean legs still wet from where she'd been messing in the cave water. He laid her there and smoothed her hair and put her hands to her side. It was hot and he looked at the fan which wasn't turned on, and he looked around the room, I imagined, for some sign of himself, some sign of the time he had been there, but he didn't find it, cause Mamaw had got rid of every sign of him, like he was a catching disease. I'd been there when she done it.

Nicolette stared at Mamaw. I stared at Houston. Houston stared at the door and then went back down the stairs, walked out the back door, and got in his car and started backing down the driveway. I ran out after him, caught him before he got to the end of the drive, got ahold of his arm through the open window, said,

He said, "Got to go to the apartment."

I said, "What for?" Said, "What are we supposed to do with her?

Houston said, "I got to go, honey. You can leave her here. She'll be all right. You can follow me. If you want. Get the baby and follow."

I took my hand from around his arm. Nicolette ran up to me and asked could she ride with Houston. I looked at him and he looked at her and I nodded my head, goofy with what the day had become. Houston and Nicolette backed out the driveway and I went back and turned the air condition on and locked the house. I caught up quick to slow-ass Houston creeping down the mountain, and we all went to the High-Rise, to the apartment where Houston stayed.

GENE

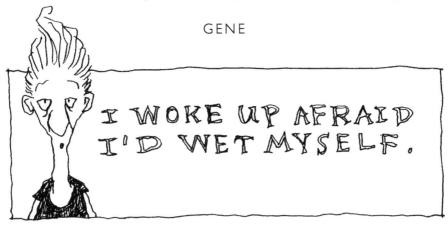

But I was dry. The sun come angling in the side of the little house. Sister had paper blinds on the windows, turned the light yellow, made you feel like you was floating in a bottle of pine cleaner.

My head was swimmy and I needed to wash my mouth out. Felt like I'd been eating them chunks of grass that pack in on top of the blade of your mower. It occurred to me that brick of grass'd taste good to a cow. Be like one of them power bars That Woman give me to eat. Power bar for a cow. Never thought of that.

Sister blowed her head off again in my dream. Just like she did in the kitchen in the big house. Back Easter. I pushed my feet down to the floor. The recliner folded back up. That Woman's dog slept on the rug beside me. Her paws twitched. I hoped she fared better in her dream than I had in mine.

They was two Walmart bags in the chair with me. One was full of dog food That Woman give me to feed her dog till she got back. The other had a stuffed gorilla you squeezed to make a gorilla noise. That dog would chase that thing long as you'd throw it.

They was also a dog brush in the bag. I seen That Woman use that brush on Pharoah one time. That Woman sat up on the edge of a rocking chair, leaned over, a sprig of hair trailing over her eye like a pea vine. She run that brush across Pharoah's back with one hand, caught up the fur in the other. That Woman had a shirt on made her look like a lady slipper. It come down low in the front and even through the screen door I could see how peaceful it was down inside that shirt, darkness real soft, a little night place you could go to dream right.

When Pharoah woke up, I brushed her like That Woman had. The hair come off in wads, come off like dog hair cotton candy, piled up enough there on the rug to make another Pharoah.

It had got hot in Sister's little house, and even though Pharoah'd took a chunk out of my hand the day before, she seemed to like that brushing. She panted till her tongue dripped and finally lay down at my feet, went to sleep. I picked the fur out of the brush, brush wiry in its bristles, a red felt bottom to it.

My daddy had a hairbrush, hard brown plastic brush, plastic bristles. He didn't care to take the bristles to you. Or the back neither, if you didn't get what he said the first time. But what I thought of was the bristle side, side Sister used to slick back my hair even after I was grown, Daddy's dandruff down under mine, same hair, same coming-off skin.

A train come through down by the river, empty and squealing. I held That Woman's dog brush, tried to imagine it in her hand, imagined her fingers on it, and then imagined me a dog brush, me riding through Pharoah's fur, me with That Woman's hand around my neck, and then me turning back into me, her still there, her still having ahold of me.

Brother come knocking at the door. I was supposed to have met him an hour earlier over at the High-Rise where we was weedeating. He come in the house and the train's squeal got louder. Brother said, "What the hell you doing?"

The dog went to barking at him, barking so loud you couldn't hear the train for it. I give Brother the brush. Brother took off his hat and run that dog brush

through his thistly hair. Three times he pulled it through. Then he smiled like he
thought he ought to be on TV, paying no mind to the dog barking. I got my
thumb in that dog's collar, pulled her back to me. She quieted.
I said in her ear where she's the only one could hear,

MUST BE NICE TO BE ABLE TO COMB YOUR OWN HAIR.

Brother said, "You coming?"

I said I hated to leave the dog in that hot house and Brother said to turn
her out and I said I couldn't do that and Brother said, "Well, chain her to the
porch," and I didn't have no chain, so I just told Pharoah I'd be back soon and
not to worry and put two big bowls of water out.

We went over to the High-Rise and started weedeating, it the evening,
the cooling of the day, hateful High-Rise boss not there to tell us it was
too late to weedeat. It felt good to be there with Brother, not so hot, able
to remember him and then Sister, all of us when we lived together with
my granny, the closest thing to me ever having a family. I remember Sister
and Granny showing me and Brother how to play Rook, and me taking the
longest to get the hang of it, but finally getting it, finally understanding what it
meant for the red two to be worth twenty points, same as the rook, which is
boss, but for the red two being able to take a ten card but not an eleven nor
nothing bigger, me finally understanding the difference between power and
value. Got all that and pop in a bottle, two pops for the four of us, Granny
not drinking but a sip, and it not high summer yet, the baby frogs peeping out,
excited about growing out legs and being able to jump.

I was thinking on all that, my weedeater rolling back and forth, hypnotizing
me, not so many vehicles in the parking lot, me edging beside the pavement,
me daydreaming about card playing and pop drinking when I heard this woman
saying, "Hey! Hey!" When I looked up, she was hollering at me, telling me
not to throw grass on her vehicle, which was a great big black Tahoe, which I

had already done where it was parked, and hadn't gotten a speck of grass on her vehicle. She was pointing a painty nail finger at me and I knew what she was telling me not to do and I knew she was threatening to have me fired if I didn't do what she said and so I didn't turn off my weedeater and in fact kind of thumbed up the gas so it run a little louder, and then there was some kind of ruckus behind her—I didn't hear what it was—and she jerked her head around and looked up like stuff was falling out of the sky and I went back to weedeating, thanking Jesus for whatever it was took the Tahoe woman's mind off me.

DAWN

When we got back to the High-Rise, Houston and Nicolette went straight upstairs, left me sitting in the car. I seen Gene and his brother walking towards me, both packing weedeaters, and Gene a can of gas. I got out and got inside so I wouldn't have to fool with him and by the time I got inside I'd worked myself up, agitated at how Houston wasn't talking to me about Mamaw's body, about what to do, which I felt like he should be the one, not me, figuring out how to do for her. I thought, if he doesn't say anything about it when I went in there, I would just call her family out on Drop Creek, her brother and them, even though they didn't much fool with Mamaw, and let them deal with it. So when I walked in Houston's apartment and he had his music turned up loud and was at his shelves messing with his boxes of cassettes, it flew all over me. I said,

Houston did not look up. He kept rooting through a case held twelve cassettes looking for the one Nicolette wanted. The one had the song Mamaw called for when she died. "Darlin' Cory."

Papaw set down the box, looked at Nicolette sitting cross-legged on the floor. He had a cassette in his hand. "I got two versions, sweetheart. One by Roscoe Holcomb. One by Doc Watson. Which you want?"

"Nicolette," I said. "Don't do that. God Amighty." She was picking chewing gum off the bottom of her tennis shoe.

"Roscoe," Nicolette said.

A little brown bird landed on the windowsill. Houston took the cassette from the case and put it in the player. He fast-forwarded and reversed till he found the spot. The bird on the sill tweeted and Nicolette turned to it. Houston held the cassette case close to his face, read the single-space cap-lock typing on the handcut slip of paper. He pushed play. He fast-forwarded and reversed. He pushed play.

I said, "Houston, I need you to talk to me."

Houston hummed.

I said, "What did Mamaw want us to do with her body?"

The brown bird's tweets turned into more like a song. Houston pushed pause on the player and started to sing: "Little Birdie, little birdie. What makes you fly so high?"

Nicolette joined him singing. I snatched the box of cassettes off the table and threw it out the window. It crashed on the parking lot two floors down. The bird was gone. The singing and music stopped. Nicolette looked at me like she wondered if she could throw stuff out the window, too. Houston looked like I stuck a knife in his ribs.

I said, "What's the matter with yall?"

Houston took a deep breath through his nose. His hair stood on end like silver grass. His shoulders were drawn high and stooped. "Your grandmother and I," he said, "were not supposed to court. Her father thought I wouldn't be able to provide. He thought me too tender to shoulder a man's burden." Houston lay his hand on the table, his fingers spread like a colt's legs. "So we had to sneak. We would plunder through the mountain, all up and down Blue Bear. She would name the plants and trees, copy the calls of birds and name them too. For a boy from town, it was a revelation." Houston sat down at his table with its boomerang top. "Then," he said, "I didn't listen to any music but what was on the radio. Popular music. Knowing all this," he said, waving his hands towards shelf after shelf of cassette boxes of old-timey music, "came from knowing her." Houston turned his head to where the bird had been. "One time me and her were in a cave, found a human skeleton on a rock shelf. I wanted to tell someone about it. Your grandmother wouldn't have it, said, 'leave it lay.' I always suspected she had an idea who it was. But what she said was, 'We don't know but what it was a choice to be left here.' She said she wished she could die her body left aboveground, go to bone in open air. 'Just the bones,' she said, 'the rest carried away or rotted down.'"

Houston stood and walked to the open window. "She didn't speak of me, of where I was to be. Did she want me, when it was my time, to come lie down next to her?" Nicolette moved to her knees. Houston said, "We will put her with her people, on Blue Bear." Houston put his hand on the window sash. "I can't do what she wanted," he said.

Nicolette came and stood at Houston's side. She hooked her finger in one of his belt loops.

I called Mamaw's brother and told him what had happened and he was sorry and we talked and it felt like family and I told him to go ahead and dig Mamaw's grave at the family cemetery on Tallow Creek, deep on Blue Bear Mountain. He said he would. Houston wiped his face and we went outside and picked his cassettes up off the parking lot and all were fine except for one got run over by a woman in a black Tahoe and Houston said it was OK, the cassette was mostly the Blue Sky Boys, who he said he never much cared for anyway.

I said, "Houston, I'm gonna go."

And he said, "You got it worked out with Denny and them?" I said I did and he said, "They're gonna call and get somebody to fetch her body?" I said they were and he said, "I better get back up there."

About then Weedeater come up behind me, said, "This yall's?" and it was one of Houston's cassettes, the one had "Darlin' Cory" on it. Houston took the cassette from Weedeater, looked at it, and give it to Nicolette, who took the cassette, which looked big in her little hand, and Weedeater said, "Nice night" or something like that and Nicolette said, "My granny died in a cave today."

Weedeater said, "Cora?"

Nicolette nodded and Weedeater said, "I'm sorry," and said she was a real good woman, and I said thank you. And Houston told Weedeater who he was, and Weedeater went back to weedeating and me and Nicolette went to Tennessee and didn't come back till the day of Mamaw's funeral.

GENE

Me and Brother finished the High-Rise right after dark. I come back to the house and sat and wished I had a bowl of ice cream. Sister's husband come in my little house without knocking on the door. His hair wadn't setting where it usually set. His face was flush, red in places a face aint usually red. He'd had him a pill. I was in my drawers, washing a plate at the sink. He come around the counter and up behind me before I could get turned around.

He said, "Gene, I got to have some rent. Five hundred a month if you're gonna stay here." He said it fast and gravelly to the back of my head.

Me and Brother got fifteen dollars each for the High-Rise. That Woman paid me sixty dollars to mow her yard. She was my best-paying customer. I was already into one of them payday loan places for I believe it was twenty-four hundred dollars. Only way I was keeping my head out of water was not having to pay rent. I asked Sister's husband when he thought the rent-paying would start. He said him and Sister talked about it before she died. He hadn't said nothing before, he said, on account of us both grieving.

I stopped wiping my plate. I didn't say nothing, but turned to face him.

He said, "I was thinking we'd start with May. So for May and June," he said, "you owe a thousand. And then July be due by the middle of the month. Next Friday. So," he said, never stopping staring me down, "fifteen hundred by next Friday." He unwrapped him a piece of chewing gum and put it in his mouth without taking his eyes off me. He said, "That make sense to you?"

It didn't make no sense to me at all. Sister had had that house before she'd married this man. It was what she'd got when she divorced her first husband. She'd had to fight tooth and toenail to get this new man to let her stay. He'd wanted a fancy new house. She'd had to bow down to him pretty heavy to get him to move in there.

I said, "Well, I understand what you're saying."

And he said, "All right then. I'm glad you going to be a man about this anyway."

He said it like they was other things I wadn't being a man about. I reckon where I wouldn't work for him in the coal mine.

He give me one more good hard look and then he left, his feet on the floor like a horse's, his big old dress-up work boots like an army going through your country, eating people's food, burning down their places, doing ugly things to the women and livestock.

MADE ME FEEL SMALL.

DAWN

The drive to the cemetery was hot and bright. The sun bounced off a string of empty coal cars standing on the siding below the road like angel coffins. A black dog chased a yellow dog in and out of a field of corn. A boy with the sleeves cut out of his four-X black T-shirt stuck his burrcut bullethead out of a mostly white Corsica. He looked at me like he'd give anything for me to be an ice cream cone.

Blue-headed flowers strung on long stems down the side of the road as me and Nicolette and Houston in his Caprice, Albert and Hubert in Albert's yellow truck, a stout, silverheaded man and his wife in a Camry, and two of the organizer girls in June's red Honda passed. Mamaw didn't want church in her funeral, so there wasn't.

At the funeral tent, a beat-to-shit Subaru pulled up and Willett and Kenny got out. I dried my tears on my shirtsleeve. Nicolette ran to her father. Willett's mother come out in a blue dress, dark and quiet, with little white buttons down her leg. Mamaw's brother Fred and his family rolled up in a blue Durango, and Fred's son Denny came in a Silverado I stole once when I was fifteen. All them come and stood with us under the tent. They didn't say a thing, just nodded.

A short man in scuffed brown shoes come smiling and stood by Mamaw's coffin, which was decked in country-looking flowers June and Houston had picked out on Blue Bear. I should have gone with them. Nicolette did. There was no reason for me not to. When they went I set at Mamaw's house and would have till they come back but I got afraid Momma would show up, so I walked out behind the house past the pile of poison ivy not yet withered down and headed up the hill.

I went out to the ridge, which was pine-tree hot. I saw bugs and snakes and toads and lizards running to hide from the heat and blowing wind. When I broke from the trees, free from everything but the stone and the open air, I was alone. I saw Mamaw's chin gouging out into the air off the edge of the rock sure as if she had been there. She stood there not afraid to act mad at the world. Mad at the people and the mistakes they made. She wouldn't back up from being mad. Not even in her coffin, which she didn't want open, but they left open, even then they couldn't make her look peaceful.

When I thought of that, I put my face against my knees and cried and the hot wind dried my tears.

Even when I thought she would, she didn't.

~~~~~~~~

AT THE funeral tent, the smiling lawyer in the scuffed-up shoes said my mamaw was a giant. Said she was a legend. Said she spoke against strip mining before there were organizers, before there were people raising money to pay people to fight against strip mining. She stood in front of bulldozers when there were only a handful doing it. And then he called the names of them had been there with her. I hadn't heard of any of them, but the stout silverheaded man smiled. He nodded his head. Aunt June come up behind me and took my hand and squeezed it.

"And had they not stood up," the little lawyer said, "we wouldn't have gained what we've gained, would never have protected nine thousand acres of Blue Bear Mountain. Would never have protected the settlement school. And now," the little lawyer said, his tears shining his cheeks like apples, "when the gains are one by one taken from us, the importance of a Cora Redding only grows."

The scuffed-up lawyer smiled when he brought his glare down on us. He looked at the empty chairs one by one, making a list of the names of people should've been there. He looked out from the tent at the five vehicles we brought, at the hearse, at the backhoe and the pile of yellow clay that would soon be between us and Mamaw and he smiled as the tears rolled down his cheeks.

"Lord help us," the brown-shoed lawyer said.

~~~~~~~~~

THE LITTLE crowd broke up fast after the brown-shoed lawyer stepped away from the grave. Willett stood in the sun outside the tent holding Nicolette's hand. The back of her other hand was against her eyes, which were closed against the afternoon light. Nicolette whined like a cattle gate, opening and closing over and over, grinding rusty squeak on misery's breeze.

I stayed in my fold-up chair under the tent, staring into the Astroturf hole where Mamaw's body went. My cousin Denny sat down beside me. Denny worked in an underground mine. His dad was Mamaw's brother. He's ten years older than me. When I was in high school, he used to put liquor in my Mountain Dew at Thanksgiving. He is all right. He leaned forward on his elbows, looked across me at Nicolette, who was slouching against Willett's legs. Nicolette slumped to the ground. Willett picked her up by the armpits. When she went back to the ground, he lifted her above his head and set her on his shoulders, even though he knew how good a way that was to throw out his back.

Denny said, "She's getting big."

I nodded.

Denny stared into the Astroturf hole. He said, "She was a tough old bird."

I didn't say anything.

Denny said, "I admired her."

I said, "Why?"

Denny said, "She cut her own path."

I stood up, stepped to Mamaw's hole, saw the zinnia stems June had thrown on the box, saw Houston's daisies on top of them. I thought of funerals I had been to where people had thrown themselves on the box, or on the body, wailing and drowning in sorrow. I felt dry as a bird skeleton I found in Mamaw's attic one time. It made a sound like stepping on Rice Krispies when I crushed it in my hands, and when I showed Mamaw what I'd done, she folded the bones up in a paper towel and sent me to wash my hands.

Nicolette was asleep, her head on Willett's head. I said to Denny, "You wish you were like my mamaw?

YOU WISH YOU WERE LIKE CORA REDDING?

Denny bowed his head, didn't say anything. The door to his father's big pickup opened and shut. His family was loading up to go.

Denny said, "Heard you all were doing good in Tennessee. Heard Willett got a job."

Denny's father's truck started.

I said, "You wanting him to get you one?"

Denny said, "No. I want yall to be all right. You deserve it."

Willett ducked coming in the tent so Nicolette's head wouldn't hit. Willett said, "I'm going to take her to Mom's for the night."

I said OK.

Willett said, "You staying here with June?"

I said I was going to Mamaw's.

Willett nodded, asked Denny how he was doing, and Denny said all right.

I said, "Go on if you're going."

Willett said, "I'll call when we get there."

I said, "Well." I asked him when he was going back to work. He said he wasn't sure. Said Monday or Tuesday.

I said, "You better get it figured out."

He said he would.

I looked at Denny and tried to make my eyes two bottomless black Astroturf holes. I don't know why I did that. I left without saying goodbye to anyone else.

GENE

The sun sunk behind the ridge where That Woman's COALTOWN! sign was
to go. I was on the road above her house, walking Pharoah on a shiny red
leash. Pharoah was wanting to get down the hill, back to That Woman, who'd
come home. We ducked through the poison ivy running across the path down
through That Woman's yard. The bugs was out in the dwindly light. Every tree
and bush was droopy and full.

The blue flower balls of Cora's hydrangeas bushes glowed and made
me sad she was dead. Made me sad she would never tell me why them
hydrangeas was a big deal to her. Made me sad she wadn't never gonna tell
me what to do again.

That Woman didn't answer the door. Pharoah set on the doormat. The
weather was good and hot. I leaned back in a rocking chair and nodded off. I
had a dream of Cora scared out in her backyard. She kept falling, couldn't get
up. Kept tearing the blooms off the hydrangeas, throwing them up in the air.
Sister come out to comfort her. Sister was nice in the dream to the old woman,
trying to pick her up. But she wasn't no comfort and the old woman started
screaming. Screaming and screaming at the top of her lungs. Sister looked at her
like she was going to slap her. Then Sister started screaming too, kept it up till I

had to wake up to get away from it, to make it stop. When I woke up, I thought the dream was real, that they were in the backyard. I was blinky in that rocking chair, sweating and sleep-drunk in the sunshine coming through the screen.

Another vision come on me, this time a true story, a memory, Sister screaming at me not to do what Brother was egging me on to do, which was to hit a dynamite cap with a hammer. I was leaning towards doing it, cause Brother said he'd done it a hundred times. I had the hammer raised and Sister come flying from the other end of the porch and knocked the hammer out of my hand. And then our cousin Gus, who always showed out in front of Brother cause he thought Brother hung the moon, grabbed the hammer and laid a good lick on them dynamite caps, and the explosion knocked all four of us over. When we set back up, the claw of the hammer had blowed itself down into Brother's thigh and Gus had his hand up in front of his face, all his fingers gone. I buried my face in Sister's chest, held onto her tight, till she had to shuck me off, so she could get the bleeding stopped and Gus to the hospital.

I fell off to sleep again, and when I woke, That Woman was there on the porch, had the telephone pinched between her ear and shoulder, her knees together, a Megamart bag full of corn shucks rolled open in her lap, an ear of corn in her hands.

Pharoah laid a paw to the screen door, dragged her nails across the screen. I was about to tell That Woman I'd take her out. That Woman raised a finger, pretty as a half-runner fresh off the vine, made me hush.

That Woman said into her phone, "How big a jail they got? You think we can fill it?"

I thought, you don't need to go to jail while I'm around. We can go on the run. I wished I had money for a muffler. Be a lot quieter on the run with a new muffler. Maybe we should take her car, I thought, if we were to go on the run.

That Woman said, "And she talked to the reporter at the Charleston paper? He's going to be there? Good."

I took Pharoah outside and she barked. That Woman wrinkled her face. She waved us in. I come through the screen door, dropped Pharoah's leash, and she click-clicked into the house to get some water. I set down on the rocker.

That Woman said, "I'll leave tonight. How long does it take? All right. See you soon. Bye." That Woman pushed a button on her phone and laid it on a wicker table next to her rocker. Pharoah came back out on the porch. That Woman took her leash off of her.

I said, "You going away again?" My hand was shaking. I was hoping That Woman didn't think I was drunk. She scratched Pharoah on the top of her head.

That Woman said, "I'm going back to West Virginia, Gene. I don't know how long I'll be there. You can take care of Pharoah?"

I said I could. Asked did she want me to go tell her class anything. She said she didn't need that. Pharoah sat back down on the doormat.

With her doormats and her rocking chairs and just her cleaning cleaning cleaning, That Woman was making a home out of her pillhead sister's house. She said, "You can water the plants? Take the trash out? I'll make a list."

I said I could. I asked her why she was going to West Virginia.

That Woman said, "We're taking some people from New York and California to look at strip jobs. People who haven't ever seen them."

"A person could take them out to the lake," I said. "Pretty there, specially at the end of the day. Me and Brother go out there near the mouth of Chigger Creek. Catch more smallmouth than you could eat in a month."

That Woman said, "They aren't coming like that, Gene. They're coming to see how bad it is. See the mountains tore to pieces."

"Hunh," I said.

That Woman said, "We hope they'll help us put pressure on the state and federal to stop that kind of mining."

I said, "That mountaintop removal?"

She said, "Yes. Exactly that."

I hated to see That Woman mixed up in such as that. I'd heard Sister's old man talk about people who was against mining. He hated them, talked about doing awful things to them. Shooting them in the face, cutting them up, feeding them to coyotes, throwing their bones in the sludge pond. Scared me to hear him talk. He scared others, even some mining people, but they was enough thought like him that I'd of been glad to see That Woman not take no part in it.

I said, "I was sure sorry to hear about your mommy."

That Woman kept her eye on her corn, said, "Thank you, Gene." She shucked an ear and laid it aside.

I said, "You want me to get the strings off them?" Her corn was still pretty stringy.

"No," That Woman said. "They're fine." She pulled back the shucks, broke off the worm-eat part, said, "My mother loved the land, Gene. Loved it more than anything."

I cleared my throat, said, "Is that why you're going to West Virginia? Cause of her?"

That Woman looked out over the town, said, "I don't know, Gene."

Sister's husband called people like That Woman treehuggers. Her neck stretched out pretty as a child's truth, made me want nothing so much as to hug a tree myself. Kiss one. Wouldn't care a bit to kiss a tree for That Woman.

"Well," I said, "I reckon she'd be proud of you trying to do something."

That Woman turned to look at me. Her face was a flower blooming and a Roman candle going off at the same time. It was also a smooth stone in your pocket, your thumb running over it, almost feel the grains of sand that made it, but not really. Just a smooth feeling. And ice cream. Looking at her reminded me of ice cream. Melting in a bowl. My point being, my mind went kind of wild when That Woman looked at me. It's embarrassing to tell.

She said, "Hard to know another's heart."

I said, "Hard enough to know your own."

That Woman took my hand. She sure did. Shocked me. My hand in hers.

She said, "They're going to be some famous people there, Gene." She dropped my hand like wadn't nothing to it.

"That right?" I said.

She said, "Mm-hmm."

"Well," I said. "That'll be good." I was nervous and jumpy and wanted to go. But I didn't. Sat there hoping she'd tell me more. Maybe take my hand again.

It got dark. That Woman turned to the folding leg table where she did her eating and drinking and writing and listening to music. She lit a long purple candle stuck down in an empty gin bottle. Made the evenest old-timey light. Made me think of Granny who took care of me and Brother. Granny was forever looking down while she was talking to you. Looking at something she was working on, some piece of clothes, a broke bucket handle, potatoes needed peeling—and when she stopped moving her hands, that's when you knew you was supposed to look up—cause she had something she wanted to tell you looking in her eye.

That Woman stopped shucking her corn and I looked up. Tears pumped out of her eyes like flood water under a trailer door. She looked out over my shoulder, out at that ridge where they was going to put her COALTOWN! sign.

The more I looked into That Woman's eyes, I seen she wasn't just looking at where that sign was going to go, but at something else. I wanted to turn around and see what it was cause it might've just been an interesting bird or a bunch of bats or something. I couldn't look away from her. Her eyes settled back down on me and she said, "I feel like an orphan child."

I said, "Honey, your daddy's still up there on the ridge."

That made her laugh.

That Woman stood up and said it was OK for me to go.

DAWN

When I got back to Mamaw's after the funeral, I cleaned the flowerpots out of her bathtub. I lay my pants off on the commode. I wiped my tears on my shirttail. I should have got a dress for Mamaw's funeral, but I don't like dresses. I don't like my legs out there, but I wished I hadn't worn black church pants looked like a preacher's. Wished I had worn something other than a black blouse with its big blue flowers made me look like I was in a Hawaiian band on some boat trip. I took off my underwear. I stood there naked on the detergent box towel. I sat down on the tub. My bottom melted down over the sides.

Before Daddy died, Momma would gin up reasons to wear a dress—go to weddings of people we didn't know. Go to every little picnic and dance party the coal company or school put on. She liked party dresses. She liked everyday dresses too. Dresses with no sleeves in them. She'd wear them with little sneakers like old women did back when Mamaw was young—dresses with quiet stripes running up and down them, washed-out flowers, dresses pale as nursing home legs.

I used the black hula blouse to wipe the flowerpot dirt out of the bathtub. Threw Ajax powder on it. Rinsed that out. Started the water.

Mamaw didn't wear dresses much. She liked being out in the weeds and up in the woods. She needed pants.

Towards the end, Mamaw got scared of her old pink bathtub, got scared to take a bath. Said if she was going to break a bone, it wasn't going to be in the bathtub. So Mamaw was most of the time a little funky—like clothes forgotten in the washer or raw chicken should have been thrown out.

I lay back in Mamaw's bathtub. The water was cool. I scooted down in the water, tried to get my nerves to settle. I was too big for the bathtub. I was too big for everything. I splashed water on my front, wished I loved Willett like I should. I wished I could make a nice life for him and my baby.

But I couldn't. I puffed out my breath over and over, puffing and blowing like my mouth was a whale hole. I wished I knew what would make me happy. I don't know why though. I didn't much care for anybody around me called themselves happy.

The house was hot and close. I hadn't turned on the air conditioner. Hadn't opened a window. Being married is hard. You don't know who to put first. You don't know who you're living for. They give you words to say, promises to make, when you get married. Vows. But that isn't how people live. I wished I had more stick-to. I was a blade of grass spinning down a creek.

I looked down at myself, where I stuck up out of the gray water.

I WAS CURVY. I LIKED MY CURVES

I covered them up most of the time, but I liked them. I liked keeping them for me. My body cheered me up that day. Even my scabby banged-up shins, my bruised thighs and feet, my chipped-off nail polish on my dirty-ass toes—I liked how I looked that day. I put my hands on my fat rolls, squeezed a big bunch of me. And my nerves settled.

Then there come a banging from upstairs. I sat up in the tub, water splashing out on the floor and Mamaw's bathroom rugs. "Who's there?" I said.

Whoever it was come down the steps. "Who is it?" I said, and stood up in the tub. It was slick and I slipped, busted my behind against the soap dish, banged my knee hard against the tub.

I was on my knees, my head down, my elbows balanced on the edge of the tub when Momma said, "God Almighty, Dawn, I never seen nobody could tear up a bathtub."

Pills had mashed Momma's curves flat and whittled her down to a stick you could've cooked a marshmallow on. The circles round her black glass eyes was red as bricks. She looked me up and down like she was trying to figure out what she could get for me. Everything to her then was what she could get for it.

I reached past her, got a towel, tried to act like I didn't care she was there. I had no questions for her. Had no urge to get her to do anything. Had no urge to shame her for blowing off her mother's funeral.

Momma said, "Was it nice?"

I said, "What?"

She said, "The funeral."

"I reckon," I said. "It was a funeral."

Momma said, "There aint no need to be hateful, Dawn."

"What do you want, Momma? Why don't you just get whatever it is and go? Get you something you can get your money for and go."

Momma said, "I don't need nothing here," but her eyes couldn't help but cut around the room, make a list of what was to hand.

I said, "Momma, you make me sick." I got out of the tub and shouldered past her.

She said, "Be nice if you could think one minute about what this day must be like for me. Course that would mean you'd have to think about somebody other than yourself for a second." Momma put her hands in front of her face like she was crying. Then she said, "I wish Calvin was here." Then she made a bunch of big wet sobs.

I stomped up the stairs still with that towel around me and got in the bottom dresser drawer in the upstairs bedroom and got out the turquoise Chinese box with the dragons stitched in gold on it, and got out Mamaw's rings, gold bands plain and with chips of ruby in them and one little diamond ring that was supposed to be mine, and I took them back down to Momma and said, "Here you go," and I threw them rings right off her face. "Stick that right there up your nose."

We stood there glowering at each other. I could see her twitching to pick them rings up. I went in my room and slammed the door behind. Pink light filled the room. The kitchen door opened. Then the storm door snapped back in place. I let the towel fall from me. My skin lit up the color of bubble gum. I didn't cry.

I WAS dressed and dry by the time Evie come in Mamaw's.

I said, "Knock, why don't you?"

Evie said, "Where's June?"

I said, "You tell me. She's your teacher."

Evie said, "Well, she's your aunt."

I wanted to pinch off her peapod head. I said, "Leave me alone, Evie."

Evie turned on the TV set on the counter and watched the closed circuit from the courthouse like it was her own personal soap opera. Which it pretty much was. She said, "Watch him lie" when this cousin of hers from Gilders Branch told where he was when a swimming pool got stolen out of a man's yard in Fulby. "He tried to steal it with the water in it," Evie said. "They should shoot him. Just for that. At least tie his tubes."

I said, "Evie, I got to go."

"Well," she said, "go on, then." She put her feet on the kitchen counter.

A new man stood in front of the judge on TV. "Look at him," Evie said. "He's purty."

Evie also watched the court channel like it was Match.com.

I said, "Evie, get out of here."

"I can stay here much as you," she said. "I'd come see Cora all the time while you was in *Ten*nessee."

When I wrapped my arm around Evie's head, her ear was right in the crook of my elbow. When I threw the storm door open and flung her out on the patio, she went skating across the concrete like a water bug on a creek eddy.

"You got mean down there in Tennessee," she said, jumping up. "You didn't use to be like this," she said.

I thought marrying Willett would calm me down. I never seen him mad. He always had an open-mouth smile on, like in an old magazine ad where somebody's trying to talk you into how good their cough syrup tastes. Bullshit smile. Willett wasn't bullshit exactly. He really was sweet. I thought Willett being so different from what I'd known he'd knock down some of that wanting to fight in me, that wanting to get redneck on everything.

Evie popped me in the shoulder with the flat of her hand. "Say," she said. "Why you acting like I aint even here?"

I popped Evie in her shoulder with the flat of my hand.

Evie said, "You think you can just walk off. Move to Tennessee and nobody say nothing. Well, you can't."

I said, "How much pill you take, Evie?"

Evie said, "You think can move away and won't nobody notice? Don't work that way, Dawn."

I said, "You want me to stay here till I'm crazy as you? That what you want, Evie?"

Evie stood there long enough for me to actually look at her face. Her nose was pretty. It's a thin nose. Long. Her eyes are nice, the color of fresh motor oil, golden brown with a blue and green glow when the light caught em right.

I said, "Do what?"

"Too much medicine," Evie said. "I'm quitting."

"Well," I said, "you should."

Evie said, "Tricia's the one you need to worry about. Not me. June too. All yall are the type."

I said, "Type of what?"

Evie said, "Type to take things too serious. Type to let things get ahold of you."

My phone rang. When I answered, Willett said, "Hey, baby."

I said, "What's wrong?"

"Nothing," he said. "Just wanted to tell you we made it home. And that I love you."

"OK," I said. "I love you too."

Then he told me the baby was fine.

"I know," I said. "That all?" I said. "I'm doing something."

Willett said bye, and that he loved me, which he'd already told me.

"Was that Willett?" Evie said.

I looked at her like she was stupid.

She said, "He got fired from his job."

I said, "No, he didn't."

"Yes, he did," Evie said.

"Aint no way," I said. "He just started."

Evie said Hubert said Willett made such a mess the first day—tore up a piece of equipment, almost killed a guy—that they had to send him home.

I KNEW WHAT SHE SAID COULD EASILY BE TRUE.

"Shut up, Evie," I said. "You don't know and neither does Hubert."

"Call out there to where he worked," Evie said. "They'll tell you."

I went back in Mamaw's house, closed the door and locked it. Evie stood out there and cussed me a while. Which to tell you the truth, I didn't mind. Least with Evie, jacked up as she was, I knew what was what.

9

~~~~~~

ALREADY DEAD

GENE

The place where they decided to put That Woman's letters was on the hillside behind Beautyspot. Beautyspot was a couple rows of houses against the bottom of the hillside on the other side of the railroad tracks. New 38 cut Beautyspot off from the rest of town. They was one house way up on the hill, right next to where they was wanting the letters to go, and it was owned by a man named B. C. Fowler. When we was kids, we used to call him B. C. Powder.

The original plan was for the words to be "THIS IS A COALTOWN!" and the part said "COALTOWN!" was spose to be on BC's hill up above the right side of Beautyspot. Beauty Branch ran down into Beautyspot, cut it into two parts, and on the hillside on the other side of Beauty Branch, that's where the words "THIS IS A" were spose to go. And when it got clear that the county, which had lined up a contractor to build the supports—the phone poles and 6 × 6 crosspieces we were going to hang the letters on—wasn't going to have time to get all that support stuff built before the president got there, the decision got made to just do the COALTOWN! letters there on the west side of Beauty Branch.

The contracting outfit the county hired with June's grant money cleared trees and brush and planted the posts and put the crosspieces in place so when those younguns finished with the cutting out and painting them letters, all that would be left to be done was to screw the plywood sections onto the frame.

That Woman laid Brother off when she did me, and he didn't like that not a bit. So he went up to the contractor building the frame at Beautyspot and said me and Brother would be willing to work on that frame, and be willing to work cheap. We didn't say nothing to that contractor about how we had been working for That Woman down in town, and we didn't say nothing to That Woman about how we was up there on the hillside above Beautyspot working for that contractor. That Woman, she didn't much come up on that hillside, and if she did, it was usually after that contractor's workers was done working for the day. I know because a lot of times on them after-hours trips, I would go up there with her, cause I was still her yard man and she didn't mind having somebody with her on that mountainside with a broad snake-killing background like myself.

So it was that when they were near finished with getting the letters together, I was up there looking at the frame the letters was going to get hung on, and I was there to hear That Woman say she was going to tell that contractor the next day that what she was going to be needing next was some way of covering up them letters so that when the day come of the big ceremony, they could give a sign down at the podium where the bigshots were, and the cover would fall away and reveal the fine job we had all done to make this monstrous sign.

That's when I told her how Brother knew a man had a billboard business down in Corbin and anymore them billboards is printed on vinyl and when they get done with them, Brother would buy them cheap and sell them for boat covers or truck covers or covers for people's woodpiles and stuff and that's why sometimes when you was driving you'd see a doglot tarped with some man's face asking you to vote for him for sheriff or a bass boat covered with a dentist talking about cheap dentures or a knocked-down wall covered by a special on some kind of biscuit at Hardee's. And I told That Woman we could probably get some of them old billboards to cover her letters.

That Woman said that sounded perfect and then after a second said oh wait, we can't have a bunch of advertising hanging over our letters and I told her we could put the back side facing out and so that next day That Woman told the construction foreman about her billboard plan and then me and Brother sold them his whole billboard collection.

DAWN

I was sitting in Hubert's big green truck in Mamaw's driveway the morning after the funeral when he told me he knew where Momma would be and that we had to go get her.

I said to Hubert, "And do what with her?"

Hubert said, "Get her out of here."

So we went to Causey. Causey was where railroad people used to live. The houses in Causey were packed tight, block after block. Cinderella told Hubert Momma was coming to Causey to have it out with Belinda. He told Hubert Momma said she was tired of being scared of the Coateses. Belinda had an apartment in Causey across from a gas station where you could get breakfast. Hubert said we would wait there for Momma to come get after Belinda.

I was going to ask Hubert about Willett being fired when we got to the breakfast place, but when we walked in Evie and Albert were already sitting side by side in a hard-back booth, Evie trying to get Albert to stop popping open ketchup packets with a plastic pepper shaker. I would have sat somewhere else, but Hubert sat down with them, so I did too.

I stared out the window while Albert spun the ash out of the stamped aluminum ash tray, took apart the card advertising meatloaf sandwiches, and started tearing it into pieces.

The waitress brought Hubert a foam clamshell box. All three compartments were filled with potato wedges. She set a bottle of hot sauce and packets of mayonnaise down next to the potatoes.

As soon as the waitress was gone, Hubert said, "Dawn, go get me some coffee."

I got up, went to the counter where the coffeepot set on an eye next to the cash register, brought it back, poured Hubert some.

Evie said to Hubert, "I can't believe you let that man get away with all that money, Hubert. That's fucked up."

"Yeah," Albert said, "That don't seem like you at all."

I said, "Shut the fuck up, Albert."

Two men talking about lawnmowers at the next table stopped talking, stopped laughing.

Evie said, "Leave him alone, Dawn. God Amighty."

I said, "I don't know why you two are here. Didn't nobody invite you. Don't nobody enjoy your company."

Albert said, "Dawn, why are you such an asshole?"

I said, "Why are you?"

Them two made me so much dumber. God, I wished I was a witch. I'd have witched them into tiny chunks of meat in some old man's gravy. Him sop them up and eat them on a biscuit and them be gone.

Hubert slid out of the booth. He said, "There she is."

Across the way Momma got out of a shit Bonneville. Her and that Calvin.

<div style="text-align:center">~~~~~~~~~</div>

PAINT PEELED off the steps up to Belinda Coates's apartment. Greenish mold climbed up the front of the building. Weeds stuck up through the broken pavement. There were paintball splatters and stains could be blood, could be chocolate on the tongue-pink walls. Syringes on the ground. Tampons. You wanted a nuclear waste cleanup suit just to walk over there. Nasty.

PERFECT SCENE FOR MOMMA & BELINDA'S BULLSHIT.

Momma was inside by the time we got across the road. The bony store woman hollered after us to pay for our biscuits. There was already yelling coming out of the apartment.

"Go back and pay," Hubert said. I went without saying anything, but two steps away said, "I aint got no money."

He give me ten dollars, said, "Go on," when I kept standing there. The yelling kept on, both Momma and Belinda going at once. Puke come up in my mouth. I bent over and spit it out.

Evie and Albert were gone when I got in the store. Hadn't paid. I didn't have enough money. I gave the woman the ten dollars, told her I'd go get some more and before I could get out of the store, a basket of laundry come flying out the door of Belinda Coates's apartment, T-shirts and panties all over the parking lot. The store woman sparked her lighter and lit a cigarette said, "Better hurry."

I run across the road, had to duck a red coffee tub come flying off the steps. When I got to the top, Hubert came out with Momma wrapped up in his arms. I backed up and they come down, Momma's feet not touching the ground, her knees thrashing, her hands opening and closing, her arms pinned to her sides by Hubert's come-along strap arms.

Momma said, "I aint scared of her. Let me go." She was screeching, a bird caught in barb wire, bloody feathers, beak broke off.

Hubert's face was a nothing. His hat was knocked almost off his head. There was pain in his eyes, in how straight he held his lips through Momma's kicking and flailing. Belinda came out, flung a no-stick skillet, hit Hubert in the small of the back, and his eyes went cold and hard. He threw Momma into my arms and picked the skillet up and headed back up to Belinda's. Momma almost slipped away from me, but I got her around the hips. Evie and Albert ran past us up the steps, and Momma started trying to reach around behind herself, trying to claw me. I pinned her arms to her sides, but I tired out quick.

"Momma, stop," I whispered in her ear. "Please stop, Momma."

And she didn't. Didn't stop for a minute. I held her as long as I could. I couldn't keep her. It was like a dream where you don't have all your strength. I let go of her.

Momma ran in the apartment. I went after her, and when I got to the top of the steps, Momma had her face up in Hubert's face, up in Belinda's face. There were couch cushions on the floor, covered by a sheet. Momma was bouncing on them. She said, "Aint none of yall got no say over me. Aint none of yall gonna boss me. I'm tired of it. I'm done with it. Hell with every one of you."

I wanted to put her down, like they do a mad dog.

She said, "I got me somebody I can count on now."

I looked around for Calvin, Momma's new rock and redeemer, but he was nowhere to be seen.

Belinda Coates put her finger up in Momma's face, said, "I don't give a fuck what you do cause you're already dead anyway, Tricia. You're dead. You hear me?" Belinda squeezed Momma around the throat. Momma put her fingernails into Belinda's face and started clawing.

About that time the police pulled up, not the sheriff but the Causey police, a young cop, said, "Hold on now, everybody. Just slow down here. Let's stop a minute."

I was so pissed I had got caught up in this.

Evie said, "Chucky, this aint nothing. Just playing cards. She tried to cheat me. I got hot about it, but it aint no thing."

Chucky looked around for cards. There weren't any. Everybody stood there looking like the bullshit lie they were, Momma's shirt collar stretched, her neck red. Hubert's combover was blown all over his head, up in the air.

Chucky said, "Whose stuff is that all over the parking lot?"

Belinda said it was hers.

Chucky said, "It better be gone when we come back around."

Evie said, "It will be."

Chucky took another look around and said to nobody in particular, "Don't make me come back here. Cause if I do, everybody here's going straight to Big Violet."

Which is where the jail is.

Nobody said a thing, nobody moved. Chucky left, and Momma stomped through the apartment hollering for Calvin. She found him back in the back bedroom in his sock feet, sitting up on Belinda's bed watching some kind of dirty movie. She hollered at him to come out, but he didn't move.

Hubert said, "Tricia, let's go. You don't need to be here."

Momma ran to the end of the hall and locked herself in the bathroom. She hollered at us to leave. She said she didn't need us anymore. She said we were ruining her life.

Hubert told me to go outside and make sure Momma didn't jump out the window and run away. I went down the steps to the end of the building. I turned the corner to the back of the building and Momma's legs were hanging out the second-story bathroom window. She pushed herself out, all the time yelling at Hubert how worthless he was and that she never loved him and he wasn't half the man my father was, and not a quarter of the man Calvin was, until she dropped out the window and landed on top of the dumpster in the parking lot. She climbed down off that and took off running, crooked and clumsy towards me, not my mother at all. I pushed back around the corner and let her run right past me. My phone rang and it was Willett. Momma didn't turn around when the phone rang. She cut across a backyard and went running through the slides and swing sets at the little park there, and headed down towards the river. My phone kept ringing. I pushed the button to answer and Calvin walked down the steps, calm as ice, and got in his Bonneville and drove off in the opposite direction from the way Momma ran.

Willett asked me where I was and I said, "Don't even ask," and he said he needed to talk to me and he said it was kind of serious and I said, "What is it?" and he said, "I don't want to work at the plant. I want to go back to school."

Hubert came down the steps, said, "Where's your mother?"

I pointed the way she'd gone.

Hubert said, "You were supposed to watch her."

I said, "Willett, you got fired, didn't you?"

There was a long quiet on the line, and then Willett said, "Yeah. I did."

Hubert took off through the playground. I walked after him. I said to Willett, "How could you do that?"

Evie and Albert came down the steps, crossed the road to the store, got in Evie's Cavalier, and went in the same general direction as Hubert and Momma. I sat down on the swing set in the park and said, "Willett, why can't you do anything?

Willett said, "Don't be mad at me."

I said, "Who do you want me to be mad at, Willett? Tell me who I'm supposed to be mad at, and I swear, that's who I'll be mad at."

He made some noise like he was about to cry, and I cut the phone off. There was a dip down to where the floodwall was and a little gate through it down to the river. I seen Hubert go through the door to the other side of the floodwall. To the river side.

I SAT there in the swing set, in the butt stirrup, in the park above the floodwall, and rocked back and forth from my toes to my heels. I was too big for the swing. Way too big, but I had Mamaw's pipe and a bag of her tobacco in my pants pocket. I had her lighter too, so I scooped out a bowl and lit it and smoked Mamaw's pipe and waited for some neighborhood watcher to call the police and send Chucky over to ruin my day some more.

A red-and-gray Astrovan went past and stopped and backed up. The van belonged to Evie's mother Hazel, and she backed onto the sidewalk between the park and the road and she came bowlegged, hobbling over to me.

She said, "What do you say, old girl?"

I drew on the pipe and said, "Not much."

She said, "Sorry about your grandma."

I said thanks. She leaned in over me and breathed deeply through her nose. She took a second to make sense of what she smelled. Hazel said, "You aint seen Evie, have you?"

I said, "No, not for about fifteen minutes."

Hazel said, "Where did you see her?"

I said, "Up there raising hell with Momma and Belinda."

Hazel said, "What kind of hell?"

I said, "Pretty much the standard kind."

Hazel leaned against the swing set, said, "Where you reckon she is now?"

I said, "Well, last time I seen her, she was heading that way." I pointed the way Evie and Albert had gone.

Hazel looked the way my finger pointed across the bridge, over to Railroad Street, looked so sad and give up as if I'd pointed down a rathole or off down the China Road.

I said, "I'd say she'll turn up, Hazel."

Hazel said, "The fragile promise of tomorrow."

I said, "Aint that the damn truth."

Hazel looked like she wanted to sit down in a swing with me, but she didn't. Hazel had three or four different limps and she grimaced and groaned a fair amount, not looking for attention, but I think because she really hurt. I'd heard her say she used to run with bikers, and that she'd had any number of motorcycle crashes and car wrecks and domestic incidents, and all told, I'd heard her say, that all she had was a limp was a blessing.

Hazel said, "Dawn, you say she was up there in them apartments?"

I said yes and she said, "Was you up there too?" and I said I was and she said, "Well, you reckon you could walk over there with me, see if we can find out where she might be?"

I wasn't much interested in that, for all the reasons you might imagine, but Hazel had never done nothing to me. In fact, Hazel had always been pretty good to me, so I flung myself out of the swing and said, "Yeah, let's go."

When we got around front of the apartment house, the one where Belinda Coates stayed, there was Belinda Coates, sitting on the stairs, a milk crate filled with the stuff that had been all over the parking lot between her legs. She sat with her head in her hands, and it was obvious she had been crying. In fact, she still was crying when we come up on her. I aint one much for pity, especially in the case of Belinda "Asshole" Coates, but with her knuckles rough and red covering her face, and her stressed-out hair pulled back in a ponytail, and her tanktop and her pajama pants as sour and house-dirty as could be, she was about as far from beautiful as I'd ever seen her and fairly pitiful looking.

I said, "What are you crying about?"

Hazel said, "Belinda, you seen Evie?"

Belinda Coates looked up at Hazel and said, "She went out to shit and the hogs ate her."

Hazel said, "Belinda, honey, are you all right?"

Belinda Coates said no.

Hazel set down on the steps, a couple down from Belinda, said, "I always wanted to be a lady astronaut. I always wanted to experience weightlessness. Especially after that wreck got me all this metal in my leg." Hazel rubbed her thigh, said, "You know what else?"

Belinda Coates looked up from where she had her head on her knees and said, "What?"

Hazel said, "I always wanted to be the first person to smoke in space."

Belinda Coates said, "Weed?"

Hazel said, "Well, yeah, weed would be good, but I was thinking even a cigarette would be way cool."

I said, "It would be cool," because I always had a thing for astronauts and spaceships.

Belinda Coates said, "I'd quit smoking if they'd put me on a rocket ship out of this damn place."

Hazel said, "You still seeing Courtney?"

Belinda said, "When she's not totally hateful."

That surprised me. I didn't know Belinda Coates went with girls.

Hazel said, "So was Albert with Evie?"

Belinda Coates said, "Yeah," said, "I think they said they were going up Drop Creek."

Hazel said, "I always did like that Courtney. Many a night I seen her pack a drunk man out on her back to his wife when she was bouncer at the Overhang Club."

"Yeah," Belinda said, "she is broad-backed."

Hazel said, "Dawn, how did you get here?"

I said, "Rode with Hubert."

Hazel said, "Where is he?"

I said, "Down there by the river trying to get ahold of Momma."

Hazel said, "What's she doing down by the river?"

Belinda Coates stood up, said, "I'm going in."

Hazel said, "Well, honey, I hope you feel better."

Belinda Coates nodded, went up the steps and in her apartment.

Hazel said, "You want to go look for Hubert and your momma?"

I said, "Not really."

Hazel said, "You want me to take you somewhere?"

I said, "Canada."

Hazel said, "You know why I'm wanting to find Evie so bad?"

I said, "No."

Hazel said, "I had a dream of a white buffalo."

I said, "That's cool."

Hazel said, "It came up and snorted on me in my sleep. Snorted out death."

I said, "Hunh."

Hazel said, "I woke up knowing it was Evie's death."

I looked in Hazel's eyes, knowing she was high, and thought to myself it was a dark-ass time of life. I said, "You don't want to take me to Mamaw's, do you?"

She said, "Could you help a little on the gas."

We got Belinda to loan us a few dollars for gas and Hazel took me up to Mamaw's and not much happened on the way except Hazel told me she also was hoping one day to have sex in outer space and I laughed and told her I'd be glad to go on a space mission with her some time and she laughed and put me out at Mamaw's and it felt good to have something like a normal conversation with somebody for once in my life.

GENE

The next morning I had fifty dollars in my pocket and I shouldn't have. I should keep my money somewhere safe, somewhere I aint so likely to lose it. And generally I do. But I can tell you why I had it. I can tell you exactly why. That hand-holding thing That Woman did with me threw me into a swirl of emotion. I knew better than to get caught up feeling like that. Hadn't never any good come from me feeling a bunch of stuff and that fifty dollars was a perfect example of what I'm talking about.

After she took off for West Virginia, the time where she caught me about to touch her face, I'd given myself a serious talking to. I'd told myself I'd better straighten up, that there wasn't no love to be had between me and That Woman, at least not no passion nor matrimony or anything like that. She wadn't going to be fixing my coffee every morning and I wadn't going to be asking her "how was your day" every evening. I had to tell myself to get ahold of myself and for the most part I had.

But then when she took my hand when we were talking about her momma and the purpose of life and all that stuff before she went to West Virginia the next time,

THAT LED MY HEART TO BACKSLIDE

Which brings me to that fifty dollars.

I'd got fifty dollars off this doctor's wife lived over in Falstaff Acres where a deer had come in her backyard and died and she needed somebody to get rid of the deer and all the kudzu where it had fallen. I did that and she paid me and I got to looking at that fifty-dollar bill and I let myself imagine me and That Woman going out on a date, maybe us going down to Middlesboro and that steakhouse buffet they had, and then after, maybe there'd be a concert out in some gazebo, us sitting on the grass, happy and full of steak and baked potato and jello salad, talking about how pretty each other's eyes are.

So me packing that fifty dollars in my pocket when me and Brother went to do our biggest weedeating job, which was the whole riverbank behind the floodwall in Canard—took us all day to do it—that was so I could pretend it was Friday and when we was done weedeating I was going to go pick up my girl, which was That Woman. And I was going to spend that fifty on her like I was a normal person, out on a date with someone I loved, someone who loved me.

Back in reality of course what happened was at the end of the day not only did I not have a date with That Woman, I'd lost my fifty dollars somewhere, which I needed to pay down my debt to not only the payday loan place, but also Sister's husband. And of course, the craziest part of the whole thing was it wasn't Friday when it happened. It was, if I'm not mistaken, a Tuesday.

Me and Brother went looking, back over where we'd been working. I walked through the mown grass that run all the way down to the river. The river curved, the grass ended, and weeds stood waist-high above a bed of rick-rack, big chunks of limestone like they use in retaining walls and below sludge ponds. I knocked through the cut grass looking for that money. I peered down in the dark between the rick-rack chunks. Knocked over a vienny can, wished I had me a can of viennies, wished I had my fifty dollars. I sat down on a limestone slab. We had just been there. Grass blades was still floating in the puddles. But my fifty was gone.

I kept walking, kept looking, where I'd been working down the bank where there wasn't no rick-rack, where it was green and soft and looked like rich people. An oak tree rose like a giant hand and spread over the river. I had worked in its shade.

Tricia was rolled over on her side, curled up in the tree shadow. It looked a nice place to take a nap and when I when I first saw her, I wished I was her. I wished it was me lying there sleeping a little bit in the warm of the day. I wished I could leave her curled up.

Thing was, Tricia was dead. I should've known before I lay my hand on her shoulder. But I didn't. I didn't roll her over or anything like that. I didn't need to see her all sprawled out, staring blank at the sky. I left her on her side, her hands out in front of her like somebody was about to give her something.

I SAT DOWN BESIDE HER.

A tree limb cracked. Belinda Coates sat, her legs crossed, on a stone slab bench further down the river. She broke a twig into pieces, first long as a pencil, then half as long, then half as long as that until she had a double handful of wood pebbles. She threw the wood at the water. The pebbles landed in a crowd.

Belinda Coates stood up and walked off.

Brother was beside me, said, "She dead?"

I said I believed she was.

Brother got in the truck and set for a minute and then blowed the truck horn. I didn't do nothing, just set there. Brother pulled the truck around to where I was sitting, put it in park. Brother said, "I'll be back." He put the truck in gear, said, "Don't touch her." Then he said, "You hear me?"

I said I did.

Brother drove off, left me down there with Tricia's body. I set with her a long time. Before I knew it, I was talking to her. I started off of course telling her I was sorry she had to die. I said I wish I knew how it happened. I told her what a strong youngun I thought Dawn was and how I'd try and help her and her brother Albert all I could. I set there some more, kept thinking Brother would be back, kept thinking I was going to get to stop keeping that dead woman company. But Brother didn't come and didn't come.

And it got dark. And I started talking to Tricia's body about her sister and how much I cared for her. I told Tricia about how I liked the way That Woman's hair fell. How I liked how tender she was with people. How I liked the colors she picked out and how she made the places she lived in so calm and gentle. And I called her by her name. I said, "Tricia, I love your sister June."

It was good and dark by then, and a truck came down through there and I thought, well, finally this is Brother. He's brought somebody to help us. The truck kept coming, all headlights and lack of concern, and I got a little afraid it wouldn't see us and that it would run over Tricia's body. So I started walking towards the headlights, and when the truck stopped, it wadn't Brother nor anybody that had talked to Brother.

It was Sister's husband. And he was higher than a Georgia pine.

He said, "Where the hell you been?" and before I could say a thing he said, "And where is my money, you worthless sack of shit?"

I said, "They's something we need to tend to . . ."

And before I could finish he come up and pushed me and said, "Your sister was right about you. They should have drowned you when you was a baby. You are too stupid and too sorry to live."

He knocked me down when he said it, but I got up and said, "Sister never said that."

He said, "She sure as hell did. And I tell you what else she said. She said she was glad she wasn't your real sister. Said she was glad yall had different daddies, that she didn't have a monster daddy like the one bred you and your brother. She said she was glad not to have that garbage blood of yours."

And I said, "She never said that. Sister was too good to say such."

And that animal said, and it kills me to repeat it, "She was good at sucking my dick. That's all she was ever good at." And then he said, "Now where's my goddamn money?"

I threw my hands around his throat and I thought I'd snapped his neck in that first grab. I didn't, but he went down backwards trying to get away from me, and all my hurt came pouring down through my hands, like hot black

asphalt, all the hurt of Sister's shooting herself, and never having no mother nor father, and Granny dying, and never getting ahead and never having no one to love, it all came out and I was dead sure
I was gonna kill that man,

AND I WAS DEAD SURE I WAS GONNA FEEL BETTER WHEN I DID.

DAWN

It was late at night when Belinda Coates called me, said Momma was messed up. Said I needed to come get her. Said she was down by the riverbank in downtown Canard. Right near where the bypass went over the river. So I went down there, and when I got there, Weedeater had a man down on the ground, had both hands around his throat trying to strangle him to death.

The man Weedeater was strangling thrashed his legs and squeezed Weedeater's face. It was dark by the river, the only light the gray pitched by streetlights on the other side of the floodwall. Weedeater gasped like it was him getting choked, and then he started moaning. The guy getting strangled hammered Weedeater in the side of the head with his fist, and Weedeater tried to swat away the hammering hand. When Weedeater did that, the getting-strangled man rolled over on top of Weedeater, but Weedeater flung him off, even though Weedeater was a hundred pounds littler than the man he was strangling.

I walked off down the riverbank. I found a chunk of pallet four feet long and solid, hefty but easy to handle. When I got back, the mud under them two made sucking sounds as they wrestled. I waited for a minute to see if they would wear each other out. Weedeater pinned the other guy's arms down with his elbows. He went back to strangling. Daylight popped the ridge and I could see Weedeater's thumb gouging down into the other man's Adam's apple.

I said, "Gene. Stop."

Weedeater shook his head like I was a bad memory. The getting-strangled guy's eyes showed all white. His arms and legs flailed slower. I raised the pallet chunk and brought it down on Weedeater's head. The first lick dazed him but he only turned loose of that man's neck for a second and then went back to strangling.

I popped him again. Weedeater went over into the mud on his side. The getting-strangled man was on his back and rose up on his elbows, breathing like a freight train, eyes nightmare wide. He was a big old dude. He had on khaki clothes, looked like something some old papaw would wear. But this guy had plenty of hair, mostly gray and wiry. Some might have thought him nice-looking, like a guy in an Old Spice commercial. But he didn't look like no Old Spice man lying there beside the river. He looked spit out of the front crack of some wild-haired mud momma.

Weedeater got up on his hands and knees. His head hung between his shoulders. His hair trailed off his face. The khaki man looked like he might kick Weedeater, but he just rolled away from him, got on his hands and knees, too. The morning light turned pink. The two of them both started crawling around. They looked like cavemen bred for little dwarf cavemen to ride the back of. I was afraid they were going to go at it again. I picked my pallet chunk up out of the mud.

The khaki man veered off from me and Weedeater towards a wad of driftwood and garbage piled for burning. Khaki man rose up on his knees and stood and walked over to a khaki Dodge pickup, got in it, started it, and drove off without saying nothing else.

Weedeater walked down the riverbank and I followed him. It was about the only time I'd ever been with Weedeater that he didn't talk. He staggered along like the most tired person ever. I had to stand him up one time when he went to his knees tripping over a tree branch mired in the river mud. Then he took me to Momma's body, lying on its side in the grass.

I got on my knees beside her and put my hand in Momma's hair. I put her T-shirt sleeve between my fingers. I hadn't been there two minutes when an ambulance came. They asked who I was. I told them. They asked did I need to call somebody. I called June on my flip phone. She was in West Virginia. I called Houston, and he got there before the ambulance was gone. I left a message for Willett.

They took Momma to the hospital. When we got there, Evie and Albert were there.

Evie said, "What happened?"

Albert said, "Where's Momma? Where's she at?"

He acted like he was going to do something about something.

Hubert came in and hugged me, hugged me good. I let go into him. He pulled me tight.

Hubert whispered in my ear, "Where's Belinda?"

Evie stepped to us and said, "Where's that Tennessee garbage?"

And I wondered where Evie had been. Where was she when Momma died?

GENE

It's not everyone has tried to choke another person to death, where it's illegal and where when you start, it's hard to keep going. It aint like changing a tire or giving a dog a bath. They're fighting you. Sometimes a dog'll be hard to bath. That Woman's dog, where it was a rescue dog, found tied up and starving, scared of everything, I had to take it out in the yard to bath it, put it on two leashes, one on each of my wrists, and still I like to never get it wet with the water hose. She'd spin like a tornado and bite me every time I'd get my hand down near her mouth and still that was an easier thing than strangling Sister's husband.

When I strangled Sister's husband, he gouged me in the eyes and kneed me in the privates. I didn't much blame him where I was doing my level best to kill him. I can tell you about it now cause I aint mad like I was. I calmed down about a week after it happened. Had to count pennies every morning for a hour, every day for fourteen days. I have a canning jar of pennies I count for calming. Stack them out in stacks of ten or stacks of five, depending how many pennies I got.

I stacked till I didn't think no more about the stuff Sister's husband had done to Sister. Not his cheating on her. Not his getting on pain pills and taking up with people scared Sister, women with laughs like spent fan belts and dudes with no tomorrow in their eyes. Fourteen days before I forgot what he said.

I didn't never shake hands with him, or tell him he was fine or nothing like that. But we did come to agree that it was best for both of us for me not to kill him.

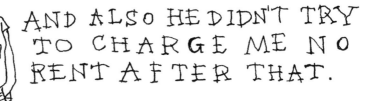

AND ALSO HE DIDN'T TRY TO CHARGE ME NO RENT AFTER THAT.

DAWN

When I was fifteen, my mother got baptized at the church of Goldie Kelly, the sister of Keith Kelly, a man my mother used to go with before he died in a wreck. Keith Kelly was the first one any of us knew to OD on Oxy. That's what caused him to wreck. That was six years ago. By the time Momma died, seemed like there were people overdosing every week. And it didn't seem like it would ever end. One day they were normal people—some of them nice, some of them mean, some of them funny, some of them quiet—and the next day they was zombies or acting wild, acting so different to whatever they had been before. It would be like you hadn't ever met them, and then the day after that they was dead. And you were left sitting there missing a person you could barely remember.

I always thought she did it to get out of whatever trouble with the law she was in when it happened. Evie told me that wasn't true, that my mother thought God would help her, that she really had faith.

Anyway , the church Momma got baptized in was where the funeral was. It was out on Drop Creek, close to where Mamaw grew up. The church wasn't big, but it was pretty full for Momma's funeral. People always liked my mother. She had been fun. Sweet, people told me she was. Evie and Albert had done most of the getting the funeral together. I let them scan a couple pictures I had, but they did most of it. They were the ones put together the giant posterboard collages on either side of the coffin. They were the ones set up the flowers people sent. They were the ones talked to the church people and the funeral home people.

And when I say "they," I really mean Evie. She seemed like my sister-in-law then. She seemed like part of the family. It didn't make me exactly happy she was. But it was mostly a comfort, at least at the time of the funeral.

Houston was there. I felt sorry for him. He looked way older than he did when I took Nicolette to see him with June right before 4th of July. His prediction had come true about Mamaw dying, and now a thing everybody predicted, Momma dying, had come true, too. June had got word that they were going to hire her permanent at the community college, and she and Houston paid for Momma's funeral.

I sat there on the church pew, being sadder for Momma than I thought I'd be, but also worrying about money, worrying about how I was going to make it. I looked up at the homemade painting of Jesus with his arms spread standing on the water. The painting was on the wall behind the baptismal hot tub. I apologized to Jesus for thinking on the things of this world when I should be torn up over Momma.

Albert wasn't having no trouble being torn up over Momma. Ever since the hospital, he had been on a tear—ping-ponging back and forth between how everybody needed to get off drugs and how he was going to kill Belinda or Calvin or whoever it was responsible for Momma dying. Cause everybody who knew said Momma couldn't stand needles. That somebody else must have shot her up.

I didn't know my mother's drug-using ways. I didn't care to know. Nicolette sat beside me and looked at the people who went to Goldie Kelly's church. There was a woman playing piano had hair a yard long. Nicolette took in her songs, her lips moving like ninety, her eyes darting back and forth watching the long-haired woman play. Nicolette was storing up that church's songs in her mind like a woman like to quilt storing up fabric scraps. Willett sat on the other side of Nicolette. He shifted from one butt cheek to the other. He drummed his fingers on the pew. He scratched his head and ran his fingers through his hair. He was aggravating. I wanted to throw him off. Get shed of him.

Hubert came in and tapped me on the shoulder, had me to scoot over. He was late and I asked him why. He shook his head. I knew why. He'd been out in his truck crying when we got there. I looked across him. On the pew on the other side of the aisle set Evie and Albert. Albert cried into his hands. Evie patted him on the back, not with much spirit to it, doing it cause she was supposed to.

On Evie's other side sat June. She was still, her back up straight. She had a rolled-up handkerchief wrapped around her knuckles. She cried without any fuss. Kenny was beside her looking like he don't belong on a front pew, looking like he didn't belong in his dark blue suit, no tie, his orange curls against his shirt collar, rubbing his hands against his thighs.

There was no sign of any Coateses, just like there hadn't been at the visitation. Which suited me fine. Willett, June, and some others wanted to talk to me about how the Coateses killed Momma. They probably had a hand in it, but I was looking for Calvin, who hadn't been seen either. That's where I thought the problem was. That's whose eyes I wanted to look into.

Others were there. Hazel was there. And Decent Ferguson. Willett's parents. Them two, especially Willett's dad, softened my heart toward Willett. I was glad Nicolette had the Bilsons for grandparents. I hoped Willett's father lived a big long time. He was quiet and strong like my daddy in my memory. I don't really know what my daddy was like anymore. People get gone and you have to work to keep their memory. You got to keep polishing it up to keep it from getting covered with everything that happens. The dirt and fuzz and dead leaves of all the different daily angers and hurry-ups and disasters and getting the baby ready and putting the food on the table and the house halfway clean and all that causes you to forget who they were.

The other person at Momma's funeral was Momma. Looking at her funeraled up was hard. Her face looked like instant potatoes been in the fridge a week. Making us look at her in the open coffin seemed pointless, but maybe it wasn't because it sure did make me know she was really gone.

Goldie Kelly's preacher come in. He was a good hundred pounds bigger than he had been when Momma got baptized and his hair was thinner and he had a look about his mouth like he thought he was a lot smarter and better of a person than he used to be. He started right in, not knowing Momma that well, least I don't think he did, but he called her Sister Tricia and talked about her relationship with the Lord, talking about it like him and the Lord and Momma had spent a day at Dollywood together. Preacher said how when Momma wandered, he had prayed so hard for Sister Tricia, but that, you know, friends, it's hard to know another's heart, and it is hard to stay on the path and that's why it was important to stay in the church, to keep your church family close.

Somebody said, "Amen," and the preacher said it a question: "Amen?"

And more people said, "Amen," and that warmed the preacher up and he kept talking on being lost and he got louder and started making that "HAAA" sound about every tenth word and everything was about the salvation and it made it hard to think of Momma, but I made myself.

I thought of how when we still lived at the trailer, after Daddy died, but before Momma fell apart, Momma used to keep flowers on the kitchen table. Momma took a hippie skirt she'd got at the mission store and cut it open and used carpet tacks to tack the skirt to the ceiling, turned the tube lights orange and blue, hippie shapes like tears and microscope slide one-cell animals met your eye when you looked up. When I was little, Momma liked to light candles and old globe lamps. She liked to make things magic, especially at night, especially when we were waiting for Daddy to get home from work, and

even after Daddy died she did things to keep the light orange and golden, and
everything warm and brown, and she'd play Linda Ronstadt and Fleetwood Mac
and I thought things might be OK and I remember thinking that life could still be
fun. I remember food tasting good and loving all kinds of weather and not being
able to wait to put my clothes on and get going in the morning. And things were
OK. Pretty much. Until they weren't.

Goldie Kelly's preacher, he didn't talk about none of that, he didn't tell the
stories on Momma that would make you smile, make you warm. It was just
Jesus Jesus Jesus and hell if you didn't like it. He went on and I wondered did
he even remember he was doing Momma's funeral. I didn't have much else to
think about while he went on. Didn't no other Momma stories come to mind. I
just sat there toughing it out.

Finally the preacher did his "does anybody want to get saved" thing and
Albert got up, his face still in his hands and he got down on his knees and kept
his hands over his face like he was ashamed and wailed on and on, wailing like
he was trying out for a play and all I could think was how stupid Albert had
always been and how everybody thought somebody dropped him when he was
a baby and wouldn't admit it, or maybe he'd swallowed something, cause he
was stupid in a different way than   the other stupid people in the family.

The preacher put his hand on Albert's shaking shoulder and said, "Brother,
are you ready to accept Jesus Christ as your personal Lord and Savior?"

Albert put his hands down on his thighs and nodded his head. The preacher
nodded at some of the dudes at the front of the church and they took Albert
in the back and the preacher nodded at the piano player and she pounded out
a come-to-Jesus song and the regular church people began to clap and sing,
getting louder and more driving, and then Albert came back out in a white
getting-baptized outfit.

They led him around to the back of the baptismal hot tub and took him into the water and turned on the jets. The preacher was already there at the tub when Albert got in, and he said some Jesus words over him, and then they lay Albert back in the water, kept him down there for a good while, and he come up gasping and the bass player and the drums joined in with the piano player, and the air got all stirred up.

Albert tried to climb out the front of the hot tub. The preacher had to grab him by both shoulders to stop him, and they got him out the back, the way he'd come in, but he tried to bolt. The men held him, didn't let him go. Albert dragged them up the church aisle, him sopping wet, his hair mashed flat. The church women who'd brought out towels to comfort and dry him couldn't get at him, and he looked people dead in the eye first this side of the aisle, then the other. Albert reached out and touched the faces of the people closest to him. He looked so plain without his usual hip-hop car-racer bullshit on, without his leather bracelets, without sunglasses and a sideways ball cap on his head, without his chunky boots not like people who work wear, just stupid unlaced boots—he didn't have none of that on. Only thing messing up his pure paleness was his black drawers showing through where his wet robe clung to him. Finally then when he calmed down, them guys let him go. Albert went to the back of the church, turned around, and said, "You know I see you."

He started back up the aisle said, "You know what I see when I see you." He stopped and pointed at Terry who was just out of jail. "Terry, you know you need to slow it down." He pointed at another one. "I see you, Kyla. You know what all we done together." He got another one around the shoulder, a boy named Roy Lee Daniel. He said, "Roy Lee, come here." He led Roy Lee to the coffin, said, "Look there, Roy Lee. Lay down the needle. Or you're going to end up like Momma. End up in a box in the front of a church before your time, Roy Lee." Roy Lee looked embarrassed, but like he'd been embarrassed before, and slipped away from Albert back to the back of the church.

Albert lay his hand on Momma's coffin and said, "You think they're going to do anything about this? This is just another one off the list."

Albert's shoulders hunched up and he stalked up and down the church aisle like a tiger in a circus ring you wasn't sure was going to obey the tiger man. People backed up away from Albert as Albert pointed his finger first this way then that. He said, "Cilla, you know I aint no better than you, but you need to lay it down, girl. Playing with fire on Dum Dum Knob. You know you are." Cilla just stared at him like she'd like to kill him. Albert kept pointing and said, "Aren't you?" Cilla Stacey turned away.

Albert made his way back up to the front of the church, turned and faced us. He said, "Jesus touched me. He laid his hand on me. And it took this woman here dying." Albert pointed at a picture of Momma laughing in short pants, smoking a cigarette with her legs crossed in summertime. "Took her dying for me to feel His hand on my shoulder. You got to lay it down, Danny. You got to lay it down, Cilla."

Albert stood there teetering. Albert was the most horseshit person I ever knew. I loved him, I guess, but what you need to remember as you think about all them people crying over what Albert said and thanking him and petting him as they took him out to dry off and get his clothes back on is that we found Albert cold and blue stretched out dead on the table in Hubert's kitchen right before Christmas, dead of the same thing took Momma.

GENE

I knew I was going to go to Tricia's funeral, where I had set out with her body by the river and because she'd come to me in a kind of vision after that, but I don't much like going to funerals so it took me time to get it in gear to go. I come in during the middle of it, stood near the back door off to the side where they was two or three big dudes and a couple women all with their hands in the pockets of their jeans, all looking like they'd been through some rough times, all black-ringed eyes and dyed hair.

I come in while Albert Jewell was stampeding up and down the aisle, calling people out for their bad habits. He was making such a show, I didn't notice a gray-haired woman steal up beside me. She come to my shoulder with short hair all fixed up, color of dirty snow. She touched me on my shirtsleeve and bid me follow her. I looked at her and she nodded in a way reminded me of Granny and put me at ease.

She was Calvin's mother. I remembered her breaking up beans on her porch when we brought Calvin home after he stole that money the first time, after he'd locked me in the trunk of his Bonneville. I remembered how tickled his mother seemed to be to see him when we brought him home, how sweet a feeling I got to put Calvin back with her, and that's who I was following out into the gravels of the Drop Creek Church of God parking lot. When we got out to her car, which was a Chrysler, a Newport, I believe, from years ago, but in very good shape, better a shape than I'd maybe ever seen a car that old. And when she lay her hand to the door handle, she turned and said,

IT'S A LONG WAY HERE, AINT IT?

And I said, "Yes, ma'am, it is. From about anywhere."

She said, "I come from Kingsport. I brung yall something."

And it was what I figured it was—that red bag of money, that red bag about all of us had handled.

I said, "Ma'am, that aint my money."

She pressed it to my chest, said, "I seen you. And Calvin told me about you. And I believe you're good. I believe you're the one to get this money where it goes." She pulled the money back away from me, said, "Are you?"

Before I thought, I said I was.

She put the red money bag in my hands.

I said, "I'll do my best."

And she said, "I don't know how much is already gone."

I said, "Well."

She said, "It doesn't matter to me. I brought it to you freely. But if you choose not to say where you got it, that wouldn't bother me."

I said, "Well."

She smiled and said, "Thank you, Eugene," which nobody but Granny called me.

And I said, "Goodnight, ma'am."

And I reckon that was that.

DAWN

When Momma's funeral was over, we went to the graveyard out Tallow Creek where Mamaw was buried. Didn't hardly nobody go with us. Which was fine. But Gene went. When the burying was done, I went up to Gene, there with his brother about to leave, I said, "Gene, what are you doing here?"

He said, "You reckon Hubert's around?"

I said, "I reckon he is."

Gene said he had the red money bag.

I said, "You," thinking Gene had got the money, but then I was like, aint no way. My thoughts that he had something to do with stealing that money, those thoughts were my own meanness.

WEEDEATER WASN'T A THIEF.

GENE

Hubert walked up. I told him what I told Dawn, that I had the bag of money. He said give it to him. I told him I didn't have it, which was true, I'd hid it before I come to Tallow Creek. Hubert asked when he could have it. I said I was working at That Woman's the next morning. Said I'd have it then. Hubert said he'd like to get it tonight. I said I'd be at That Woman's early as he liked.

DAWN

Next morning I lay on the bed at Mamaw's and I thought of Nicolette. I thought how it was my job to put flowers on her table, my job to help her make a world she wanted to get up in the morning and run out into.

I got up and went in the front room. Nicolette had made herself a tent between the sofa and the television, a pink blanket with a pink satin trim, a blanket I'd made a tent of when I was little. I got on my hands and knees and looked into the pink air of her tent. She set, her legs folded under her, giving a bunch of little plastic monsters a talking to.

"Now you got to work the mule," she said to a monster that turned into a spaceship when you took it apart, "and you," she said to a purple monster with bottom jaw fangs sticking out, "you got to churn the butter." She had a hundred tinfoil balls from Hershey Kisses lined up by color, red and green and silver foil.

I said, "What are those?," pointing at the foil balls.

She said, "Hey, Mommy. Do you want to come in my tent?"

I crawled in a little on my elbows.

She said, putting her finger down along the rows of tinfoil balls, "These are the tomatoes and these are the cabbages and these are the onions."

Her face was flush as a peach.

I said, "I thought onions grew under the ground," said, "and I thought tomatoes grew on a vine, a whole bunch of tomatoes on every plant."

She looked at me, a monster in each hand, and said, "They're monster onions, Mommy. Made of silver. And the cabbages are emeralds."

I said, "And the tomatoes rubies?"

Nicolette said, "The tomatoes are just tomatoes, Mommy."

I said, "Who is that?," pointing at a redheaded princess action figure.

Nicolette said, "She's the country music singer witch."

I said, "Country music singer witch?"

Nicolette said, "She sings on the radio and it makes people be nice to each other."

I said, "She's a pretty witch."

Nicolette said, "She don't care about that, Mommy. She wishes she was ugly."

I said, "Does she?"

Nicolette nodded. I said,

She said, "With baloney on it."

I went and fixed her a baloney and tomato sandwich and she ate it in her tent, her lips smacking, me listening from a stool at the bar between the living room and the kitchen, and that's how I got through that morning, got through till it was time to go to June's and find out about the red bag of money.

GENE

Next morning I got to That Woman's just as Dawn did. It was raining hard. A froggy strangler, Granny would've said. I sat in the car, thinking it might let up. Dawn jumped out of her mamaw's Escort. The rain mashed Dawn's hair flat. She looked like misery itself. I wanted to put Dawn and That Woman together somehow. That Woman's mommy dead, Dawn's mommy dead. They needed one another. But they was at odds. They didn't need to be.

The horn blew on a coal train when the train crossed the bypass and cut through the floodwall and across the river. A hundred train cars full of coal rolling by, stopping everybody on the bypass. The coal was flying.

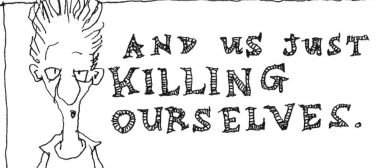

AND US JUST KILLING OURSELVES.

Killing each other. All that anger present in the world all the time, about to pop out like frozen biscuits from a roll. You shudder to think about people who don't have people to stop them doing crazy things.

DAWN

June met me at the door with a big thick bath towel. She dabbed it on my cheeks with both hands and put it up over my hair and kissed me next to my lips and pulled me in close to her. The wet on me made spots all over her.

Mamaw always gave June a rough way to go. June did stuff like going to those protests in West Virginia because she thought that's what Mamaw would have her do. I never could understand why Mamaw had so much fight in her, fight for something bigger. June was big fight too, but I thought maybe she did it so she'd look right. I don't know. Maybe I was wrong. June just always seemed to care more about what she looked like than what she was doing. Seemed to always disgust Mamaw, seemed to me, caring what you looked like. Course Mamaw always cared a crap ton about what she looked like—not so much her clothes or hair, or what people said about her out in town, but more what she saw when she looked in the mirror, which you might think is better than caring what you look like to others. But it's still caring what you look like.

AINT IT?

After June dried me off, she looked down the hill, saw Weedeater sitting there in his Sentra. June said, "What's he doing?"

I said, "Saying goodbye to that money, I reckon."

I went upstairs to see what Momma left. Which was next to nothing. She didn't have a box under her bed full of stuff she wanted to pack out if the house caught on fire. She didn't have rings or CDs or books. She didn't have a pile of makeup bottles and lipstick tubes and little eyebrow brushes and all kinds of nail polish. No pictures on the wall or sitting on furniture, or stuck in the mirror frames. Momma died borrowing off everybody, wearing whoever's clothes were in the place she fell. I sat on the mattress in her room, smelled her dirty clothes, breathed in her rancid-butter-smelling sweat soaked down in the cotton. I picked up the blood-pink Kleenexes scattered around the bed, threw them away, and listened to the air conditioner moan.

Aunt June came in the room, said, "This was something your mother made."

Aunt June came back from Kingsport to save my mother, save her from herself. In the end, I don't feel like she tried very hard. Saving my mother wasn't nine to five enough for her. It was an on call all the time job. I didn't blame her. But my aunt didn't look beautiful to me anymore.

June held a clay cup out in both hands like it was sacred. It was a heavy thing, glaze dripped on it by somebody didn't really know what they were doing.

Aunt June said, "That is real good for a first pot. Real good."

I smiled, acted like I was glad to see it, like the pot was going to be some treasure I was going to pass on to my daughter. When June handed it to me, I just let it fall, let it smash on the floor.

June picked up the pieces and said, "We can fix it."

After all that, I truly wondered did she really believe we could fix it.

She was standing there holding the pieces when Hubert's voice come booming from downstairs. He was laughing.

Me and June went downstairs. Nicolette, Weedeater, and Hubert sat at the kitchen table.

Hubert said, "That's exactly what we ought to do with it," and laughed again.

~~~~~~~~

TURNS OUT there was a hundred and fifty kids from Drop Creek Elementary School who were supposed to go to Dollywood as part of a summer program and they lost their state money. And somehow Weedeater heard about it, and he told Hubert. And Hubert said he would pay for all them kids to go to Dollywood out of the waterfall money. And then he said anybody who wanted to could go and he'd pay for them too, until the waterfall money ran out. And that's how in the middle of the last week of July in 2004, over five hundred people from Canard County went to Dollywood on the same day. Me and Willett and Nicolette went. Albert and Evie. June and Kenny. Hubert. Houston. Gene and his brother. Hazel went. Decent Ferguson went. All the people in June's class. Everyone in this story who was still alive went, except Sidney and Belinda Coates. And Calvin. They didn't go.

Everybody from Denny's coal mine went, all their families. They were already going, before Hubert said he'd pay. And then after people heard Hubert was paying, there was a bunch more. Big gang from Goldie Kelly's church. Bunch of women from where Hubert went to get his hair cut. I mean, seriously. It was like all of Canard County.

When Gene got that red money bag back, we didn't know what to do with it. Cause Hubert never wanted it. He only took it out of the waterfall to try to get Momma out of trouble. Then Sidney wouldn't have it, and then Momma was gone anyway. So Hubert said why not, tell them all we'll go to Dollywood.

Hubert told people to show up that morning at the store he run across the mountain and told them to get them a tank of gas. They were lined up back up the hill almost to the gravel quarry.

People were happy too, telling Dollywood stories about kids that got lost and kids that got found and music they'd seen. They laughed about throwing up on too much kettle corn and they talked about how good that frozen lemonade was going to be. It was nice after all that dying, all them funerals, to see everyone glad to be up in the morning, glad to be going someplace.

We convoyed to Dollywood, the cars and trucks and minivans with their Canard County tags strung down 11E like it was a high school football road game. Hazel said she was scared the Astrovan wouldn't make the trip, so she rode with me and Willett. She sat in the backseat with Nicolette. Me and Willett sat up front. We were outside Morristown when Hazel leaned up and said, "Listen. Evie told me about the money for this trip."

I said, "Did she?"

Hazel said, "I know where that money come from." She said, "I'll tell you if you want to know."

I said, "All right."

She said, "Before yall was born, back when most everybody here worked in the mines was union, they had elections in the union. Back when I'm talking about, the big man for the union was named Tony Boyle and he didn't like the man running against him, man named Yablonski. Boyle didn't like that man saying he was a crook. Which he was. So Boyle paid these boys in Cleveland to kill Yablonski, paid with union money."

Willett said, "How'd they do it?"

"How they done it was they put a bunch of money out in Canard to pay retired miners to campaign for the union candidate for judge-executive. But those boys never campaigned for nobody. They cashed their checks and give the cash back to the union for them to pay the killers. A hundred men, three hundred dollars each."

I said, "I never heard nothing like that."

Hazel said, "Cause none of them dudes ever said a word. Them old coal miners, ones that fought for the union in the thirties, knew how to keep their mouths shut. And didn't care to do anything the union said do."

I said, "Why you telling us this?"

Hazel said, "Cause your great-grandpa Scratch was the union dude collected all the money. He's the one had it."

I said, "So?"

She said, "That's the money behind the waterfall."

I said, "How do you know?"

She said, "I know."

I said, "So how is the money still here? I thought you said it went to the killers."

Hazel looked at Nicolette, who was looking out the window counting cows, acting like she wasn't listening. Hazel said, "Never made it. Them guys in Cleveland was such screwups the law caught them before they got paid. And after they got caught every FBI agent east of the Mississippi showed up in Canard, up in the business of every union miner, every official, everybody could spell UMWA."

"Wow," Willett said.

I said, "That many law and they never found the money."

Hazel said, "That's right."

Nicolette started humming to the music on the car stereo. I didn't say nothing. My questions were for Hubert. Why hadn't he spent the money before? Why did he want to give it away?

Nicolette's nose smeared against the glass as she sang low, "Love is like a butterfly, a rare and gentle thing."

Willett said, "I read about this."

"Yeah," Hazel said, "but this is true."

I said, "So the man didn't get killed?"

Hazel said, "Oh no. They killed him. Him and his wife and his daughter too. Middle of the night on New Year's Eve. They just never got paid."

I said, "And where were they from?"

Hazel said, "Who?"

I said, "The killers."

Hazel said, "Cleveland, Ohio. But their people were from Tennessee. Around LaFollette."

I said, "Are they still alive?"

Hazel said, "That I don't know."

We drove a hundred miles in silence, me trying to think of something rare or gentle in my life.

WHEN WE finally got to Dollywood, people were pouring across the parking lot, kids excited, old people on the shuttle buses smiling and pressing their teeth back in place. When we got to where you go through the gate, there were groups from other places, dumping out of their tour buses, all wearing the same-color T-shirts, listening to people tell them when and where they needed to be back.

The Canard people all went tear-assing up to the gate where Hubert stood with a fistful of tickets thick as a brick, handing them out to everybody who stuck their hand out for one. Soon as we got in, Willett starting telling me stories on all the Dolly Parton songs playing over the loudspeakers. At the museum we saw the rag coat Dolly had when she was little, her coat of many colors, and we saw her report cards, and all that kind of went over Nicolette's head, but she loved the birds, the big bald eagle sanctuary. While we were standing there looking at the eagles, Decent come up eating a turkey leg and told us how her sister got proposed to right on the spot we were standing. And then June told us about a girl she knew in school who got proposed to on the Ferris wheel in the carnival part of Dollywood.

Hubert got one of Dollywood's motorized wheelchairs and went around on that with two of them Drop Creek schoolkids riding on his wheelchair armrests. Albert got him a wheelchair too, told them he needed one cause he was in rehab trying to get off drugs. When he went to get on Blazing Fury, that ride where you're rollercoastering through the town on fire, I took his wheelchair back to the wheelchair checkout place and told them he was healed and wouldn't need a wheelchair no more. So then I had to stay away from him cause he would have made a ruckus cause him and Evie and Hubert were all putting liquor down in their frozen lemonade and they were getting good and drunk and I found out how good and drunk when I told Hubert I'd ride Blazing Fury with him and he started crying saying it reminded him of when he worked in the mines, all that darkness and fire, and when the ride was over he kept on crying and wouldn't get off and told the dude that told him to get off because there was a ginormous line of people wanting to ride, Hubert wouldn't do it. He told them he was a disabled coal miner and that every gray hair in his beard was a friend he'd lost or a rockfall he'd been in. He told them all that even though he hadn't worked in the mines since I'd been born.

When Hubert finally got tired of riding Blazing Fury, I pushed him out in his wheelchair. I wanted to ask him again about the money, cause now I could tell him I knew about the blood money, and he might tell me something.

I said, "Hey Hubert," and he said, "What?"

Right then Evie and Decent walked up. Evie said, "That's enough."

Evie and Decent had been talking, and Decent, who didn't realize how drunk Evie was, said to Evie maybe she ought to take Hubert on home.

Evie said, "Come on, Hubert. Dolly says you need to go home."

Hubert said, "She never did."

Evie should have never mentioned Dolly, cause Hubert got stirred up about it, wanted to see her, wouldn't turn loose of his wheelchair, but they eventually got him out of there, and Evie and Hubert left, with Evie driving Hubert's truck.

~~~~~~~~~~

NEXT WE went to Splash Country, which is the water park at Dollywood. They had a little kid area with a wave pool and Echo and the Bunnymen and Simple Minds and all these people June liked were playing over the loudspeakers, so I left Willett and Nicolette there, shivering wet with a corndog in each hand, and I went and got in the line for the water ride where you rode on a mat down through a tube like in a science fiction movie.

The line was awful, standing there in your bathing suit dripping with a ton of other people all wet holding those slimy mats. I was there by myself with nobody to talk to, and I heard these girls a couple turns ahead of me in the line, and I don't know what they were talking about exactly, but I could tell they were talking about drugs and they were going to the outlet mall, and you could see they weren't up to no good, and they were mean to each other and especially mean to this one girl and that girl kept saying fuck you, fuck you, her voice thick and slurry and loud, all messed up, and I realized it was Belinda Coates, there at Dollywood with a bunch of girls I hadn't ever seen before.

Good thighs. Strong calves. She had forearms like she chopped wood. But she was standing there in a bikini, looked like she hadn't eat in a month. I stood behind a bunch of young tall guys all pimples and lies and wished I could hear what Belinda and them were talking about. They had gone from picking on each other to scheming on something. The line moved and all the girls Belinda was there with screamed like crazy when they went down through the tube.

The thought of taking revenge on Belinda Coates made me sick to my stomach. I usually wasn't much into what other people thought was fun, but going to Dollywood that day listening to all them people at Hubert's store getting their gas and their cigarettes, everybody keyed up just to get out for a day and ride rides and laugh and eat what they wanted, it was so good. Especially all of us being together for it. I didn't want to do nothing mean. I didn't want to hate Belinda Coates.

Which was crazy, because I had hated Belinda Coates for such a long time. She accused me one time of trying to steal her boyfriend when I was in sixth grade, which was stupid because her boyfriend told me I was ugly for a boy, much less for a girl, but Belinda wouldn't get over it, and carried my bicycle down to the river bridge down the road from the Pine Knot School where I went to grade school and she threw my bicycle in the river and when I went down to get it, I laid my foot open on a piece of metal roof down in the river and had to get a tetanus shot, plus I got pneumonia right after that cause it was February, the dead of winter, and I'd fell in the river barefoot and icy. Plus on top of that, I'd also got some kind of eye infection off the nastiness in the river and missed a whole lot of school and almost failed sixth grade and was always kind of behind after that, I swear, all the way through high school. I never really thought about that till now, but yeah, that's where my troubles began in a way—when shithead Belinda Coates threw my bicycle in the river over stupid jealousy cause she was too much of a retard to realize that her boyfriend really did think I was ugly.

Then all through high school, me and Evie hated her, and we fought her and a bunch of other girls one time, and jacked her up good, and got kicked out of school for three days. And then the kicker to my hating Belinda Coates was her stealing Evie from me as a friend, and then maybe killing my mother to boot. So all that was going through my mind as I went swirling down that tube, and because it was, I didn't get in no big hurry to get out of the landing pool. I just kind of bobbed there, my chin barely out of the water. People came and went, a whole bunch of them, spitting out of the tube, splashing around for a second, leaving. But I just stayed there relaxing.

Then some asshole kid said, "That's lady's pissing in the pool," which I wasn't, but the twerpy churchy Dollywood girl said, "Ma'am, you need to clear the pool."

I did, went to the ladies room, and was sitting there in the stall, weird to be peeing in my bathing suit, and Belinda Coates come in there, said, "Dawn?"

I said, "Yeah?"

She said, "What are you doing?"

I said, "Peeing."

She said, "Somebody done that to your mother."

I said, "You."

She didn't say nothing. I pulled up my bathing suit, but didn't leave the stall. Belinda Coates said, "It wadn't me."

I said, "Who was it, then?"

She said, "I don't know. I wadn't there."

I said, "Who was?"

She said she didn't know and I said,

And some mother come in with her little boy, told him not to touch anything and he took forever peeing and I thought maybe Belinda Coates had left, but when that little boy and his mother finally left, Belinda Coates said, "Sidney said for me to stay away from your mother."

I said, "Then what was you doing down there where they found her? Why was you the one to call me and tell me she was dead?"

Belinda said, "Evie called me. Evie was there."

I said, "So what happened?"

Belinda said, "They fucked up partying. It was an accident. That's what Evie said."

I know that could be right.

I said, "Who are them girls you're with?"

Belinda said, "Girls I knew from when I lived in Corbin."

I said, "When did you live in Corbin?"

She said, "Don't you remember when I went to Corbin in sixth grade? When my dad broke my arm for making out with Shawna Parke in the basement?"

I said, "Sixth grade?"

She said, "Yeah. I went not long after Christmas and when I come back that summer was when I started living with Sidney."

"Sixth grade?" I said.

And Belinda said, "What can I say? It's how I do, Dawn."

I said, "Is one of them girls Courtney?" I was remembering Hazel asking after Belinda's girlfriend when we were at Belinda's apartment in Causey.

Belinda said, "No. Courtney won't have nothing to do with me."

Then there was a ruckus, a trash can got knocked over and then loud girl laughing, giggling, cussing, and one girl saying, "Goddamn, Belinda. Did you fall in?"

I peeked through the crack in the door in time to see one of the girls crush up a pill on the stainless steel tray above the sink, not even caring there was somebody they didn't know who it was in the stall. One of them said, "Get you some, B," and Belinda Coates did and they jabbered a minute more and then they were all gone.

~~~~~~~~~~

WHEN I got back to where Nicolette and Willett were, I was shaken up and never did quite get the easy Dollywood feeling back, even though the people were still running around, still eating, little kids still wanting one more time on this ride or that. And I couldn't help but smile through my sadness when Denny come up and said, "Yall get over there," and about thirty Canard people, my baby and my papaw two of them, gathered around me and they got some preacher from Virginia to take a picture of us with every single person's camera or phone in front of that big butterfly made of flowers, and when we were going home I fell asleep listening to Willett teach Nicolette the words to "Jolene" and in between awake and asleep I went up to Dolly Parton standing in a grocery store where she was giving away weenies stuck on toothpicks of many colors and hugged her and she hugged me back and in my little almost dream I turned around and everyone I had ever seen in Canard County was behind me, and I stepped out of the way and stood there next to Dolly and everybody hugged her, not like she was a celebrity, but like she was a relative, like she was in the receiving line at a funeral, and knew how to do, and about halfway through Dolly Parton took my hand and held it while all those people hugged her and thanked her for doing Dollywood and asked about her family and told her to come see them next time they were on Drop Creek or in Causey or out Tallow Creek or Bowtie or Pine Knot or wherever it was they come from. And Dolly Parton squeezed my hand and I could tell she knew about everything and hadn't forgotten anything and I could tell that it was hard to be Dolly Parton, but that Dolly Parton had decided to be Dolly Parton anyway. And that helped me.

GENE

I didn't stay there at Dollywood long.

It's too big a crowd and too much pavement and too many hollering kids and church people and men in short pants. The food is too high and mostly I just don't like being inside a fence. Brother worked it out to ride back with Denny Stack and them, so I drove the Sentra back to Canard, got my weedeater at Sister's, and went out towards Bowtie where Brother had a lawyer paying us to weedeat along where he kept his horses and everything out through there at his luxury home. His house was like a castle, had a gate around it, that man so rich he had his own cell phone tower. They said he was trying to be like them horse people down in Lexington, and maybe he was. Cause far as I was concerned, he might as well been one of them horse people, hard as he was to find when it was time to get paid.

But I was out working part of his property out on the state road, two-lane blacktop, a straightaway hundred and fifty yards long. Hubert's big green truck come in the other end, jerked to the left. The back end of that truck heaved to the left, and Evie, who was driving for some reason, jerked the steering wheel back to the right. The truck come fishtailing towards me. I stood there staring at it. I thought, "Well, she's gonna get that thing straightened out before she runs over me." But the truck kept jerking back and forth across the road, even as the front end began to point back towards the far end of the straightaway. The truck rocked up on its side on two wheels and the front tire clipped the edge of the road. The truck flipped in midair and landed with a crash, bottom side up in the ditch that ran beside the road.

I walked up to the truck, crouched down and looked in, eyeballed the gas tank and the front end of the truck wondering if the truck was about to explode.

I said, "Hello," and there was no answer. I said, "Hello," again. Said it louder.

Coolant ran out of the radiator into the ditch. Hubert's back pressed against the cracked back window of the cab. He moved and junk clattered in the cab.

A woman in a bathrobe stood at the other end of the straightaway. She said, "I called the police."

The truck sizzled and the passenger door creaked open. Hubert crawled out, blood on his temple, his clothes twisted. I reached my hand out to him, but he didn't take it. His brow was bent and he looked aggravated and confused.

I said, "You're a lucky man," and Hubert rolled his eyes.

I looked in at the driver's side. There was blood on Evie's jeans, soaked into her pink hoodie. Her arm was twisted and her face crushed. Her sweatshirt rode up on her and bared her ribs and stomach. She had some kind of wire on her. At first I thought it was from her mp3 player, but I saw something turning, a little wheel. It was a tape recorder, still recording. I laid my fingers on her neck. Evie was dead.

The woman in the bathrobe was talking to Hubert, drawing the hair back from the cut on his temple. The tape stopped, and when it did, the duct tape holding the recorder to Evie gave way and the recorder fell, bounced off the roof of the truck and fell into the ditch. I snatched it out of the standing water, gathered it and its wires, and put it in my pant pocket.

THE WAIL of the ambulance bounced off the hillsides on both sides of the straightaway. Hubert smoked with shaking hands. The thin hair on his temples was swept up and he looked like Little Caesar on the pizza box.

HE SAID, GIVE IT TO ME, BOY.

The state policeman's shiny leather shoes clicked across the blacktop towards us. The state police motioned for Hubert to step aside with him. I heard Hubert say that he was talking with Evie and she got distracted and the curve come up on her too quick.

Two cars came down the straightaway. Both asked if anyone was hurt and asked who she was and then they said they sure were sorry. Evie's body was out of the truck, but the state police were still poking around, taking pictures and measuring.

"Sir," one of the state policeman said, "what did you see?"

I put my hands in my pockets, wondered if the police would notice the spots of blood at the pocket's rim. I told the man what I saw, he took my name and address, and went back to talking on his radio.

I asked could I go, and the man said I could.

When I got back to the house, I sat down in my chair and thought what to do with that cassette. It kind of felt hot in my hand. I called That Woman. I knew she was still at Dollywood, but I had her cell phone number and when she answered she couldn't hear that good for the Dolly Parton music playing and the rollercoasters and such and I'm pretty sure I got it across to her I needed help deciphering something and could I come over in the morning. And I'm pretty sure she said that would be fine but not to come too early where they was getting in from Dollywood so late.

DAWN

I liked Weedeater's house. It was little, but it was a real house, with a real porch and roof and windows. Not a trailer. I also liked it was a one-person house. I'd seen it from the road when we put him out there the day we picked him up from that wreck, the day we met him.

I went to Weedeater's the night Evie died, when we got back from Dollywood. I knew Hubert was over there, knew something was jacked up. Knew I needed to be there.

When Willett was letting me out, he said, "You sure you don't want me to go with you?"

I said, "I'm sure."

He said, "It could get weird."

I said, "It already is weird."

He said, "Are you going to walk home?"

I said, "If I aint, I'll call you."

Nicolette said, "Bye, Mommy."

I said, "Bye, baby."

I got out of the car, told Willett I loved him through the window. Walking up the hill, I felt like Batman or a movie detective. I felt like a dark avenger. I was glad to be a female dark avenger.

THERE NEED TO BE MORE FEMALE DARK AVENGERS

Hubert and Weedeater were sitting on the porch when I got there—Hubert on the steps with his back to the rail, Weedeater on a swing. A cassette tape clicked in Hubert's hand as he spun it.

I said, "What are yall doing?" and sat down on the low wall.

Hubert smoked.

Weedeater said, "You want a pop?"

I said yeah. Weedeater went inside.

I said, "What the hell, Hubert?"

Hubert shook his head, said, "She was trying to be smart."

I said, "Decent should never have let her drive."

Hubert nodded, said, "I'm out, Dawn."

I said, "Out of what?"

Hubert said, "I'm going over to that store and sit there and sell toilet paper and cigarettes and baloney and nothing else."

I knew what Hubert was saying. He wasn't going to sell drugs no more.

I said, "OK."

Hubert said, "That's what she wanted."

I said, "Who?" Weedeater come out with a can of Pepsi. I popped the top, said, "That's what who wanted?"

Hubert said, "Evie."

I said, "What happened, yall?"

Hubert said, "She wrecked is all. She was hollering at me to stop selling pills and she wrecked."

I said, "And that's all there is to it?"

Hubert said, "What else would there be to it, Dawn?"

Something, I thought.

Weedeater said, "Dawn, you want anything else? You want me to open a can of soup? Make you a grill cheese?"

I said I was all right.

Hubert stood up, said, "I'll be glad when this damn month is over," threw his cigarette in the grass, and walked off.

Me and Weedeater sat there, first time we'd ever been alone together.

Weedeater said, "Four people dead in a month."

I said, "Who's the fourth?"

Weedeater said, "That man in the Buick."

I nodded, said, "What the fuck, Gene?"

Weedeater said, "My sister killed herself Easter."

I said, "Yeah."

Weedeater said, "It's a lot."

I said, "If Evie was here, you know what she'd say?"

Weedeater said, "What?"

I said, "She'd say, 'How long you gonna feel sorry yourselves?' She'd say, 'That was yesterday. That was forever ago.'"

Weedeater said, "Little badass."

I said, "She was."

Weedeater said, "She was recording people. Talking about drugs."

I said, "Do what?"

Weedeater said, "She had a tape recorder going in her pocket when she wrecked."

I said, "Does the law know?"

Weedeater said, "I don't reckon. I got the recorder off her before the troopers showed."

I said, "I'll be damned."

Weedeater drank his pop.

I said, "That's the cassette Hubert had."

Weedeater said, "Yep."

Weedeater said, "I reckon."

I drank my pop.

Weedeater said, "I think I'm gonna need more time with all this. I aint over it."

I nodded. I went in Weedeater's little house and got us both another pop.

GENE

I'm glad I told Dawn what Evie done. She cried a little, but I'm still glad I done it. She sat there a long time letting the tears run down her face, not saying a thing. She made a noise in her throat every once in a while, sniffed and wiped her nose. Finally she settled down, and I asked if she wanted another pop. She shook her head, looked around like she aint never seen the world before, and said, "I got to go."

I said, "All right. Thank you for coming by."

She walked down the steps, started across the yard, stopped, and said, "Thanks for telling me."

I told her just like I told you—

I'M GLAD I DID.

DAWN

I went back to Momma's house. June and Nicolette sat in the back room watching *Hee Haw* reruns. I said, "Where's Willett?"

June said, "He went back. His daddy is having a bad night."

I said, "Are yall all right?"

Nicolette nodded. June got up, come and hugged me. She said, "What do you need?"

I said, "Nothing."

She said, "You sure?"

I said, "I'm going to bed."

June said, "All right, Sweetie."

I said, "I don't think I can go to Evie's funeral."

June said, "I think that's OK."

I went upstairs. Momma's door was closed. June's was open. Her pretty quilt, her pretty IKEA lights, the pretty blue paint she'd put on the walls soothed me. I went and lay down on the air mattress in the room at the end of the hall and stared at the walls June had painted pumpkin orange. I tried to think what the point of myself was. I fell asleep before I figured it out.

~~~~~~~~~

FIVE DAYS after Evie died, the doorbell at Momma's rang and it was Decent Ferguson. Decent Ferguson told me I had to come to her floathouse. Told June she had to come too. She tried to get us to go with her after Mamaw died, and she tried again after Momma died, but when Evie died, she came and got us. June's sign was finished and her class was over and we were just waiting for the president of the United States to get there, so Decent Ferguson said there was no reason for us not to come with her to the floathouse.

Decent got us each under the arm, and said we didn't have no choice. Decent tried to put us in her car, but we convinced Decent we'd go if she'd let us take our own vehicle. When Decent left, I said, "June, I got to get us a bathing suit."

June said, "You want to go to Megamart?"

I said, "No. I'll go see if Hazel has one."

~~~~~~~~~

EVIE'S MOTHER Hazel sat in a lawn chair under an umbrella at the roadside sale between the cutoff to Ridge Road and the place where Rooster the tree trimmer lived. She was sitting with a woman with a crewcut. Hazel's friend had on a yellow tank top and was selling baby clothes, statues of black Jesus doing different Jesus things, and framed pictures of unicorns flying over enchanted cities. Hazel had a white bandana with black paisleys wrapped tight against her skull, hiding her snow-head of hair. She had on short pants that came to her knees, pants full of buckles and straps and extra pockets. She had on a tie-dye T-shirt had the sleeves cut out, and seen me before I seen her out of her little round mirror sunglasses.

She said, "Misty Dawn Jewell," said, "come here and give me a hug, girl."

I was sorry then I hadn't gone to Evie's funeral.

Hazel said, "How are you, darling? I have had you on my mind."

I told Hazel I was OK. She raised her sunglasses and looked at me with peppermint candy eyes and talked about how sad she was and how she wasn't sleeping.

Hazel said, "She loved you, Dawn Jewell. You should have heard the way she talked about you."

I said, "What did she say?"

Hazel said, "She thought you hung the moon."

I said, "Well."

Hazel said, "What about Calvin and Belinda?"

I said, "What about them?"

She said, "Are yall going to do anything?"

I said, "About what?"

She said, "Most folks figure one of them killed Tricia. Folks are wondering what yall are going to do."

I said, "Nothing, I reckon."

Hazel took her cigarettes out of her pant pockets, said, "My heart is jacked up. I'm supposed to walk the track at the park. I don't. I'm supposed to give up my caffeine. I don't. I'm supposed to give up my cigarettes. I don't."

I said, "You think we should do something to Calvin and Belinda?"

Hazel said, "That aint for me to say, honey." Hazel's hand shook and sweat beaded on her lip and forehead. "I just want you to know I'm here for you."

I said, "Yall got a bathing suit fit Nicolette?"

Hazel said she might. She didn't, but a woman two trucks down did. I got Nicolette a purple bathing suit with pink polka dots. It matched her water wings.

I said, "Hazel, you ought to go with us to Decent Ferguson's floathouse on the lake in Tennessee."

Hazel said, "Sweetheart, the last thing I need right now is to be out on a lake."

I said, "You sure?"

Hazel hugged me tight, said, "You stay close, you hear?"

I said,

Hazel pulled back, held me by the shoulders, said, "When you coming to see me?"

I said, "Before the end of the month."

Hazel smiled and said, "You bring the beer. I'll have the weed."

10

FLOATHOUSE

DAWN

Decent Ferguson's floathouse didn't really float. It was anchored in a lake down in Tennessee. The floathouse had been a little party house for TVA bosses. At least that's what Decent Ferguson told us. She bought it from a friend of her father's.

Decent Ferguson was broad-hipped and lived in Tennessee. She was a school principal at a special school for bad kids. She had lived in Canard for most of her life. She'd gone back to school to get her principal papers when her kids got old enough. She used to live out on the Trail. People used to go to her house to party, but not bad party. Fun party. She'd have parties where people play music, tell funny stories, bring all their junk mail and cardboard boxes and set fire to a stump she was trying to burn out in the backyard. People would sit around the fire in camping chairs and Decent Ferguson's big black dog named Angus would chase all over the yard. Angus would chase a stick straight into the fire if you threw it in there, but that didn't happen more than twice a year.

Decent Ferguson's house in Canard had been her granny's, and she always had way more stuff than she could ever eat stacked up in the kitchen. Cases and cases of pop and cases and cases of ramen noodles. Bags and bags of Grippos. Her refrigerator she'd had in Canard was covered with refrigerator magnets of places she'd been and magnets made out of pop bottle tops. Decent Ferguson had an aboveground swimming pool and sometimes people would jump in it in their underpants. People wouldn't get naked at Decent Ferguson's house.

Decent Ferguson left Canard one day, said she wanted to see how the rest
of the world did things, so she moved to Tennessee, left her son in her granny's
house, didn't hardly bring anything with her but some clothes and a couple of
pots and knives. There wasn't a place for what she called her art collection—wild
animals and famous women in history made out of painted gourds, all kinds of
paintings with stuff stuck on them with a hot glue gun. She didn't take her music
collection. All she took was a portable CD player she set in her kitchen window.

THE ROAD to Tennessee was green woods and red clay, block-set houses
tucked against slopes, lowhill cows lined out against blue skies, church signs
and old gas stations still in business, still selling beer and worms and Styrofoam
coolers. To get to the lake, to Decent's floathouse, you didn't go the Kingsport
way. You went the Knoxville way. Doing that, you went right by where we seen
that man die. Where we'd first run up on Weedeater.

It was me and June, Nicolette and Pharoah, in June's little red Honda
car. Nicolette made Pharoah nervous, so Pharoah set far away as she could,
dragging her nose across the car window till June cracked it open. June talked
about me going to school, and whether I was sure nursing was for me. She
worried I wasn't going to be fulfilled.

I think she thought I couldn't do it. The classes would be hard, but the way
I figured it, if Willett was going to get fired from every job he ever got, I didn't
see how being fulfilled was really an option for me. Not if I wanted to be the
one do for Nicolette. Not if I wanted to keep her from being raised by Willett's
mother. I should have asked June about the tattoo business. But I didn't. I was
too chicken. It used to feel good for June to advise me. But by that day going to
Decent's floathouse, it seemed we were going in opposite directions, seemed

I had to strain to hear what she was talking about. And when I did hear it, it seemed to make a lot less sense.

There weren't any flowers on the road sign where that man's Buick hung up, on the spot where he died, but none of us needed reminding where it was. June slowed down and Nicolette made a crashing sound and I could see in my mind the people piled up at the scene, could see how white that man's hand had been against the blue velour of the Buick seat, how yellow-white his eyes were rolled back in his head, how red-black the cave of his mouth was. Part of me wanted to come out there and ziptie plastic flowers to that sign.

June said, "Evie was wearing a recorder when she died. She was recording what she and Hubert were talking about."

I asked June how she knew. She said Weedeater told her.

June said, "Why you reckon she did that?"

I said, "Cause she was a snitch, I guess."

We went through the tunnel into Tennessee. It was hotter in Tennessee. Brighter. We went down the four-lane through Harrogate, the Abraham Lincoln college on one side of the road, Hardee's and Dollar General and the IGA on the other. June pulled into a beer store. She went in. Me and Nicolette sat out in the car. Nicolette snored in the backseat, baking in the sun. Pharoah leaned against the opposite door, whined. June came out with plastic bags full of beer and Funyuns. She already had two big bags full of wine and fancy crackers and cheeses, weird grainy salads with lemon juice and parsley. June packed like she was wanting to have fun, but there wasn't much fun in her eyes.

June said, "When are you going back to Kingsport?"

I said, "I aint in no hurry."

We turned on a long, straight road, ridges on either side of us, barns had GET RIGHT WITH GOD on their roof. I said, "You should have got whoever done that barn to help you with your sign."

June explained who the man was had done the barn sign. He did those stone markers you see beside the road say "PREPARE TO MEET GOD" and "JESUS IS COMING SOON." June said the man lived on the road we were riding. It's hard to get ahead of June in knowing stuff like that.

We got on the interstate for a while and then get back off the interstate and wound around the lake before we got to the boat dock, where we took a boat out to the floathouse where Decent Ferguson stayed. The boat was a johnboat, didn't have much motor, so it was slow going. We motored past a bunch of party boats like you see on *Miami Vice*, boats with dumb names like *Aqua-holic* and *Ship Happens*, and the names of the people who own them and the places they come from painted on the side. There were a few people out, a woman with long legs all wrinkled and brown piling up pool toys and a big-belly man with silver hair and a beer in a hugger at 10:30 in the morning.

Decent jumped out when we got to the house and tied the boat to the deck. We had to crawl around the boat and pass her the rope and hold each other's hand as we got out. Nicolette wore a orange life jacket that about swallowed her up. She liked the life jacket, said it made her feel like she had big muscles.

Decent's house was one room, with a kitchen where you came in, a bed in the center, and a bench with cushions around the wall. After we got settled in, Decent set out the crackers and cheeses June brought, and sausages and olives in little bowls, on a table on the deck. Decent and June drank their wine and Nicolette and I drank pop. Nicolette liked all the stuff they had to eat. I ate cheese on crackers with pickles a woman worked at Decent's school had put up and give to her. The lake was ringed round by hillsides. The lake was there cause the river had been dammed by the TVA. It was weird knowing you were floating over what used to be people's houses and farms. Where it was Sunday morning, there weren't many people out, just a jet ski or two. A pontoon boat went by every now and then. Nicolette chased Pharoah around the deck until I told her three times to stop, and when she did, Pharoah pooped right there on the deck.

June said, "I'm so sorry," and jumped up.

Decent said, "Honey, that aint no problem. It'll give me a chance to show you how the toilet works."

She took us to the back of the house and showed us the closet of a bathroom. The commode was almost dry. You had to poop and then flip an old-timey metal switch and then there was a garbage disposal grinding sound grinding up your poop as it went down and I wondered did your poop just go out in the lake and Decent said no, said it went in a tank and said you called this woman and told her it was full and these guys came in a boat and pumped out your tank into a tank on their boat and hauled it off.

Decent threw the dog poop wrapped up in toilet paper into the commode and turned on the grinder. We went back on the deck. I got in the water with Pharoah and Nicolette and her life jacket. Pharoah paddled around a while and then she decided she'd had enough. She needed help getting out because the deck was four or five feet above water level. Pharoah got scared when we tried to help her out, and tried to bite all of us, but we eventually got her out.

Me and Nicolette stayed in the water, hanging onto a purple pool noodle. She chattered on about wishing she could bring all the dogs in the world to the lake and let them swim, all at once. She kept chattering until she ran out of talk, until it was just her teeth chattering. Nicolette wanted to climb the ladder by herself, but she wasn't strong enough yet, so June and Decent hoisted her out, swallowed her up in towels, and June held Nicolette while she and Decent rambled on and it was just me floating in the water.

My legs hung off the purple noodle down into the cold cold water. I let myself be alone. My elbows draped across the noodle and my chin rested on it and I felt safe and let go of how scared I was of how lonesome I was going to be without Mamaw and Momma and Evie. I got mad at myself, saw myself for how foolish I was for thinking I was tough, for thinking I was independent. I'm an idiot.

But I didn't want to break in new people to help me, didn't want to have to get used to a new bunch of whoever to talk to to figure things out. I felt like a noodle myself, like a bowl of school lunch spaghetti, too full of water, nothing to keep me from sliding off the fork except getting into a twist.

I closed my eyes and the water lapped me, and my mind went off on its own. I turned into a dark hollow room. I heard Willett's voice. He was real

happy. He was looking for me and he wanted me to come do something I
didn't want to do, something he thought was fun. I thought I'd lost something.
I wanted him to help me look for it. He said it was at the place he wanted me
to go. I couldn't get mad at him. I wanted to, but I couldn't make myself do it. I
didn't like not being able to get mad at Willett.

"Dawn," June called to me from the deck and woke me up.

I said, "What?"

She said, "I'm going with Decent to the store. Her neighbors are coming
over tonight."

I said, "To do what?"

June said, "To have dinner. Sit around and talk."

I said, "Lord."

June said, "You want to go to the store with us?"

I said, "No."

June said, "You want us to take Nicolette with us?"

I said, "Where is she?"

June said, "She's in there on the bed asleep."

I said, "Leave her there."

June said, "You sure you're going to be OK here?"

I said, "I reckon."

June said, "We're going to take the boat. You won't have any way off the
lake. Are you sure you want to stay?"

I said, "Yeah. You're not going to be gone that long, are you?"

June said, "It'll be a little while."

I said, "Well. Go on if you're going."

June looked at me a minute, then her and Decent puttered off.

I went in the house and checked on Nicolette. I took a drink out of a bottle
of bourbon sitting on the counter and went back outside. I sat with my back
against the house. I watched bats weave around between the lake and the
shore, listened to bugs buzz. I lay on my belly, still wet from swimming. I rested
my cheek on my hands. I stared off over the water, drowsing. Before long I
heard something paddling. I opened my eyes and there was that damn Calvin,
sitting a little lower than eye level in a kayak.

I sat up and said, "What the hell are you doing here?"

He said, "Dawn, I need to talk to you."

I said, "No, you don't."

He said, "Dawn, it's my fault your mother is dead."

I said, "Get out of here, Calvin."

He said, "Dawn."

I said, "How did you know I was here?"

He said, "Dawn, it was me shot up your mother. It was me killed her."

I said, "Why? Why would you do that?"

Calvin said, "It was an accident. Please believe me." Then he said, "Can I come up there and explain what happened?"

I said, "No. You can't come up here. You stay down there in your stupid boat. Just go away."

That's what I said, but by that time I was thinking that if what he said was true, then I needed to keep him there. I needed to get him where we could get him arrested, get him on his way to prison. So I said, "You want to come up here?"

He said, "Yeah."

I went over to the door, pulled it shut, said, "Come on up."

Calvin started talking before he got his boat to the ladder, said, "Your mother, buddy, me and her got along great. I aint never seen a woman so sweet. She didn't care. She laid herself out there. Emotionally. You know what I mean?"

I took a deep breath. I couldn't believe my mother went with this man. Calvin grabbed hold of the ladder, said, "We were partying, Dawn. Me and her and your brother and that little redneck girl he goes with."

I said, "Evie."

Calvin said, "Evie. Yeah," said, "I heard she didn't make it." Calvin said, "Anyway, so your mother said she wanted the needle but was scared to do it herself, said she wanted me to do it for her and I told her I would and I did, and I'm sorry that's how it ended, Dawn. I wouldn't have done it for the world. I loved your mother, Dawn."

I stepped over and blocked him getting off the ladder. I said,

Calvin tried to step off the ladder. I shoved him, said, "Where did it happen?"

He said, "Dawn, let me off this ladder and I'll tell you."

I said, "You tell me now."

He said, "Dawn, it was an accident."

I said, "Where did you do it, Calvin?"

He said, "Dawn, it don't matter."

I shook the ladder and Calvin goes, "Dawn, honey, don't do that. I can't swim."

I said, "Where'd you do it, Calvin? Where did you kill my mother?"

He said, "Dawn."

I shook the ladder again and he said, "Up there at that apartment. In Causey."

I said, "How did she end up on the riverbank?"

Calvin said, "Dawn, it was so crazy."

I said, "You took her down there, didn't you?"

Calvin said, "Dawn."

I said, "Say it, Calvin. Say you dumped her body like it was a bag of garbage."

Calvin said, "Dawn, it wouldn't have done no good . . ."

Before he could finish, I shook the ladder and kept shaking it and he slipped on it, got his leg caught in it. One side of the ladder come loose and he went down into the water headfirst, his leg still hung in the ladder. He sputtered and gagged, and I said, "Say it, Calvin."

He said, "Dawn, get me up."

I said, "Say you dumped her like she was a bag of garbage."

He said, "We were going to go back and get her. I swear on my mother's grave."

I said, "Calvin, your mother aint dead."

I lifted up the other side of the ladder and cut the whole thing loose to sink to the bottom of the lake, take Calvin with it. When it started sinking, Calvin started really flailing. He couldn't get loose. He was fixing to give up, fixing to go down with the ladder, when I'll be damned if Weedeater didn't come puttering up.

GENE

That Sunday, I come to clean the toilet of a bunch of them boats and little houses in that corner of the lake. When I come down through there and seen Dawn knock that worthless Calvin off the ladder down in the lake, and he started thrashing, and went down with that ladder, I stopped thinking, I guess, about how bad I hated Calvin, cause the water went even and quiet where he went down. If I'd come up five seconds later, I wouldn't even have known there was a Calvin under there. I could have gone back and pumped out the toilet tank and wouldn't have known Calvin was gone.

But as it was, I stopped thinking and jumped out of my boat and tried to get over where he was and the thing I stopped thinking is how I can't swim too good and by the time I got close to where he'd gone under, I couldn't keep the water out of my own mouth and well,

DAWN

When Gene tried to dogpaddle to Calvin, he didn't get anywhere. Then Gene went under and came up choking and spitting out water. About that time, Nicolette came out on the deck, yawning and wobbly. She perked up quick enough when Gene started hollering, "AAAAAAAAA" and "GAAAAAAAAA."

I didn't want to explain to Nicolette, or anybody else, two drowned men and why I didn't do anything to help them. I said to her, "Reckon I better get in there."

Nicolette said, "You can do it, Momma."

I threw on a life jacket and jumped in the water right next to Gene and threw my arm around his belly. He grabbed ahold of me around the neck, and it wasn't too hard to hold him. Nicolette threw the pool noodle in and Gene's brother, who also couldn't swim, pulled up close enough to reach a hand down and I got Gene on that noodle and then his brother got him out.

About that time, up bobs Calvin, totally freaked out. He'd been under a good minute, I guess, and he was thrashing and flailing way way worse than Gene had been. He grabbed at me and I thought he might take me under. He poked me in the eye, slapped me in the face, and generally was a big baby.

I hooked him the same way I had Gene, but he was less agreeable than Gene had been. I got him pinned down and Gene's brother reached me his hand and we got Calvin up out of there. Gene's brother reached his hand down for me, but I didn't want on their funkyass boat, and I swam back for the ladder, but of course the ladder was gone.

Nicolette said, "Here, Mommy. I can pull you up," which she couldn't.

Gene's brother said, "Come on, Dawn. Come over here," his brown hand stretched out and crusty like a five-finger pretzel.

I swam back, and Gene's brother pulled me on that stinky boat. I sat there catching my breath with Gene and Calvin. Calvin looked at Gene and said, "Pew-wee" and made a face about the stink, which it did stink, but I don't think Calvin had any call to point it out, so I told him so, said, "Calvin, this damn boat saved you from drowning. I don't think you need to be criticizing how it smells. We could always throw you back in the fucking lake if you think you'd like it better, you damn pillhead."

Calvin said, "I'm aiming not to be a pillhead anymore."

I said,

Gene said, "That'd be good, buddy. That'd be good if you could." Then Gene said, "Lord, buddy. Look at your leg bleed."

Calvin had laid his leg open getting out of that ladder, gashed it open in a way you knew was going to need stitches—flesh flapping over the shinbone. It was gross. Of course, Calvin looked at it and passed out right there on the boat.

Gene's brother said, "We might ought to get him to somebody could sew that leg up."

I remembered how Gene's brother didn't want Gene to get looked at after he dropped that concrete on Gene's head. I said, "What are you going to do, take him to the vet?"

Gene's brother said, "You want to get your little girl before you go?"

I said, "I aint going nowhere. I aint got a vehicle, and besides that, I don't care what happens to him."

Gene's brother said, "Well, you got pretty bad cut yourself," and pointed to my forehead, which I touched and my fingers come back all bloody from where Calvin had clawed me up.

I said, "I'm staying here. You can take him if you like. It aint no business of mine."

Gene said, "Are you sure?"

I said, "Why doesn't anybody think I know what I want? Why does everybody ask me, 'Are you sure?'"

Gene said, "I only asked you the once."

I said, "Put me back at that house."

Gene's brother put his honeyboat in reverse and eased it right up next to the house. I got out and stood there as they left, kept standing there until they were gone out of sight.

GENE

It took eighteen stitches to close up Calvin's shin. While we waited on Brother to bring the vehicle around so we could take Calvin where he wanted to go, Calvin sat in a chair in the emergency room, a long strip of gauze trailing off behind him towards the treatment room. His lips moved like he was scheming or gone in the head.

Calvin said, "You know, I give three hundred dollars for that little kayak."

I said, "Did you?"

Calvin said, "I bet I don't never see it again."

He went on like that, making a list of all the grievances he had against Dawn—that she'd tried to drown him. That it was her fault he'd had to get stitches. He wanted me to consider it was her fault her mother was dead.

Calvin said, "She used to agitate Tricia. Drove her to drugs. I ought to take Dawn Jewell to court."

I said, "Hunh."

He said, "I should. She thinks she's such hot stuff. I'm gonna do that."

I said, "What do you think you're going to get off her?"

Calvin said, "Everything she's got."

I felt like Calvin was kind of on his high horse. Felt like maybe I should try and get him off it. I had hate in my heart for Calvin. I wanted rid of it. Calvin glared off at the checkerboard tile on the emergency room floor like he was playing life-and-death checkers. I leaned over, my head below my knees, so I could see his eyes.

I said, "I love you, Calvin."

At the time, I didn't know if it did no good or not.

DAWN

When Calvin and them left, Nicolette said, "What was that, Mommy?"

I said, "That was why you're getting swimming lessons soon as we get home."

Nicolette said, "Where's Aunt June?"

I said, "She went to the store."

Nicolette said, "When she's coming back?"

I told her I didn't know, told her to come in the floathouse with me. When she did, Nicolette said she wanted a sandwich. When there was no bread, I asked did she want a piece of baloney plain, and she said she did. She ate it slow, lying back on the bed.

I said, "Nicolette, sit up before you choke."

She sat up and I sat on a stool in the kitchen and thought how I was there when Mamaw stopped breathing, how I was there for her last breath, but wasn't there for Momma. Wasn't there for Evie. I thought how much me there isn't. How much me isn't there when it should be. I thought about there being more of me, multiple copies of me, so I could be more places, and

Nicolette got up and got her another piece of baloney. She lay on the bed like I told her not to. As I was fixing to fuss at her for it, she rolled up her piece of baloney into a breathing tube and stuck it in her mouth. She breathed through it and the baloney made a whistling sound as she slowly worked it down in her mouth, eating it bit by bit without using her hands.

I said, "That aint gonna stop you choking if it gets caught in your windpipe." She sat up, said, "Can we call Daddy?"

I looked at my phone, said we didn't have service, even though we did.

Decent's boat pulled up and June and Decent made their way across the floathouse deck with bright-printed cloth bags full of groceries. They come in yakking about couches, leafy green celery stalks and carrot tops sticking up out of their bags printed with flowers and the names of conferences they'd been to. There were bottles of oil and vinegar with labels in French and Italian. There were two whole chickens, short and fat, plucked and naked like storybook kings, like headless magistrates.

Decent unwrapped one chicken, held it up by the legs, said, "Put your pants on and get me a load of gravel, you damn naked magistrate." Then she laughed, and coughed, and said, "Lord. I'm out of breath. You'd of thought I paddled out here."

Decent lit a cigarette and Nicolette said, "They was a man out here in a paddleboat."

June looked at me and said to Nicolette, "Is that right? Who was it?"

I said, "Calvin come out here acting like he done something."

June said, "Acting like he done what?"

I looked at Nicolette and told June, "I'll tell you after while."

Nicolette said, "Calvin said he give Momma Trish a shot."

June looked at all three of us, one by one. Then she looked at us all three again. Then she went to setting the groceries out of the bags and on the counter. "Did he now," she said.

Decent opened a high cabinet full of board games and pulled out a green-and-yellow ball with spikes sticking out of it, some kind of puzzle. Decent pulled all the spikes out of the ball and said to Nicolette, "Put them back in there for me. You got to do it just right or it won't work."

Nicolette picked up a spike and stuck it in the ball and when she stuck the second spike in, it wouldn't go. She said, "Oh," and then she sat down on the floor and started fooling with the ball. Decent waved me and June outside. We sat at the deck table and June said, "Tell me what Calvin said."

I said, "He says he shot up Momma and killed her. Says it was an accident. Said they was partying and she asked for it and they just fucked up."

June said, "Did she die right off?"

I said, "He didn't say."

Decent said, "Chickenshit Calvin."

June said, "So Belinda didn't have a hand in it?"

I said, "Not to hear Calvin tell it."

My phone rang. It was Calvin.

He said, "Dawn, I need my kayak."

When I didn't say anything, he said, "Dawn, I'm going to go down to the police and tell them what happened."

My breathing got short. I kept my mouth shut and air pumped through my nose.

Calvin said, "Are you there?"

I said, "Yes."

He said, "Do you care if I come get my kayak?"

I said, "What do you need a kayak for? If you do like you say and tell the law what you done, you won't need a kayak, cause you'll be in jail."

Calvin got quiet. Then he said, "I guess that's right."

I said, "I'm giving your boat to the next person I see and I dare you to say a thing about it."

Calvin went quiet again and then said, "Please tell June I'm sorry."

I said, "You better turn yourself in, asshole. Cause if you don't, I'm gonna come find you and when I do, you're going to wish you did turn yourself in, cause I will fuck you up my own damn self."

I hung up the phone before I heard him say anything else. I sat there breathing hard. My head pounded and spun like a honky-tonk mirror ball. Nicolette stuck her head in the window screen above the bed, which she must have been standing on despite me telling her not to do that. She said, "Mommy?"

I said, "What?"

She said, "Can we call Daddy now since the phone's working?"

Right then the neighbor women paddled up in a canoe, and Nicolette got distracted by all their bringing groovy food and the female hubbub of getting it all set out and the table set and the wine opened and the candles lit. And then Nicolette got distracted by all the big talk that kind of women talk about politics and natural products and gardening and adopting babies and women getting better jobs or not getting better jobs. And then it was Nicolette's bedtime and I put her to sleep, and I lay down with her, and I went to sleep and I guess maybe she never did sleep, cause the next thing I know, Nicolette rolled over top of me off the floathouse bed, stood with her hand on my face, knob-kneed in orange shorts and no shirt.

I said, "Where are you going?"

She said, "Out there with the women."

I said,

YOU STAY AWAY FROM THE EDGE.

She padded across the floor.

I said, "You hear me?"

She answered with the slapshut of the screen door.

I slept through the start of the cleanup, cause next I knew, dinner with the two women from the next floathouse was over. Dishes rinsed and piled but not washed sat stacked by the sink. Empty wine bottles stood on the counter like they wished they could lie down, like they wished they were in the garbage. I could hear the women talking outside. I could hear Nicolette talking on the phone.

I was lying down. I had had enough. Enough of a day. Enough of the four women talking. Enough of organic garden talk and native ornamental talk. Enough of vitamins and herbal tea talk. Enough of free range and fair trade. Enough of victims' rights and patients' advocates. Enough of making connections and rinsing colons. The dead air of the floathouse suited me. I did not care it was cooler on the deck. I did not care to watch my child. Plenty of nurture on the deck. What was one mother more or less?

I slept and turned to mud, to thickness without air. I slept while my phone rang, woke enough to see it was Willett calling, woke enough to know when my phone stopped ringing and June's started, that Willett had moved on to her, that Willett had heard the message that Nicolette left for him earlier that night.

I gave up waking for sleep, for dead hot sleep. I woke to Pharoah groaning on a rug beside the bed. She shifted in her sleep and groaned again.

I said, "I know, baby," and she quieted.

I slept again, not rolling over when Nicolette shook me, not rolling over when she kissed me on the back of my head, not rolling over when she said,

"I love you, Mommy," not rolling over because I heard the puny motor start and I knew that Decent was taking Nicolette to her father, where she would be fine. I didn't roll over though I wanted to. Then I cried. I cried fat and alone,

11

~~~~~

COALTOWN!

DAWN

The day after we got back from the floathouse was the day the president of the United States came to Canard. It was the day June's giant sign got revealed. I didn't want to go down there. Dudes in mirror shades and hearing aids had been talking into their wrists, poking in stuff, turning stuff over, looking at people like they were stupid or terrorists all week. Local politicians walked around puffed out and proud like they done something just cause the president came to get his picture taken in a place where people would vote for him cause he said he was for coal. All of them gathered at the parking lot below the new courthouse, proud of themselves for getting federal money to lock people up in their new jail big enough for the busted and snitched on from counties far and wide, not just Canard.

And June in the middle of it, all arted up in a fancy scarf trying to look hot, good with everybody cause she'd been doing all her hippie protest carrying on three hours away in West Virginia and nobody here knew what she was up to.

When I got there, the stupid president was already sitting on stage, squinting, like he didn't know we were there. Or didn't care. Or like he knew we were watching him and he thought he was worth watching.

I wasn't watching him. I don't know what his name even is. The kids in the high school band were down in front of the stage. They played a song and a fat man standing in front of me turned around and said, "Why they playing that? That's a Texas song. "Yellow Rose of Texas." They should play a Kentucky song." The woman with him, his wife I guess, said "You got ketchup on your face," and wiped it off with her thumb.

The band kept playing and the muckety-mucks piled in, men in shirtsleeves and neckties, women in bare-armed dresses and done-up hair. And down on the ground, everyone else struggled in, mouths open, fussing and pushing each other along in wads. Woman said to her child, "Johnny, you know what's good for you you'll get over here right now." Bible camps of kids rolled in, all in matching shirts. There were people with hand-markered signs—"THANK YOU FOR LOVING COAL" and 'YOU ARE THE MAN" and "CANARD HEARTS COAL AND THE PRESIDENT" and "GOD BLEASS OUR LEADERS. AND COAL"—and people with signs printed up by the coal companies and the politicians saying "COAL KEEPS THE LIGHTS ON" and some with just the names of the politicians, all the printed-up signs matching size and colors with each other. Churches had tents set up and sold hot dogs and rice krispie treats dyed red white and blue and pops for a dollar and a half each.

A girl's baby set in crying next to me. The mother was churchy, long hair straight and dull brown like old chocolate. She was shushing that baby, saying, "Shhh, Jesse, shhh. You don't want the president to hear you crying."

That baby got on my last nerve, crying like a lawnmower running on bad gas. I looked around for somewhere else to stand and seen Calvin standing up front talking to these women I knew Momma and Evie partied with, and I said, "I'll be damned," and that church girl literally covered her baby's ears. I wanted to say to her, "It's done gone in what I said. All you're doing is holding it in there like that," but I didn't have time to get into it with her. I took off through the crowd turning sideways and saying excuse me a thousand times and was close to where Calvin was when he saw me and left and I looked at them Secret Service guys, and I saw Calvin cross the highway that run alongside where the river used to be over to the all-night sitdown Kolonel Krispy.

There was a shorter way than the way he was going, so I went the shorter way and just about caught up with him without having to even act like I was in a hurry. I was afraid them Secret Service guys might be watching me, but when he looked back and seen me and ducked around the far corner of the Kolonel Krispy I couldn't help it no more and took off running.

I ran across the highway without looking. A paint-flaking pickup truck full of rusted-wire tumbleweeds, bedsprings, and bent sheets of metal screeched its brakes. It about hit me and the boy in the back of the truck lost hold of the bucket of paint in his lap. The bucket of paint sailed out of the back of the truck and hit the pavement and the lid come flying off and the swimming-pool blue paint inside jumped out of the bucket, and when it did it was like my head flooded with water and I went to my hands and knees on the road.

The woman driving the truck jumped out to check on the boy and the paint. A coal truck stopped behind the woman and a little white car with mold all over it come the other way run straight through the paint on the highway and splattered it all over itself and the road and kept on going and I could hear the man and the woman inside the moldy white car arguing with each other like they were going to live forever. The woman driving the truck come over to me said, "Are you hurt?"

I had gone from being on my hands and knees to also having put my forehead down on the road and before I got her answered, I looked up enough to see two dull black boots worn by a city police and he squatted down said, "Ma'am, do you need an ambulance?"

I looked up at him and the idea of riding in an ambulance and laying up in the hospital and eating Jello and scrambled eggs in a gown with no back to it sounded pretty good, but I said, "I don't need no ambulance." I stood up and he stood up and I said, "Am I in trouble?"

He looked at me, trying to decide if I was high. A big round of applause went up from over where the president was talking and the cop squinted like he was smelling a cat-pissy house and he shook his head, and so I turned and went over to Kolonel Krispy where Calvin was.

I should have got that cop to arrest Calvin but I didn't. And when I didn't, it felt like I planted a seed of stupid in me, like I'd done a stupid thing and it turned into a stupid seed and it stupid sprouted and stupid grew, and before I knew it, my whole life had petered out for lack of light under

Calvin set on the railroad track on the far side of Kolonel Krispy. He had on short pants and flip-flops. He had a new tattoo of a red woman with devil horns and a pointy tail riding an anchor. It was so new, there was a shaved spot on his skinny white leg with its black hairs, and the tattoo still had Saran Wrap on it. Calvin had on a tight little tangerine T-shirt had "HOTTIE" written on it in cursive. He was smoking a cigarette in green wraparound sunglasses with yellow lenses. He looked like a pawpaw, turning brown, ripe for getting stomped.

Calvin threw his cigarette into the railroad gravel and stood up. He stubbed his butt out against the sole of his flip-flop and stood there like him and me had an appointment, like some secretary had set it up for us to meet at whatever time it was on the railroad tracks behind the Canard Kolonel Krispy.

When I got up close to Calvin, I put my nose close enough to smell him good. He smelled like stale beer and raw onions, like sawdust soaking up vomit, like horse manure and Dr. Pepper. Like Tennessee.

He said, "I'm right here," said, "Do what you got to do." Like I wouldn't anyway.

I said, "I don't need your permission to do."

He said, "I know it. You just need to know I aint going to fight you."

I said, "Now you going to tell me what I need?"

He didn't say nothing to that.

I said, "You fucking dumbass."

He didn't say nothing to that either.

I said, "Why didn't you turn yourself in like you said you would? Plenty of cops here today."

When he didn't say nothing to that, I didn't know what I wanted to do. I'd promised him to beat his ass, but I stood there, looking at two of myself in Calvin's sunglasses, wishing hard I was somebody else, wishing hard Calvin was somebody else. Cause I didn't know whether I was glad Momma was dead or not.

About that time, a big train horn blew and train bells started clanging. A coal train came groaning and grunting down from Drop Creek like a gang of elephants. Me and Calvin had to step off the tracks and the train stopped. The wind gusted like it don't hardly ever do in July, and even though it was clear and hot you knew it was gonna rain that night, and it was chilly and Calvin asked did I want me some of them chili cheese fries they got at Kolonel Krispy.

Before I could say, that train started backing up, wheezing and making a metally echo-y sound. The coal cars were empty. And before I knew, the train had backed up out of sight. Me and Calvin looked to where the train would have been going and we seen a bunch of cars out on the bypass, a motorcade, the president in it I reckon, red lights spinning, cop car lights spinning, and it all silent and quick. They got gone fast, like something had gone wrong.

Everything had gone quiet in the direction of the bandstand. Where there had been all kind of racket, band playing, different full-of-themselves politicians getting the crowd all fluffed up for the president, little kids singing in their screechy voices "You are my sunshine" and some girl from Mallet singing "Oh Say Can You See" straight through her nose, everybody hand over their heart, people clapping, people whistling—then there wasn't nothing but the sound of metal foldup chairs getting stacked up.

Calvin said, "Well. I'm going to the house."

And I just let him go. I couldn't do it. I don't for the life of me know why. I went back across the highway. There were all kinds of people coming towards me, some people shaking their heads, other people acting like everything was just the same as always. I waded through them to where the president had been, looking for June.

June was on the bandstand with two local politician dudes. One was young and short in a shirt the color of an orange push-up pop, had on a baby-blue tie and a bunch of product in his hair. He stood there with his hands on his hips while a tall man with a silver hair combover and the back of his hair brushing his shirt collar and a belly big as a truck tire. His mouth flapped open and closed yelling at June, yelling at her like a mad hog, yelling at her way too much, way too rough.

All them Secret Service guys were gone by then, and so were all but a few of the crowd. Dudes in blue county work shirts folded up chairs and stacked them with a clatter. Nobody was looking up at the mountainside. Nobody was looking at June's COALTOWN! sign she worked so hard on all summer. I know I wasn't looking at it. I was looking at that silver combover, moving toward him, trying to hear what he was saying. I couldn't understand his words, and I was about to holler at him that he better tone his self the fuck down, talking to my aunt like that.

He raised his arm, pointed back behind him, back at the mountain where June's COALTOWN sign was, never stopped hollering, never missed a beat being pissed off. When June looked up, I looked up, too. June's COALTOWN! sign didn't say COALTOWN! It said, "COAL = OXY."

I stood there in the parking lot and looked up at the words and thought how big and real they looked, how much bigger and realer they looked saying something like COAL = OXY, something that said something, than they did saying something stupid and nothing like COALTOWN!

The empty coal train, the one that backed up for the president, started through town. It clang-clang-clanged across the bypass and through the gap in the floodwall, clang-clang-clang, a hundred empty coal cars. The train blew its horn long and flat and I waited, thinking something was about to change in me, thinking that if I took that moment to let everything sink in, let myself be aware of everything, things would come clear, like city tap water coming out milky and settling clear.

So I waited and waited some more, thinking love would wash over me, or my hate would turn solid, or there would be a direction lit up, obvious for me to go, and I would become either a superhero or a villain. I breathed, and I held my breath, but you know what happened?

I sat down in a folding chair and listened to that man yell at my aunt June, and I could finally understand what he was saying. He was winding down, running out of gas, even though he didn't want to, running out of gas cause he didn't take care of himself, cause he thought his man machine would run on attitude. But he wasn't no Daniel Boone. He wasn't no old school coal miner. He wasn't no real-life mountain man. He was just an out-of-shape courthouse doofus.

He said, "You think this is a joke? You think you can pull a smartass trick like this on us in front of the president of the United States? You don't have no ideal what you done. You don't have the foggiest notion."

A big white Ford pickup truck pulled up down below the stage. The man with the orange shirt and the product in his hair put his hands back in his pockets and walked down the steps at the end of the stage, not like he was big as the president of the United States, but big enough, big enough that everybody in Canard County thought they could tell him what he needed to do. He climbed in that white pickup and it sat there rumbling for a minute, windows all blacked out, rest of it white as a marshmallow. The horn blew and Combover come down off the stage, landing hard with every step, and the Hair Product Judge got out and let Combover get in the back, and they drove off.

June stood alone on the stage. She looked around at the chairs where the president and the rest of them had been. Then she looked up at her mountain at the trucks on the way to take down her sign. Then she looked at me and smiled like she'd just swallowed the sweetest thing she ever put in her mouth. And then for the first time in the longest time, I smiled at my Aunt June.

GENE

I DIDN'T WANT THAT WOMAN TO GET FIRED.

I didn't want to be the one put an end to coal mining. But I had to show That Woman I was more than grass stains and broke-off teeth. The president of the United States stood at the microphone, had coal miners lined up behind him. Orange stripes across the fronts of their shirts run together like they was one long piece of taffy, kind you get at the beach, every piece looking like the suits of a different ball team. I only had such taffy once, but it was good taffy, and I ate it all. And the whipping I took when I threw it up all over the Chrysler New Yorker of the man keeping me and Brother didn't hurt a bit, but the churn in

my belly right before I blew was the exact same churn I felt when the president
of the United States turned, looked over his shoulder, and seen what I done.

～～～～～～

I CHANGED the letters in that sign around a week before the president
come. I was walking back to Sister's house from a job Brother had got on
That Woman's street, another house with a bunch of steps. We'd been
packing coal out of the basement of this other place. They'd had a coal
furnace years ago, and even though they'd hadn't heated that way in a long
time, they still had that coal in there, and they decided to get shed of it, and
said they'd give it to whoever would pack it off. So me and Brother packed
coal out of that house, two five-gallon buckets at a time, walking up and down
fifty steps, that whole day.

I was killed, and tired of Brother. He'd been talking about women and how
he was trying to teach himself to be a taxidermist, telling me about a squirrel
he'd skinned himself and stuffed with Megamart bags, and I'd wearied of him, so
when he asked me if I wanted a ride back to Sister's, I told him I was walking.
When I set out walking, I said to myself, "Well, long as I'm walking on her
street, I might as well check on That Woman."

I come up on her without her noticing. She was sitting on the porch and
hollering into her telephone. I hadn't ever seen her that stirred up before. She
said, "All they want to talk about anymore is drugs. You can't get anybody to
come to a meeting about mining because they got to go to a funeral or they
got to drive somebody to rehab or they got to go to court for somebody or
they cant leave the house without nobody in it cause so-and-so will come rob
them blind."

That Woman was smoking a cigarette, had a ashtray full of butts in front of
her. She said, "I know it's bad. But God Almighty they are tearing this place up."

That Woman ran her fingers through her hair. She let out her breath like
she didn't need the person on the other end of the line to tell her what they
was telling her. She said, "I know. Didn't I just bury my sister over it?"

She took a drag on her cigarette, said, "You know what people should be
talking about? I tell you what. They should be talking about why. They should be
talking about why it's so easy to get all these people hooked on pills."

That Woman went quiet. I sat down on the steps leading up to the porch.
She said, "Yeah. I know they're hurting. I know they're poor. I know they aint
got nothing else to do. But what about what's going on out their window?
What's going on up above their heads? What about the fact that they're living

in the middle of bombs going off all day long? You go up on any strip job you want and tell me it doesn't look like Nagasaki."

She paused and I could hear the evening birds trilling. Then That Woman said, "I know you know. But nobody talks about that. Nobody connects the dots. Nobody . . . I don't want to calm down. You calm down. I have to be calm all day long. What? No. Kenny, that aint right."

I SHOULD'VE KNOWN IT WAS THAT DANGED OLD KENNY.

That Woman said, "It is the same thing. It is *exactly* the same thing. Coal started off something people needed. Something put people to work. Coal made factories run. People didn't know how bad it was going to be."

That Woman narrowed her eyes, kind of stamped her foot. "That's what I'm saying. Oxy started off the same. People needed painkillers cause they had pain. And Oxy kills pain."

That Woman's hand was shaking. She mopped her forehead with the back of her smoking hand, said, "The money was too good. Thing too addictive. Coal addictive. Pills addictive. You hook anybody, *anybody*, up to a lie detector, they'd tell you. Coal is bad. Oxy is bad. We'd all been better off had neither one ever come in the world."

That Woman stood still, held the phone to the side of her head, hands at her side. I thought sure she would turn and see me. "Well," she said, "that's what I think." She put her cigarette to her lips, her other hand in her front pocket, said, "You gonna try to talk me out of it? I don't reckon you should, either. Well," she said, stubbing out her cigarette, "call me tonight. Will you? All right. Talk to you tonight."

That Woman hung up her phone, fell in her rocker, her back to me. She didn't feel me there at all. I went down the green steps of the porch, started up the rock steps out her backyard, up the hill to Lovers Lane, then over back of the hill to the little house behind Sister's.

When I got there, I hated to go in. The evening was cooling off nice. Picture of That Woman's sweet fleshy arms in her cream coffee tank top come on my mind. So did her kinky curly hair pulled up off her neck, her eyes slit narrow, all stirred up talking to Kenny Bilson. I set on the swing on my bitty porch at my bitty cottage, cottage set up by my bitty stout sister. Sister's old man on them pills holding down his mine boss job wanting to charge me all that rent, dealers sucking up his boss money, so he had to wring me out, wring a pill out of me every week till I whipped his butt.

I paced that bitty porch, back and forth, felt like I was about to pop out my skin, so much dang energy, huffing and puffing like I'd run up the mountain and down. I left the porch, halfway down the driveway when I lifted my chin to the hillside rearing up across the road from Sister's mailbox, and the idea to fix that sign like I did come on me full and fine as Christmas turkey. So I went over there where them letters was at.

<center>~~~~~~~~</center>

EVEN IN the dark, I could see them letters good. They'd hung a curtain of used vinyl billboards over the fronts of them letters, the side that showed out. Out front, two stories of scaffolds, big bunch of scaffold, so's a gang could work on them, so they could get done quick. That's how it was set up. I climbed up the first set of scaffolds to think it out.

I figured if I was to change the sign to what might be better for That Woman, I'd have to change the T in "COALTOWN" to an equal sign. Then change the W to an X. Then the N to a Y. Then I'd be done. The letters was made of plywood four-by-eights. Not that hard to handle. The way the scaffolds was set up made everything easy. Them men That Woman found knew what they was doing. Brother'd got them to leave the painting of the letters to us, so we was the last ones out there, the rest of them done and gone. I had a key to the toolbox where the drills and stuff were. I could do it. By myself. All in one go. But I figured I'd do it the next night, so I climbed down off the scaffold. I was about to the ground when a voice said, "Hey" from up under a dropcloth. It was That Woman's sister, eyes sparkling like car lights off a beer bottle by the side of the road.

That Woman's sister was blue-looking peering out from under that dropcloth, which was a billboard advertising GED classes. She said, "What are you doing up here?"

I said, "I work up here."

She said, "Not now you don't." She sat up, lit a cigarette. Her eyes was the color of a storm cloud. She'd been crying.

I said, "How much you been up here?"

She shrugged her shoulders.

I didn't want That Woman's sister up there, for about a hundred reasons.

FIRST ONE BEING THAT SHE WAS DEAD.

I said,

YOU'RE A GHOST, AINT YOU?

She said she was, said "Yeah, I'm dead."

I said, "So why you here?"

She said, "Where am I supposed to be?"

I didn't know. I didn't know her that well. I said, "What's it like to be dead?"

She said, "Boring. And you're hungry all the time." She pulled on the cigarette. The smoke didn't go away. She said, "God. I'm starving."

I said, "Are you still on pills?"

She took another cigarette pull. "No," she said. "At least that's better."

I said, "I guess it is."

That Woman's sister knocked the billboard off her, sat up, hung her legs off the side of the scaffold, said, "Seriously. What are you doing up here?" She looked at me and wouldn't stop.

I told her about my idea to fix the sign. She said, "You want some help?"

I said, "Well, I wadn't going to do it tonight."

She said, "Why not? You'll chicken out if you don't."

People will tell you all kinds of things about ghosts, but if all ghosts are like the ghost of Tricia Jewell, there aint no point being scared of ghosts, cause she was way nicer as a ghost than she had been as a person—or at least way nicer than the person I had known.

The ghost of Tricia Jewell helped me fix up them letters. She could make herself glow, which we used for light. She held the chunks of plywood while I unscrewed the screws and held the screws for me while I moved things around. She helped me rearrange the pieces and pointed out how if I would trim this piece here and that piece there that it would look smoother, better, that it wouldn't look so cobbled up. She made that whole thing look a whole lot better.

When we got the letters fixed, she helped me hang the vinyl back and rig up the rope to pull to get the vinyl to fall away. When we got done with that, she ran got me a pop out of the cooler and set and watched me drink it, both of us hanging our legs off the scaffold. I told the ghost of Tricia Jewell me and Brother were supposed to take the scaffolds down in the morning and she smiled at me and all the teeth she'd had pulled come back in her mouth and she turned the rest of her glow off—she went dark except for her teeth, lit up and glowing blue-purple, lit up the color of the hydrangea blossoms and then the rest of her lit back up and she didn't have no clothes on and her body wasn't young but it was very beautiful, her curves like a stand-up bass, her skin mostly blue, the streams of wrinkles between her breasts more purple.

She pushed me at my shoulders, pushed me back on my back there on the scaffold. Then she climbed astraddle me, on her knees towering over me. She took my hand and put it on the hair at her middle, and my fingers slipped inside her and she smiled. She was cool inside. And slick. She unloosed my belt and took my pants down and let my man business out in the night air then she set on my belly and her behind so round and smooth was just the best feeling.

She lay her hands on my shoulders and leaned down towards me, her hair brushing my face, and I breathed so short couldn't catch my breath to save my life and I thought I was going to have to throw her off, but she leaned over and put her lips to mine, parted my lips with her tongue, and she breathed into me, and I caught my breath, breathed easy, and I let her do what she was going to do, which was to slide herself onto my man business.

She rocked her hips back and forth on me in a way that made me feel so natural and real. I joined in with her, rocking my hips too. She glowed a little brighter and never quit smiling but closed her eyes and I put my hands on her hips and we sailed along like that a good while and I thought about my family and squirrels and owls and big old deer and she opened her eyes just as I was finishing, just as them minnows went leaping out of me, and she watched me from on high, watched me in my pleasure, and when I calmed she put her hands to my cheeks, and she rose off me back on her knees astraddle me and she went dark again and her hands come off my cheeks and then she came off of sitting astride me and set down beside me and she said out of her darkness, "That's a good thing."

I said it was.

She said, "Why do you think I did that?"

I said I didn't know, but wondered did it have something to do with her sister.

She lit back up and sat up beside me, her arms around her knees, her face resting on them. She said, "Strange about dying the way I did. The thing in you that would have regrets and would make you wish you'd done different than you did—that part of you don't carry over. Fear is gone. Dread is gone. Worry is gone. Guilt is gone. And really, it aint better or worse. It just is what it is. And you can see everything happening but you can't change anything."

I said, "I think I'm going to have to change my drawers."

She laughed and rubbed her fingers in the man cream wet spot around the fly of my drawers. She put her fingers to her lips and said, "That's for you to decide." And then she said, "Come on," and fixed my pants and took me by my hands and stood me up and we had that scaffold took apart and stacked up in short order.

I WAS afraid I might be a witch or want to drink blood or something. None of that happened, but I did feel different. I thought I was changed. I think that's why I jumped in that lake to try and save Calvin. I thought that ghost sex would make me to where I couldn't drown. But that turned out not to be true. Maybe I wasn't changed.

After I done that to them letters, I never did go back to Canard County. I never saw That Woman again. I didn't have no call to. No urge to.

But to be honest, I did go back. I was there the day the letters got shown. But I didn't have no interest in that. I went back to get Calvin. I caught him getting in his Bonneville at the Kolonel Krispy parking lot and I went and got in the other side.

He said, "Hello, Gene," which was the first time in his life he'd ever got my name right.

I said, "Hey Calvin."

He said, "For a second I thought you were a ghost."

I asked him why.

He said cause of my white pants and T-shirt and cause he said my hair'd got whiter since we'd been in Tennessee together.

I said, "Calvin, it was you killed Tricia."

He said, "Yes, it was."

I said, "And you told Dawn Jewell you was going to turn yourself in."

He said, "Yeah. You were sitting there when I told her."

I said, "Yeah, I was."

We set there quiet for a minute. Then I took Calvin's face in my hands and kissed him. Right on his lips. Then I set there. Calvin put his hands on the steering wheel.

He said, "Will you go with me?"

I said I would.

Calvin started the Bonneville and drove over to the sheriff's office and told the little boy they had sitting there he's the one killed Tricia Jewell. Said he's the one dumped her body down by the riverbank like she was a bag of garbage. Then Calvin set down and that little fellow arrested him and handcuffed him to a hot water pipe.

I walked out of the sheriff's office and down the old courthouse steps, left out of there,

NEVER DID GO BACK TO CANARD COUNTY.

~~~~

WHERE WITCHES COME FROM

DAWN

I drew a picture of Nicolette turned into a flying fish on the hood of June's car. I drew it with my finger in the yellow dust June carried home from the West Virginia strip jobs where she'd been raising a ruckus. In the picture, Nicolette leapt out of the ocean towards a spaceship. The spaceship was shaped like a fish too.

My phone rang. I answered and Nicolette said, "Hi, Mommy."

I said, "Hey, baby. How are you?"

She said, "Good. Where are you?"

I said, "I'm with Aunt June. At her new job."

Nicolette said, "When are you coming home?"

I said, "I don't know, baby. When we get everything straightened out here."

Nicolette said, "How long is that?"

I said, "Not long."

I said, "You know I love you, don't you baby?"

Nicolette said, "I know, Mommy." Said, "I love you too."

I said, "I know, baby."

Nicolette said, "Tell Aunt June I love her."

I said, "I will, baby."

"Bye, Mommy."

"Bye, Baby."

It was hot and bright in the mostly empty community college parking lot. The car hood burned my finger. June walked up, a bag of papers on her shoulder. She walked slow and crooked, smiling like a guy just had his first kid. She come up to me and sighed. I wiped my finger on my pants.

I said, "Did they fire you?"

She said no. Said, "You want to see my new office?"

We walked between the buildings on the college campus, went in the art building. A nice lady behind a half wall said hi, and we went in June's office, which had windows on two sides, a desk with cabinets, a round table for people to sit. The chairs were solid. Everything matched.

I said, "This is yours?"

She said yeah.

I said, "All to yourself?"

She said yeah.

I said, "Dang." Said, "They weren't mad about the sign?"

June said, "They knew that wasn't my fault."

I said, "Well."

June said, "It didn't hurt either I'd got that grant."

I said, "How much is the grant?"

She said, "Four hundred thousand dollars."

I said, "And that sign is already took down."

June said, "That's right."

I looked around at the bookshelves bolted to the wall on either side of the windows. Two dogs licked themselves outside. I said, "Well. This is nice."

June said, "You ready to go?"

We left and went back to Momma's. On the way, June asked me did I want to go with her and Kenny to Johnson City to see a bunch of guys with long beards play music. I said no.

Nicolette was still with Willett. Willett was still in Tennessee. I was still in the soup. I was in a giant cookpot treading soup, wishing there was a giant floating potato for me to grab onto. Or maybe a dumpling I could stretch out on. But there wasn't. There was just me in soup getting hotter all the time. I was like the rat that fell in my friend Pete's soup one time at an interstate restaurant, the one with the checkerboards and rocking chairs. The rat fell in the soup and nobody noticed, and they put the lid on the pot, and the rat cooked, and they put the rat in Pete's soup bowl. That was me, drowning and boiling in the dark. Soup in my rat lungs and eyes and ears. It sucked.

When June left to go to the concert with Kenny, I was in the house by myself. I sat on the air conditioner stairs and called Hazel. It was the end of the month, and I'd promised her I'd come to her house. Pharoah lay sleeping on the top step above me. She hung close after everybody died. She knew. She wasn't a stupid dog.

It was the last day of July, 2004. The three main females in my life all died in the same month in the same year.

Hazel said, "What time you coming, baby?"
I said I didn't know. I didn't say it, but I didn't want to go at all.
Hazel said, "Baby, I aint going to lie to you. I'm down in the mouth."
I said, "I know, Hazel."
She said, "Don't know how I'm going to make it."
I said, "I know."
I heard somebody stirring downstairs. I told Hazel I'd be there around dark. Told her I'd be glad to stay over. And I reckon I was.

Hubert and Albert sat at the kitchen table acting hungry. I asked them did they want something to eat and they said, "What do you have?" And I said, "Baloney. Peanut butter. Cereal." Albert asked did I have Lucky Charms and Hubert asked did I have ham, and I told them both no. They both said they'd take baloney sandwiches. So I fixed them baloney sandwiches. Hubert's with tomato and mayonnaise. Albert's with mustard and double baloney. Everything seemed so shrunk up. Back to normal. But tiny.

Hubert and Albert told me Evie had been wearing a recorder and working with the police to get out of trouble. She ratted out Sidney. She ratted out Groundhog and Fu Manchu. But she wasn't trying to rat out Hubert. She was trying to get dirt on him so that she could make him quit drug dealing. She also was going to turn Albert in if he didn't stop using and selling. That's what Hubert and Albert said. Hubert said Evie had been trying to get him to stop for months. Albert said Evie flushed his pills down the commode. Hubert said she was going to get herself killed doing that shit.

When he said that, we just sat there. I thought Albert was going to cry. Pharoah came down the steps, her needing-cut nails clicking on the stairs. She lay down under the kitchen table, right in the middle of us, like she didn't hardly ever do.

<hr>

I'D BEEN thinking about Belinda Coates since Dollywood. I was worried about her. It didn't even feel strange to worry. I thought about her with her twelve-year-old self with its broke arm in Corbin. I thought about what all must have been going through her head when she threw my bicycle in the river. It crossed my mind maybe Belinda Coates had liked me in sixth grade.

Anyway. I lay around the house, read a comic book about Amazon lady warriors in ancient Greece, drew pictures in a notebook I found, one June gave me when I was in eighth grade. I hadn't drawn in it since tenth grade. I thought about my dream of becoming a tattoo artist. It seemed far away. It seemed unreal. I didn't know who would talk me into doing it.

Decent Ferguson called. She asked me how I was doing. She called me darling. I asked her how you got to be a tattoo artist. She told me about a friend of hers who had written her master's thesis on tattoo artists someplace where there was a lot of navy ships, and sailors, and because of that a lot of tattoo artists. Decent said she'd been meaning to call that woman anyway. She said she'd call her for me, find out how to be a tattoo artist.

About five o'clock, I asked Pharoah did she want to go to Hazel's. She wagged her tail when I said "go." So we got ready and went. I stopped first in Tattletown and got beer. I got a fifth of vodka and some Sunny D, because vodka and Sunny D was what Evie liked to drink.

When Momma first started getting in trouble with the law, and the judge first started sending her to Straight Like Jesus, which was a Christian twelve-step program, me and her both thought the judge had a crush on her. Whether that was right or not, one night me and her and Evie were out on the Trail, out on Long Ridge, and we ended up in the judge's backyard, ended up bouncing on his trampoline, all three of us, holding hands and bouncing till the floodlights came on at every corner of the house, and we three scattered in three different directions. That was the last time we all three did something partyish together. We were drinking vodka and Sunny D that night.

Me and Pharoah got to Hazel's house way before dark. Hazel's house was blue with black trim and sat notched into the hillside. Cats lazed on the porch rail, watching the traffic on the two-lane below. Twenty wind chimes made of hammered-out forks and spoons jangled on twenty J-hooks lining the porch. Salvaged lumber piled up on top of a wringer washing machine on the side of the porch facing the road.

I had Pharoah on a leash cause June lost her mind if you didn't keep Pharoah on the leash. Hazel had a fair number of crazy dogs, but she had them in a pen beside her house, big chain-link setup with blue tarps to keep the sun off them and dog food scattered everywhere on the concrete pad amidst flipped-over dog bowls and poop.

Sunlight filtered through oak and maple and fell through the open front door. Balls of dust and dog hair rolled across the dull pine floorboards. Sylvester Stallone shot up a village in shades of pink and orange on the hand-me-down television across the fireplace. A yellow bedsheet printed with faded flowers covered the couch. The ashes of a cigarette piled around the opening in the top of a Pepsi can. The can sat on top of a cutoff notice from the power company. The notice sat on top of a stack of library books and DVD cases. A fly fizzed in and out of the kitchen. Except for the sunlight and Sylvester Stallone, there was no light in the room. Hazel told us to come in and make ourselves at home, but Pharoah wouldn't settle down. I said,

PHAROAH, THEM DOGS CAN'T GET YOU.

She acted like she believed me, but she never would totally relax. Hazel set back on the couch and breathed out, her cheeks puffing full of air. She played a song on her tape player she said was called "Darn Well." Hazel said the song was done by an outfit called Linnie Walker and Black Merda. The song made me feel better. Hazel sat up and opened a wooden box sitting on the table. She took out a jar of weed. She took out a pipe. She smoked a bowl. She asked me if I wanted some. I took some. I don't much like pot, but I wanted to feel different than I did. I wanted to feel different than beer or vodka or Sunny D could make me feel. So I smoked a bowl with Hazel.

I asked Hazel could we call Belinda Coates, see if she wanted to come hang out with us. Said we maybe even could go to Causey if Hazel didn't care.

Hazel looked at me and said, "Lord, honey. You aint heard."

I said, "Heard what?"

Hazel said, "Belinda Coates is in the hospital. And jail."

I said, "Both?"

And Hazel said, "Yep."

I asked what happened and Hazel told me the day we went to Dollywood, Belinda and that bunch she was running with had gone shoplifting and stolen a bunch of pocketbooks in Pigeon Forge and then went to West Town Mall and stole a bunch of cosmetics, stuck them down in the pocketbooks they'd stolen in Pigeon Forge, not even pulling the tags off the pocketbooks when they were stealing the makeup. When they got out in the parking lot, they got to fighting about how to divide the stuff, and somehow Belinda got beat up and woke up in her car the next morning at West Town Mall, getting arrested with a whole car full of drugs and stolen stuff. And her buds were nowhere in sight. Hazel said both her eyes were black, her nose was broken, a bunch of her ribs and fingers were broken, she was missing teeth, and her lips were all busted and bloody. And now she was looking at being in jail a while, Hazel said.

"Jesus," I said.

Hazel said, "I couldn't do to a dog what them girls did to her."

I felt bad about all the ill feelings I had about Belinda Coates over the years. I told Hazel so and me and her smoked another bowl. Rambo was still shooting up villages on the TV. The sound was off and more soul music played on Hazel's cassette player.

Hazel said, "Rambo is a buzzkill."

I nodded.

Hazel said, "I wonder why Sylvester Stallone never made no outer space movies?"

I said, "He didn't?"

Hazel said, "I never seen one."

I said,

Hazel said, "I do."

I said I did too.

Hazel said, "My daddy thought witches came from outer space."

I said, "Do what?"

Hazel said, "He thought that's how witches could do stuff other people couldn't. Because they came from other places, other atmospheres."

I said, "Hunh."

Hazel said, "He used to read everything he could about witches. And about outer space and about time travel. He used to take me down to the mall and the public library in Kingsport and them places looking for books on witches and things. He'd have loved the Internet."

I said, "Do you think he really believed all that stuff?"

Hazel lit another bowl. She said, "He liked to believe anything can happen. He liked to believe there weren't no real rules. He used to tell me everything bends. There aint nothing fixed."

I said, "What did your daddy look like?"

Hazel said, "He wasn't tall. And he didn't have a big belly. But he was big up top. His shoulders were huge. And he kept a moustache, a big silver moustache. Had him a full head of silver hair. He never touched it after he got it fixed right, and never let nobody else touch it neither."

I said, "Did he work in the mines?"

Hazel said, "Worked at the tipple. Worked there his whole life, till the day a man he worked with fell into the coal processor and they didn't see him, and then they couldn't get it cut off and he went through the whole processor and ended up spit out into a coal gon full of coal. Daddy said that man was twisted up like a wrung-out dishrag. Daddy walked off the job that day, never went back. We lived on what his pension paid and what he got from disability."

I said, "What'd he do to get on disability?"

Hazel said, "Got his arm pulled off trying to save that man."

Hazel hit the pipe again, pointed in the kitchen, said, "He sat right in there, in his pajamas ever day for the rest of his life, smoking White Owl cigars and reading about spacemen and witches." Hazel offered me the bowl. I shook my head. Hazel said, "One day, Daddy got up from the table, said he was going to Mars to get more cigars. I thought he was fooling, so I said, 'Which of your cars are you taking to Mars to get you some cigars?' And he said, 'Buddy, them Mars cigars is ten times better that what they got in Cuba.' Then he walked down the steps and got in his vehicle, fired it up, took off, and we never seen him again."

I said, "Are you serious?"

Hazel said, "As a heart attack." Hazel got up and said, "Everything bends," and went upstairs.

While she was gone, I thought about how I had more friends in heaven or wherever than I did on earth. Hazel come back downstairs. She had on satin pajamas cut like the kind Lucy and Ricky Ricardo wore. Hazel's satin pajamas were real dark blue, like the night sky, and they had planets and shooting stars and suns and moons on them, all embroidered in gold. All real fancy.

Hazel said, "You want to go to the store?"

I said, "Can Pharoah go?"

Hazel said, "Sure."

I let Pharoah off her chain right when two dogs started fighting in the pen outside. Pharoah peeled out across the wood floor, across the broken paint of the concrete porch, down the steps and up to the edge of the fight. There she stopped unsure what to do. Hazel and I followed. The evening had turned to night, and the darkness soaked the hillsides. By the light of Hazel's flashlight, we saw the fighting dogs' yellow teeth and gums mottled pink and brown.

I gathered up Pharoah. Put her leash on. The night clouded over. The stars disappeared.

Hazel said, "Are you ready?"

I said I was and Hazel went out to her Astrovan and slid back the side door. Pharoah jumped right in. I got shotgun. Hazel got in, kicked off her slippers, said, "Put your seatbelt on."

We both did. Hazel started the van. And we took off, into the night,

NICOLETTE

The summer before I turned four, my mother saved two grown men from drowning. Saved them both at the same time on the same day. I'll never forget how strong she looked in the water. She looked like she might rise up like a dolphin and fly away, soar out into space with a man under each arm, plunge right into the sun, come out the other side, mega-strong and huge, super-tan and with the two men gone. I would watch her circle the earth, my giant super-tan mother, proud and solar-powered and titanic. And I would wave at her, and she would wave back at me with both hands, and then flap her arms and fly in circles and figure eights and loop-de-loops in and out of the clouds. Then she would fly down through the window of her house and fix me chicken and dumplings, her hair sparkling with mist from the clouds.

I've heard about the summer of 2004, especially that July, my whole life. So much happened—people dying, people going to jail, Momma getting in trouble with the judge and the president of the United States—that I understand why Momma wasn't able to keep her promise to teach me to swim.

My mother did a bunch of other things for me. A bunch. My mother told me about our family, told me what a hero my Granny Cora was, what a good sweet man my father had been, and all kinds of stories about her daddy's family. She taught me not to be scared and she told me I was smart and she'd ask me to sing for her and always told me what an amazing singer I was. She kept me out of trouble and talked to me sweet when I didn't understand something. She always remembered what my favorite things to eat are and always made me feel like I came first.

My momma gave me everything   I ever needed.

239

Acknowledgments

This is my second novel. I wrote it in between readings and workshops and interviews in support of my first novel, *Trampoline*. Having a book in the world has illuminated for me the abundant but fragile ecology supporting the written word, and I'd like to call by name people and places I've encountered over the past three years that are making the world safe for books and thank them for the joy and energy they bring to their work. In particular, I'd like to acknowledge Brent Hutchinson with the Appalachian Writers' Workshop in Hindman, Kentucky; Darnell Arnoult and Denton Loving at the Mountain Heritage Literary Festival in Harrogate, Tennessee; Pam Duncan at the Western Carolina University Spring Literary Festival; Jesse Graves at the East Tennessee State University Creative Writing Festival in Johnson City, Tennessee; The Southern Festival of Books in Nashville, Tennessee; the Virginia Festival of the Book in Charlottesville, Virginia; Books by the Banks in Cincinnati, Ohio; the Kentucky Book Fair in Frankfort, Kentucky; Jessie Wilkerson and the Oxford Conference for the Book in Oxford, Mississippi; Maurice Manning and Liz Corsun at Transylvania University; Sherry Stanforth and the Words Festival at Thomas More College in Crestview Hills, Kentucky; Gillian Huang-Tiller at the University of Virginia's College at Wise; Silas House and the Appalachian Symposium at Berea College in Berea, Kentucky; Jesse Van Eerden, Marie Manilla, and Doug Van Gundy at the MFA program at West Virginia Wesleyan College; Alice Jones at Eastern Kentucky University; Emily Satterwhite and Jordan Laney at Virginia Tech; Rachel Terman, Chris Chaffee, and Geoff Buckley at Ohio University; Glenn "Trenchmouth" Taylor at West Virginia University; Wes Browne at Apollo Pizza; Jennifer Mattox at the Carnegie Center for Literacy and Learning in Lexington, Kentucky; Carol Grametbauer and Tennessee Mountain Writers; Crystal Wilkinson and Ron Davis at Wild Fig Books in Lexington; Jay McCoy, who was then at the Morris Book Shop in Lexington but now operates Brier Books in Lexington with Savannah Sipple; Union Ave Books in Knoxville, Tennessee; Erik Reece and Kathy Newfont at the University of Kentucky; Mark Neikirk and the Scripps Howard Center for Civic Engagement at Northern Kentucky University; Nicole Drewitz-Crockett at Emory & Henry

College in Emory, Virginia; Jessica Maunz Salfia and her students at Spring Mills High School in Berkeley County, West Virginia; Natalie Sypolt at Pierpont Community & Technical College in West Virginia; Shawna Kay Rodenberg at Big Sandy Community & Technical College; Jenny Williams at Hazard Community & Technical College; Elizabeth Glass at Jefferson Community & Technical College; Sandy Ballard, Zack Vernon, and Susan Weinberg at Appalachian State University; Eric Sutherland and Holler Poets at Al's Bar in Lexington, Kentucky; Deanna Bradberry and the Wytheville Chautauqua in Wytheville, Virginia; Carter Sickels; Jennifer Haigh; David Joy; Sheldon Lee Compton; Mark Powell; Rita Quillen; Leah Hampton; Marianne Worthington; Theresa Burriss; Malcolm Wilson; FunFest, the Friends of the Kingsport Public Library, and I Love Books Bookstore in Kingsport, Tennessee; The Washington County Public Library in Abingdon, Virginia; Roxy Todd, West Virginia Public Radio and *Inside Appalachia;* 98.7 The FREQ, in State College, Pennsylvania; the journals *Bloom, Chapter 16, Electric Literature, Still, Chattahoochee Review, Appalachian Heritage,* and *Southern Cultures*; and all the people who worked with these people and on these projects.

Pat Scopa, Elana Scopa Forson, Carrie Billett, Carrie Mullins, Wes and Valetta Browne, and Amelia Kirby all read and commented on earlier drafts of this novel. Thank you. Rick Brock, Kenny Colinger, Nick Cornett, Lisa Frith, Donna Collins, Debra Lynn Bays, Clifford Pierce, Cassidy Wright Hubbard, and Devyn Creech offered great advice. Thank you. The Ohio University Press—Gill, Samara, Jeff, Sebastian, Beth, Nancy, Sandra, and the rest—have been a pleasure to work with. My brother William and his family, Stacey, Will, and Laura, and my uncle John and his family have been a great support, especially when my mother Barbara passed. Larry Gipe and his family, and in particular my aunt Jo Ann, have been in my corner all the way, as have my Buckeye cousins Susie and Jimmy Silver and all their family. Thank you. In Harlan, my Higher Ground family and Southeast Community College family are always there and I am deeply appreciative. Thank you all.